~ Unwrapping Holly ~

*A Holiday
Reverse Harem Romance*

Krista Wolf

Unwrapping Holly - Krista Wolf

Copyright © 2018 Krista Wolf

All rights reserved. No part of this publication may be reproduced, distributed, or transmitted in any form without prior consent of the author.

Cover image: Stock footage — story is unrelated to subject/models

KRISTA'S VIP EMAIL LIST:

Join to get free book offers, and learn release dates for the hottest new titles!

Tap here to sign up: http://eepurl.com/dkWHab

Unwrapping Holly - Krista Wolf

One

HOLLY

"So.... I— I didn't get it."

My lip quivered as I told him. It was a humbling admission, a shit end to a very shit day. But I felt better in saying it. Much better now that it was finally out.

"Oh honey," Malcolm said, laying his hand over mine. "That really stinks."

I took as much comfort as I could from my boyfriend's touch. The promotion was mine, by every right. Among my team I had seniority, and I was certainly doing the best job. I'd even been working tons of extra hours for it, sitting at my desk late into the evening, until my ass was asleep long after I should be.

"They gave it to Louis," I sniffed, choking back tears. All the way here, I'd promised myself I wouldn't cry. "Can you believe that? Fucking *Louis*..."

Malcolm nodded sympathetically. It was all he could do — his mouth was already full of another bite of cheeseburger.

"I—I mean, how the hell do you pick *Louis,* when he hasn't even been—"

"Holly, stop."

I looked up at him as Malcolm squeezed my hand. He handed me his napkin, which wasn't exactly clean. I dabbed the corners of my eyes with it anyway, wondering if anyone else at the greasy little diner was looking at me.

"Please, give me your keychain."

Keychain?

I blinked rapidly, driving the tears away. What could he possibly want with my—

Oh my God.

My heart soared. My whole body started to tingle. Suddenly all that nasty business at work seemed inconsequential.

He's going to ask you to move in with him!

For the first time all day, a smile cracked my lips. I reached into my bag almost reverently, pushing past my phone. The screen was still shattered of course, from when I'd dropped it earlier in the day. But none of that mattered now.

Malcolm smiled as he took my all-too large keychain from my trembling, outstretched hand.

"I— I want you to know this means *everything* to me," I said, trying once again to keep the tears at bay. But they were tears of joy this time, so I wasn't trying all that hard. "Especially after the day I've had," I sighed. "Especially after—"

I watched anxiously, waiting for him to bring it out — the key to his apartment. I'd been staying there three out of four nights a week, anyway. It only made sense for us to move in together.

Thank God.

After nearly two years of dating, of living alone in the concrete jungle of New York City, I'd *finally* have someone to come home to. And to think of all the rent money I'd save! Even after kicking in half with Malcolm, an offer I knew he'd take me up on because he was so frugal, I'd still be coming out ahead each month. Shit, this was even *better* than a raise.

More than that though, it was a sign of big progress. The advancement of our relationship. The next logical step in —

"I'm sorry you didn't get that promotion Holly," Malcolm said pityingly. "But if I'm being honest, I didn't think you would."

My eyebrows knit together. It was a cold thing to say. But that was Malcolm: brutally frank about everything, to the point of unflinching honesty. I'd thought it was heartlessness at first, but later on I realized it was only his personality.

Truth be told, I was used to it by now. Marcus approached life the same way he approached our accounting jobs: everything was all business.

"It makes this whole thing a little... harder."

I watched, trance-like, as he manipulated my keychain. Instead of *adding* a key to it, he twisted it counter-clockwise and took one off.

"W—What are you doing?"

"Taking back the car," he said simply.

"*My* car?"

My boyfriend suddenly looked uncomfortable. And he *never* looked uncomfortable.

"Holly I'm sorry," he said. "This... this isn't working out."

The words didn't register, no matter how many times my brain repeated them. I shook my head as if to clear it.

"*What* isn't working out?"

"This," he said, motioning casually back and forth. "Us. Our relationship."

The realization finally hit me — like a brick being dropped from a 90-story building. The same building we worked at together. The building where we'd met and fallen in love... or at least I *thought* we'd fallen in love, and—

"It's difficult for me to do this on a day you're already disappointed," he said.

"Difficult for *you?*"

He nodded, completely oblivious. "Yes. And that's why I feel so badly. But Holly, please, search your feelings. If you do it honestly, you'll come to the same realization I did."

A hard lump formed in my throat. "And what's that?"

Malcolm sighed gently. "This just isn't worth it anymore."

Isn't. Worth. It. Anymore.

My heart dropped into my stomach. All of a sudden I felt sick.

"B—But why are you taking my *car?*"

"It isn't your car," Malcolm shrugged. "It's a lease. A lease with my name on it."

"Yes, but I've been making the payments!"

He nodded. "You have. And on time too. I appreciate that, but—"

"You *gave* me a car for my birthday," I said, slowly raising my voice, "and you gave me a *payment book* along with it! Don't you remember?"

"Of course."

"What kind of a boyfriend gives his girlfriend a fucking *payment* book?" I practically shouted. "Who the hell *does* that?"

Now we *did* have an audience. Half the diner was staring at us, like the bloodthirsty crowd of a gladiatorial coliseum. Waiting for whatever entertainment came next. Hoping for me to slap him, or throw a drink in his face, or—

"What do you *mean* this '*isn't working out*'?" I yelled. "How long have you known? And you take me *here?* To the shittiest diner in all of Manhattan?"

The waitress topping off coffee halted mid-stride. She glared at me angrily, one dirty pot clutched in each of her hands.

"You break up with me today of all days? And now you're taking my *car?*"

"Not *your* car," Malcolm repeated simply. "It's—"

"I KNOW WHAT IT IS!"

A thousand different emotions went surging through me at once. Heartbreak. Rage. Remorse. Stupidity, at not having seen this coming. Embarrassment at having to do it in a room full of strangers.

Malcolm pushed the keychain back across the table, minus my car key and remote fob. He also pushed something else: a pair of what looked like pamphlets or brochures.

"What the hell are these?"

"City bus schedules," he offered helpfully. "And subway maps, for all the lines near—"

"You brought me *bus schedules?*" I growled.

"Mmm-hmmm," he said, almost cheerfully. "And subway maps. Look, if you leave your apartment ten minutes earlier each morning, it's real easy to just..."

His voice droned on, but I was no longer listening. My shoulders slumped. My head hurt. I couldn't believe any of this was actually happening.

Malcolm laid his hand over mine again, but now I was repulsed by it. I jerked it back like I'd just gotten bitten by a snake.

"Holly, I want you to know—"

I leapt up and threw my napkin down on the table. The tears were coming again. There was no way to stop them this time, and I didn't want anyone else to see.

Especially *him*.

The diner's bathroom was just as tiny as the rest of it. I spent two minutes bawling my eyes out, another minute feeling sorry for myself, and another staring into the dirt-streaked mirror while telling myself to buck up. By the time I finished washing my face and putting drops in my eyes, I was ready to go out there and give that piece of shit a piece of my mind.

But when I returned to my table there was just one problem with that plan: Malcolm wasn't there.

Son of a bitch!

Silently I kicked myself. I really should've known. My boyfriend was never good at conflict; he usually dealt with problems by ducking out and skulking away.

Like a coward.

I grabbed my keys, which were the only thing still on the table. They felt much smaller now. Lighter and emptier. Like my life.

I stomped past the front counter and toward the exit, wondering if my now *ex*-boyfriend were already on his way to repossess my car. If I knew him he probably was. Or better yet, he'd get someone *else* to do it. That seemed more like—

"Miss?"

The word came haltingly, almost meekly, as I pushed on the glass door. I turned around.

"You still have to... well..."

I knew the answer before even asking the question.

"Don't even *tell* me he didn't pay."

The man behind the counter shrugged apologetically. "Sort of," he said, his voice hesitant. "He, uh..."

"Let me guess," I offered, with a mad chuckle. "He

only paid for himself?"

"Well... yeah."

Fuck you Malcolm.

I opened my bag mechanically, paying with my last twenty-dollar bill. It should've been a good day. I should've gotten a raise, a well-deserved promotion. I should be celebrating with a handsome, loving boyfriend at some beautiful restaurant uptown. One who loved me enough to move in with me after nearly two *years* of dating.

Instead I was in some greasy diner, crying like a baby, paying my own bill. I'd missed the promotion, and now I didn't even have a car anymore.

Oh yeah, and my boyfriend had just dumped me. *Right* before Christmas.

Fuck my life.

I went to look down into my phone's cracked screen, to see what time it was. But when I pressed the button, all I saw was the darkness of a fully-drained battery.

Hell, fuck everything.

I pushed on the door so hard it bounced back and nearly hit me in the chin. My eyes dropped to the big PULL sign. Just as the guy behind me said the word needlessly over my shoulder.

It was just one of those days. The ones that kicked your ass, and kept on kicking you even after you were down.

At least it was almost over. At least nothing else could go wrong.

Right?

Finally opening the door, I stomped outside... into a cold, freezing rain.

Two

HOLLY

"No calls, no texts... no *anything?*"

I shook my head from the other side of the couch. The coffee shop was crowded for a Thursday. This close to Christmas, in New York City? I'm surprised we got a seat at all.

"Nothing," I said proudly. "Two whole, beautiful Malcolmless weeks."

Jocelyn pursed her lips approvingly. She took another sip of her latte.

"And you haven't even run into him at the office?"

"Nope. Remember, he works three floors above me. And it's not like I saw him a lot to begin with."

That part was a flat-out lie, and Jocelyn knew it. I saw Malcolm all the time, as much at work as outside the office. She didn't call me out on it, though. It was the mark of a good friend.

"Good for you, Holly," she smiled, raising her mug.

Very carefully, I clinked mine against it. "I'm proud of you."

In truth I was proud of myself. I'd actually gone out of my way to avoid my ex, taking a different bank of elevators and avoiding the exit near the parking garage. Hell, it wasn't like I had a car to park there anymore, anyway.

A sadness crept over me at that last thought. I really missed my little hatchback.

"So what do you think about Sunday?" I asked. "About Lincoln's... invite?"

"Sure sounds like a date to me," Jocelyn grinned.

"*Really?*"

My best friend in all of Manhattan swept a stray blonde lock over one ear. "Tell me again how he asked you."

I relayed the story one more time. The story about how Lincoln Wallace, my first and oldest personal shopping client, had asked to meet up with me on Sunday.

"Shopping and *lunch?*" Jocelyn repeated thoughtfully. "Well has he ever asked you to lunch before?"

"He's never even asked to go *shopping* before," I said. "Come to think of it, he barely makes suggestions. He's always just handed me his credit card and left everything to me."

That part was true, and it was also what I loved most about my little side business. Being a personal shopper was like getting paid to have fun. You went shopping with someone else's money, and you got to buy things you wouldn't normally buy yourself.

"How'd you meet him again, anyway?"

"I took the business over from a woman I worked

with," I said, "back when I first came to town. She was moving away and left me about a dozen clients. Lincoln Wallace was the best of them."

"You mean he *pays* the best," Jocelyn added shrewdly.

I sipped off the last of my foam. "Oh yeah. He's the CEO of his own advertising firm. And he's got four sisters and plenty of nieces and nephews. Not to mention two adorable parents back in Maine... all of whom he showers with gifts."

Jocelyn sighed wistfully. "Rich. Successful. Loves his family..." She squinted back at me. "And you said he was handsome, too?"

God, is he ever.

"Tall, dark and gorgeous," I nodded.

Jocelyn stared back at me enviously. "Well shit, Holly! If he's *not* trying to take you out, mind if I have a crack at him?"

I laughed, but my laughter came out nervous. Suddenly there was a little knot in my stomach.

Jealousy? The little voice in my head taunted. *Really, Holly?*

A huge part of me *did* want him to be asking me out. If for no other reason than to feel wanted again — to feel desired in ways I hadn't felt in almost two years. The fact that it was someone like Lincoln Wallace only made it ten times better.

But if he *wasn't* asking me out...

"Holly? Earth to *Holly?*"

I snapped back, just in time to avoid spilling my coffee

all over my own leg. It sloshed dangerously close to the lip of the mug, causing me to overcompensate and almost drop it entirely.

"Easy," Jocelyn chuckled, laying her hands over mine. "He's all yours, honey. I was only kidding."

She handed me a napkin, which I accepted gratefully. At the rate things were going, I might need a towel.

"And to answer your question, yes," she added, "I *do* think he's asking you out. Just look at yourself. You're beautiful and amazing, and now you're single to boot. He'd be a fool not to take a crack at you."

I blushed, even though it was just the two of us. "Thanks."

When it came to friends, Jocelyn was one of the better ones. Cute, funny, level-headed... and tough. New York tough. The kind of tough I learned all about when I moved out here two years ago, from my sheltered little town in Southern Texas.

"Treat it like a date," Jocelyn advised. "You haven't had one in a really long time. A good one, anyway."

"You don't think that would be unprofessional?"

"Do you really care?" Jocelyn smirked.

I thought about it for a second. "I care about losing him as a client."

She waved me away dismissively with one hand. "Shop with him. Flirt with him. Enjoy yourself for a change. If he flirts back, you know the drill. And if not?" She shrugged. "He's gay."

I laughed so hard I almost spit my coffee. "He's *not*

gay!"

Jocelyn threw me her most seductive wink. "Then go have fun with him."

Three

HOLLY

"C'mon, three more reps!"

I pushed hard, through the pain, feeling the burn in my thighs as the platform above me moved smoothly up and down. I always loved the leg press machine. The sheer amount of weight on each side made you feel like you could put up really big numbers.

"Two more..."

Except today, when I was doing it for the first time in months.

"Another two..."

"Hey!" I grunted. "You said that *last* rep!"

"Yeah, well you half-assed that one," Donovan barked. "I don't accept half-reps. If you followed through you'd be done by now."

I reached down into my core and pushed, shoving the weights away and finishing out my set. My perfectly-sculpted trainer engaged the locking clamp just as my legs went limp.

"There you go," he smirked back at me. "That wasn't so bad now, was it?"

I gave Donovan my dirtiest playful look. "No. It was absolutely perfect."

"Perfection is when I can bounce a quarter off your ass," he shot back. His look went stern. "But you already know what I'm going to say next, don't you?"

"Yeah yeah," I acknowledged. "It wouldn't hurt this bad if I came on a regular basis."

He nodded as he threw me my towel. "Damn straight."

I mopped my forehead as I looked Donovan up and down. As always he was flawless, from his square jaw and handsomely stubbled chin right down to his powerful biceps and rock-hard abs.

Jesus, did his arms get bigger?

It was the first time I'd actually seen him since my breakup. The first time I could really drink him in without feeling guilty, as if I were doing something wrong. Our playful banter was something I looked forward to during our sessions. It was cute and funny, and it also kept me in line.

"Fitness is like a relationship," he finally winked. "You can't cheat and expect it to work."

In reality I wasn't cheating. I'd been coming the last few weeks, I'd just been avoiding him.

"You avoiding me, Holly?" he squinted.

Shit, it was like he read my mind.

"No sir."

"Then where have you been?"

"Around."

"Not around *here*," he said. "At least not while I'm in the gym."

"Why?" I flirted playfully. "You been looking for me?"

Damn. That was bold! It also wasn't like me at all.

"I look out for everybody," he smiled. "But you especially."

It felt good, being able to flirt with him like this. To be free of Malcolm, who'd always thought my personal training sessions were a huge waste of money. "Why pay for something you can do yourself?" he'd argued often. "You're already paying for a gym membership. Do you really need to throw *extra* money at someone to stand over you?"

With any other boyfriend, I would've chalked it up to jealousy. After all, Donovan was *gorgeous.* But with Malcolm... not so much. Like always, he was just being cheap.

"So when did it end?"

Donovan's deep, velvety voice brought me back to reality. I stared up him curiously. "Huh?"

"Your relationship. You broke up with your boyfriend, didn't you?"

My confusion was suddenly replaced with astonishment. I was stunned.

"How do you kno—"

"Because you didn't talk about him at all," Donovan

interjected. "Not once, during our entire session. Usually you talk about him a lot, whenever I work you out."

"I do?"

"Yes," he smiled. "Nothing good, usually. He sounds... well..."

"Go on," I smiled. "You can say it."

Our eyes locked. My personal trainer hesitated, sizing me up a little before continuing. "He sounds like a cheap, controlling asshole."

I laughed as I popped the top off my water bottle. "Bingo."

"So you broke up with him?"

I wish. Suddenly I felt very foolish. As if the other people in my life could see something obvious I was totally missing. Missing for a very long time.

"Something like that."

"So then tell me," he said. "If you're single, and you obviously have more time on your hands... why are you avoiding me?"

I stared back at him, feeling like a deer caught in a pair of steel blue headlights. There was no use lying to him. He'd know immediately, before I even finished constructing the sentence.

"I— I'm kinda strapped for cash," I admitted humbly. "I don't have a car anymore, so I'm saving up for one."

His expression softened. I saw a welcome understanding in his eyes, as all judgment went out the window.

"I can't afford too many sessions right now," I said. "So I was thinking of cutting back my sessions. Maybe only coming—"

"You're a personal shopper, right?"

I blinked. It was the last thing I expected him to say.

"Yes."

"Well Christmas is coming," said Donovan. "And I've got a ton of people to buy for. Friends, family, small gifts I usually give to clients..."

His voice had changed also. It was still beautiful, still wonderfully deep and sexy. But it was smoother now. Much more casual.

"How about we trade?" he smiled warmly. "Some personal training sessions for some personal shopping?"

He had the *best* smile. It brought mine out as well.

"You'd do that?"

"I'd actually *love* to do that!" he said excitedly. "Can't tell the gym though." Donovan rolled his beautiful eyes. "It's against policy, or something equally stupid."

"O—Okay," I stammered.

All of a sudden my heart was racing. The idea of shopping for this incredible man, of getting to know him on a more personal level... there was something as intimidating as there was appealing about it.

"Gotta do *something* to get you in here," Donovan laughed. "You need an excuse to show up more."

I had to stop myself from turning about ten shades of

red.

"Maybe I need a little more incentive?"

Holy shit! Did you really just say that?

"Then maybe I should just take you out on Saturday," he countered smoothly. "How's that for incentive?"

For a couple of seconds, time stopped. It was all I could do to keep my mouth from hanging open.

"I... I work on Saturday."

Stupid! Stupid! Stupid!

"Do you work at night?"

I swallowed hard. "No..."

"Then I'll take you out then. Unless you—"

"No no," I jumped in. "I, uh... I mean Saturday night is good."

Donovan set his hands on hips as I let out a relieved breath. I couldn't believe how close I'd come to screwing things up.

"Then it's settled. Dinner, you and me, Saturday night. We can discuss the terms of our trade, and—"

"BURKE!"

We both whirled in the direction of the voice. Behind the front desk, the gym's owner — a man I knew only as Eddie — was staring daggers at us. Or more specifically, at Donovan.

"You've got an eight O'clock who's been waiting five minutes already," the owner growled.

"Yeah, we'll she's ten minutes early," Donovan shot

back.

Eddie's return scowl told me everything I needed to know next. Donovan's shoulders didn't slump an inch. He remained defiant in the face of the big, red-headed man. They stared at each other for a long moment, neither one of them willing to look away.

"It's okay," I said, pulling Donovan's attention back to me. "Go. Do your thing."

"You're my thing," he said. "At least until I'm done with you."

I smiled sweetly. "Well, are you done with me?"

"For now," he grinned back.

My stomach felt like a butterfly zoo. I couldn't believe this was happening. Donovan! Asking me *out!* And this time there was no doubt about it. This time it was most *definitely* going to be a date...

I couldn't wait to tell Jocelyn.

"I'll text you," he said, before turning away. "But remember: Saturday night, you and me."

I nodded mechanically. Like a schoolgirl being talked to by her biggest crush.

"Okay."

"Be hungry," he ordered. "But for right now? Treadmill. Thirty minutes. And I'd better see sweat when you leave."

Damn. I was hoping he'd forgotten.

"I'll do my best," I said. "Been a few weeks though, so

I'll have to go slow."

Donovan chuckled as he walked away. "No matter how slow you go, you're still lapping everybody on the couch."

Four

HOLLY

It was one of those rare glorious days, where the weather tells the current season to fuck off. In this case the skies were a pristine, cerulean blue. Totally unblemished by clouds, they were full of sunshine and warmth and promise.

Despite full winter being only days away, the temperatures had somehow climbed into the sixty-degree range. I had my ass firmly parked on a bench in Washington Square Park. Surrounded by sprawling green grass and skeletal trees that, just a few short weeks ago, had been exploding with fiery fall color.

Little things like that had astonished me the first year I was here. Simple things the locals always took for granted, like golden leaves and thousand-foot skyscrapers. Underground tunnel systems, flinging metal tubes packed wall-to-wall with people in every conceivable direction.

I had my face buried in the most boring of all possible literature: my CPA prep-book. The NYU campus loomed over my shoulder, a constant reminder that I had no less than three big finals coming up next week.

But that was okay. It was Friday. And Friday was *my* day.

Yes, it was the day I'd chosen to take all my classes. But once the morning was gone, I had the rest of the day all to myself. Friday was when I walked the streets of Manhattan, dipping randomly into shops and coffee houses and bookstores along the way. I went to museums. Saw plays on Broadway. Did anything I wanted, really, once I got my side work done and my studies out of the way.

Even then, shopping the City was like homework for my second job anyway. It gave me ideas on clever gifts to buy. I kept current on the latest fashions, just as eyeballing the millions of colorful people teeming the streets kept me up to date on the latest trends.

Most of all I loved the freedom. Malcolm worked late on Fridays — presumably so he could golf all weekend — so while we were dating I didn't even have to be home at any particular time. School aside, Fridays were my day off from everything. Especially days like today, which I considered a rare, precious gift.

I flipped the page, trying to keep my focus on more of the mind-numbing jargon. Accounting wasn't my first choice in life. It wasn't like every little girl grew up hoping to stick a pencil in her ear and maintain spreadsheets on profit/loss statements.

No, I'd wanted to do other things of course. Accounting was what happened when I took something I was already good at and added the pressing need to pay an exorbitant rent... even in a rent-controlled building.

Right now though, I didn't want to think about any of those things. I just wanted to inhale the crisp, fresh air. Enjoy the feeling of being surrounded by grass and dirt again — if only for a little while — rather than tons of glass and rebar and concrete.

I'd been on the bench nearly an hour when I saw him looking; the cute guy on the other side of the clearing. He was leaning against a tree, eating an apple. Staring at me... but not creepily. Almost as if he were looking with a certain, permissible familiarity. Which—

"*OOOF!*"

My heart nearly leapt through my chest as the jogger fell sideways against me. He came seemingly from out of nowhere. His body bounced from the bench, his momentum barely slowing as he spun away from me with an apologetic grunt and continued to run.

"I—"

Only now he was running away with *my bag*.

"HEY!" I yelled. "HEY, STOP!"

I looked around, but I'd chosen one of the more private areas of the park. The only person nearby was my apple-eating colleague, who I noticed was already sprinting full speed in my direction.

"HE TOOK MY BAG!"

The cute guy nodded as he flew past, his dirty-blond hair flowing behind him as he sprinted in the direction of the jogger. He was moving unbelievably fast. Taking long, powerful strides with what looked like long, powerful legs.

Oh my God!

A half-eaten apple went spinning to the ground at my feet. I'd never been purse-snatched before! But of course I'd read about it. Hell, I'd seen it in a dozen movies, but none of them compared to the feeling of it actually *happening.*

I whirled, looking around helplessly. There was no one else. Only the jogger and his pursuer, who was slowly gaining on him.

What if he's armed?

The thought sent shivers through me.

What if he has a knife, or a gun, or—

"*UMMPH!*"

At the edge of the clearing, both men were now on the ground. My would-be savior had made a last-minute jump, tackling the jogger around his ankles. It looked painful, the fall. The jogger landed hands first to protect his face, skidding along the cement path with a scream of pain.

The apple-eating cute guy was crawling his way onto him.

Don't just stand there Holly! Go help him!

My legs moved on their own. I was walking at first, then running over to where the two men wrestled in the grass at the edge of the path. There was a grunt of exertion, then a cry of pain as the thief kicked my would-be hero square in the jaw. He scrambled to his feet and dove into the next wooded area, stopping only once to glance back in my direction.

I gasped as we made eye contact... and then he was gone.

Holly, move!

Impotently I realized I was frozen again. By the time I ran up to help my champion, he was already on his feet.

"A—Are you *okay?*"

The cute guy, now minus the apple, was rubbing his jaw with one hand. In the other, at the end of his outstretched arm...

"My bag!"

I took it and hugged it to my body. Then I rushed forward and hugged *him.*

"Thank you so much!" I cried. "Oh my God, you saved my *life!*"

He laughed. "Well not your *actual* life," he replied breathlessly. "But your purse at least."

"But my whole life is in here!" I shot back. "Besides, I got paid today. I just cashed my check."

He started brushing himself off, and I moved to help him. Leaves and dirt fell away as my hands rubbed his chest, his arms, his back. Every surface I touched was hard with muscle. Every bit of him was in spectacular shape.

"You really carry cash?" he grinned. "I figured everyone has direct deposit these days, and—"

Our eyes met. From this distance, I recognized him immediately.

"I *know* you!"

My hero grinned back at me. "I was hoping you'd say that."

"You're in my *class*. My psych class. My—"

"Statistics for Behavioral Sciences," he grinned. "Yeah."

"That's why you were looking at me. That's why you were staring."

He laughed out loud. It was one of the better sounds I'd heard in a long time. "Was I really staring?" I watched as his skin flushed red. "Sorry, I—"

"No no," I smiled. "Please don't be sorry. You're my hero! You saved me. Saved my *stuff*."

He nodded back to the bench, where my book lay face down on the ground. "If the thief were smart he'd have left your bag alone and grabbed one of our textbooks," he joked. "They're like a zillion dollars each anyway."

He stuck out his hand. I took it, and he squeezed me firmly but gently.

"I'm Brody by the way. Brody Valentine."

"*Valentine?*" I smiled. "That's really your last name."

He frowned immediately, but I could tell he was only pretending to be offended. "Why? What's wrong with—"

"Nothing," I said quickly. "Actually it's kinda cool."

Brody guided me off the path protectively as another pair of joggers ran by. Innocent ones, this time.

"Well," I said after an awkward pause, "you have to take something."

I began rifling through my bag, but he laid his hand over mine.

"You have to take a reward for—"

"Are you kidding me?" he said. "A reward? For what? For tackling that asshole?" He grinned boyishly. "Anyone would've done that. Although I will say you got lucky. Instead of some slow, heavyweight stranger, you got one who ran cross-country all through high school."

I chuckled. Damn, he was even cuter close up.

"And on top of that we're not strangers," he said. "We're classmates."

His sparkling green eyes were almost mesmerizing. They were an incredible emerald color, flecked with the most beautiful streaks of black.

"T—That's true," I stumbled. "But you still have to take *something* as a reward. Let me at least buy you coffee or —"

"Wanna reward me?"

I nodded quickly.

"Then go out with me tonight."

It took a good three seconds for his words to sink in. "Wait, what?"

"Let me take you out," he said simply. "Or if you want, you can take *me* out." He smirked back at me proudly, and even that was cute. "You *did* say you wanted to reward me, right?"

"Yes," I said hesitantly. "But I, uh... I don't have a car."

"Then I'll pick you up."

I felt a wave of heat. Suddenly it seemed a lot more

like ninety degrees than sixty.

"Unless you have a boyfriend, or—"

"No," I said.

"Or hate devilishly-handsome men with superhuman speed, who—"

"No," I giggled. "Nothing like that."

In one swift motion he pulled out his phone and unlocked it. "Text yourself," he said, handing it over. "So I'll have your number."

It all happened so fast. So boldly, yet naturally as well.

"Uh, okay."

Before I knew it I was doing what he asked, and handing his phone back to him. Surprisingly, I found that I *wanted* to! My handsome savior looked so well put-together. So roguishly hot. So charming and sexy, and—

"And your name?" he grinned, looking down at his phone.

"Oh, sorry. That might help, right?" I extended my hand nervously. "I'm Holly."

My classmate leaned in and wrapped his strong arms around me instead. He gave me the biggest, most satisfying hug.

"Text me your address, Holly," he smiled, before walking away. He left the scent of leather and a delicious hint of cologne in his wake. "I'm picking you up at seven."

Five

BRODY

She looked absolutely adorable, standing on the corner in a pair of pre-ripped jeans and a tight white sweater. Not to mention her little lace-up black boots, which looked unfortunately new.

I could tell by the look of surprise on her face that she hadn't expected me this way. I figured that much as I pulled up. I hadn't really told her.

"A *motorcycle?*"

I smiled through my open visor and handed her a helmet. She was wearing her hair straight, so I didn't think it would be an issue.

"Ever been on one?"

"I'm from Texas," Holly chuckled, throwing one leg over the back with practiced ease. "What do *you* think?"

A minute later we were speeding uptown, her boots on the footpegs, her arms wrapped pleasantly around my waist.

Her coat was thankfully short, and buttoned up tight. Though it was dark, it was still unseasonably warm.

"Where are we going?" she shouted over my shoulder.

"For a ride," I called back.

It was incredible, being out on my bike this late in the year. Even so, I knew it was probably my last ride until spring. My last chance to get out before the snows came and everything iced over, and the dirt trucks spread enough sand over the roads to make them virtually unrideable.

Damn, she feels good!

I zipped up 5th Ave, feeling Holly lean tight with me on the lane changes. She definitely *had* ridden before. She was a great passenger, and one who didn't fight the turns.

Saving her in the park today had been thrilling. Not only did it give me an excuse to talk to her, but it made me a temporary hero in her eyes. The cute little brunette in my psych class was no longer just someone I saw on campus or studying in the park. She was on my *bike* now. Her legs spread, hugging tight against my body.

We skirted the Park, continuing north through Harlem. Christmas decorations flew by — colorful lights and wreaths, dangling from streetlights and doorways, all the way up Amsterdam Avenue. It was beautiful. Always was. Maybe even more so that I could enjoy it without freezing my hands off.

"I've never been up this far," Holly said, as we turned onto Broadway. She laughed musically. "Where the hell are you taking me?"

"Connecticut!"

I felt her thighs squeeze deliciously against mine. It gave her enough leverage to punch me playfully in the ribs.

"Alright, alright," I laughed. "Hang tight. We're almost there."

It was another half mile before Fort Tyron Park came into view. We parked and continued on foot, me pulling Holly along excitedly by her warm, feminine hand.

"Wow, this place is gorgeous!" she marveled. Her head moved like it was on a swivel. "I never even knew it was here."

"Not many people do," I said. "It's so far out of the way, it's almost not even in the City."

Cobblestone paths lead us deeper into the heart of the wooded preserve. The sounds of traffic and car horns seemed to fade with every step we took.

We walked the paths for a while, still holding hands. The two of us enjoying the silence, marred only by the steady sounds of our booted feet.

"Are you cold?" I asked, pulling her into me.

"No... I'm good."

I could see her blushing, even through her rosy cheeks. Our fingers were interlocked, and when I squeezed she squeezed back.

"If you get cold, just tell me," I said.

"Why, are you gonna give me your jacket?" she teased. When I didn't answer she shrugged. "Hmm, I guess chivalry isn't dead after all."

I couldn't help but chuckle. "Funny you should say 'chivalry'."

The path we were on opened up, and a long series of castle-like structures came into view. Holly's eyes went adorably wide.

"Oh wow..." she breathed. "What are—"

"These are the Cloisters," I answered. "A bunch of Gothic hallways and monasteries from Europe, dismantled in the 1930's and brought all the way here."

Her bright eyes scanned the ancient stones. They looked so foreign, so out of place, especially tucked away deep within New York City.

"C'mon," I said. "Let's go!"

For the next hour or so we wandered through all four of the open galleries, interconnected to form a square. In the center of the quadrangle was a lush garden that would undoubtedly be amazing in the summer. Right now it was still beautiful, but in a wintery way.

It was amazing to me, that such history could be taken apart and put back together half a world away. The interior was a breathtaking array of arches and pillars. Of colorful tapestries, stained-glass windows, frescoes and sculptures. Much of it had been decorated for Christmas, lending what could've been considered a cold place a warm, holiday feel.

Holly was a good sport, even when I made her stop several times to take different photos. I even took one of us — an adorable selfie, smiling cheek to cheek while I held the camera at arm's length.

Eventually we stopped at their tiny cafe, for a pair of coffees. Relaxing at our little table, I was able to really give her the once-over. Unapologetically, too.

"This place is adorable," Holly smiled. She threw me an accusatory look. "Maybe a little *too* adorable."

"Oh?"

"I can only imagine how many first dates you've brought here," she laughed. "I'll bet it charmed the pants off every one of them."

I pretended to look under the table.

"No wise-ass," she giggled. "My pants are *not* coming off."

"Not yet anyway," I confirmed. "But please let me know when they do."

She laughed again, and that was a good sign. Holly wasn't just pretty, she was sexy too. There was a smoldering sensuality about her that I really liked, hiding just beneath her witty surface. All I needed to do was break through.

"So how many?" she shot back. "Two? Four? Six? A girl's gotta know."

"Actually," I sighed, leaning back in my chair, "this is my first time here."

My cute little classmate furrowed her brow. "C'mon..."

"No, really. This is just one of the many places on my list."

Now she actually looked intrigued. "Your *list?*"

"Yeah, I have a list. It's... well, it's a little complicated."

"Try me."

Her eyes looked almost turquoise in this light. So pretty. So bright, even in the cafe's dim light.

"Alright," I said. "So I have this list of things to do and places to go, in and around New York City. Each month I choose one and force myself to visit. No matter what I'm doing, I just go."

She stared back at me over her mug. "That... actually sounds kinda cool."

"Right? It's my grandmother's idea," I admitted.

"Your grandmother?"

I nodded. "My grandparents raised me. My sister too. Our parents got divorced when we were eleven, and they both just sorta took off in different directions."

"Holy shit."

"That's what *we* said," I laughed.

There was a moment of silence, but for some reason it wasn't awkward. Holly's look was more one of admiration than pity — something I appreciated immediately.

"Anyway, the whole 'go someplace new' thing was my grandmother's idea. It was something she used to do, back when she could still get around."

"And you took it over."

"Yup. She's still sort of living vicariously through me now. That's why I bring her lots of photos of everything."

Holly was abruptly quiet. I couldn't tell if she was weirded out, or—

"Brody?"

"Yes?"

Her eyes looked glassy. "That's one of the most

adorable things anyone's ever told me."

Now it was my turn to blush. All of a sudden I was glad for the bad lighting.

"It's kind of silly, I guess. I mean—"

"No," Holly said sternly. She reached across the table and took my hand. "It's *not*."

Six

HOLLY

The ride downtown was a lot cozier, somehow way more intimate than the ride up. I snuggled against Brody's back, trusting him implicitly as we zipped through the streets. My hands were locked even lower around the warmth of his abdomen, which felt scrumptiously hard and rippled beneath my interlaced fingers.

God, he's so... cute.

Yes, he definitely was. But lots of guys were cute, and Brody went well beyond that. He was sexy too, carrying himself with a cool, casual confidence that made me feel safe and protected, even in the middle of nowhere. And the Cloisters had been a charming little oasis. The perfect place for a quiet cup of coffee with a broad-shouldered stranger, one with a bright, beautiful smile.

And he's definitely not a stranger, I reminded myself. *Not anymore...*

We'd walked halfway back to his bike when Brody had

pulled me against a lamppost. His kisses had been sensuous, so unspeakably hot, they'd practically melted me right there in his arms. It had been a long time since I felt passion like that. Far too long since I'd been held in a way that made me feel *wanted...* and not just superficially but with a desperate, pressing need.

We'd continued making out in the middle of the park for what seemed like a long time, oblivious to our surroundings. His hands wandered downward, over my back, sliding dangerously below my hips. I'd gasped into his mouth as he cupped my ass, pulling me hard against him. Brody merely responded with a smug smile, nibbling sexily on my lower lip.

Our mouths churned hotly, our tongues dueling as they rotated slowly against each other. All around us, the world stopped. The lamppost became our own private island; a glowing steel beacon in the darkness of the empty park. No one came down the path we were on — not a single, solitary person. It was the most solitude I'd had since leaving Texas, and for some reason it felt utterly magnificent.

Back on the motorcycle, we arrived at my apartment all too fast. I was left standing in front of my building, handing my helmet back to Brody as he comfortably straddled his bike.

"Wanna come up?" I asked boldly. "For a drink?"

I really didn't know who this new Holly was. But I knew I liked her a lot.

"Sure."

We were in my apartment all of two seconds before we were all over each other again. This time there was nothing stopping us — no inhibitions or worries about being walked up on by anyone else.

No, it was just us, Brody's rock-hard body pressing me hard up against the back of my door. His sweet mouth trailed kisses down my neck, as I helped him drop his leather jacket to the floor.

Oh wow. This is going to happen...

I swooned, clutching his head against me. Pulling him further downward, toward my breasts, even as his hands worked their way beneath my clothes to find warm, naked skin.

"I want you."

It was all he said. It was all I needed. Two strong hands rolled up along my ribs, and I raised my arms for him as he pulled my shirt and sweater over my head.

We couldn't get undressed fast enough. Clothes flew everywhere, and my eyes went wide as his incredible chest came into view. It was full and strong and hairless... and so unlike Malcolm. His shoulders were broad, tapering down to two big arms that were corded with muscle.

His face was in my chest now, buried in the perfumed valley between my breasts. I felt the welcome relief of my bra being unclasped, and then the warmth of his hands smoothing over them, my nipples stiffening in his two open palms.

"I... It's..."

He nuzzled me, dragging his lips upward. His mouth closed over my areola, and I felt the slow swirl of his tongue.

"It's been a while since..."

Brody responded by cupping me from behind. He pulled me tightly against him, our bodies molding into each other so perfectly it was like we were made for each other.

"It's okay," he murmured into my breast. An electric shiver ran through me as his palm slid downward along the flat of my stomach. Instinctively I was on my tiptoes, gasping, as his fingers pierced the waistband of my thong...

"We'll go *slow*," Brody grinned.

My mind was spinning, but my body was responding feverishly to his every touch. In a flash of clarity I realized I *needed* him, and not just his body against mine. I needed him *inside* me. Spreading my legs wide. Filling me up the way I loved and craved, the way I hadn't been filled in ages, not since before my ex-boyfriend's lame attempts at satisfying me.

I took his zipper down, and slipped my hand through his boxers. My fingers closed over his manhood, all warm and thick and heavy. The heft and weight of it was thrilling, even before it began coming alive in my palm...

Our eyes met, and Brody smiled mischievously.

"OH!"

In a whirl of speed and motion he lifted me over a massive shoulder. With one hand clamped tightly over my ass, his fingers slid deliciously through my thigh gap as he walked me across my living room.

"Bedroom," he said simply.

I was already wetter than I'd been in my entire life.

"Door on the left," I grunted.

It was slightly ajar as he kicked it open, carrying me over the threshold and into semi-darkness. Only a dim swath of moonlight filtered in through a single window. It bathed everything in a blue-hued, spectral glow as Brody tossed me onto my own bed.

Oh my God...

He stood at the edge for a moment, staring down at me like some hard-won prize. Then he dropped to his knees, rolled my panties down my thighs...

... and lowered his beautiful mouth into my warm, wet sex.

Seven

HOLLY

Brody's fingers traced lightly along the insides of my thighs, stroking the soft, sensitive skin as he devoured me. His tongue was warm and wet, his lips full and pliant and perfectly manipulative.

Oh fuck I've missed this...

It had been a long time since a guy had gone down on me. Malcolm had done it a few times in the beginning, but mostly to impress me and not with any real goal in mind.

But not Brody. He *definitely* had a goal.

Holy... holy shit...

I was staring up at the ceiling, eyes crossed, my breathing rapid.. Down between my legs, my handsome classmate dragged his tongue slowly, sensually over my outer folds. He stopped now and then to dip the tip inside, to taste and tease me. Eventually I moaned, unable to take it any longer as I rolled my fingers into his hair.

Ohhhhhhhh...

Without realizing it I was pulling him deeper, enjoying the feel of smashing him hard against me. Brody held fast as I shifted my hips in and up-and-down motion, practically washing his face with my sex.

Holly!

I was totally selfish, and wholly unlike me. And yet... that wasn't true either. It was unlike me with *Malcolm*. Somehow over the past two years I'd lost track of what I liked and disliked, what was good and what was magnificent and what I really enjoyed and wanted from a lover.

"Mmmmmm..."

The vibration of his lips moaning against me was amazing. Brody was driving his tongue now, his nose brushing my clit in the most delicious way that caused me to stiffen and quiver around him. And then I felt it; the slow rise of an impending orgasm, stirring somewhere in my belly. Somewhere in that special place *beneath* my belly, deep down at my very core.

Oh my God...

I jumped as he spread me wider... then penetrated me with one thick finger. The relief was sweet, palpable. He was *inside* me, if only a small part of him, yet my ass felt like it was practically melting into the bed.

"Brody..."

I breathed his name, tasting it on my tongue. I opened my eyes — not even realizing I'd squinted them shut — to stare down the flat of my belly... and just watch.

Look at him. He's so fucking sexy! So beautiful...

Brody's eyes fluttered open, two stunning green orbs locking with mine. I felt a flush of embarrassment, though I didn't know why. It all disappeared in a gasp however, as he winked at me and added a second finger...

"Ohhh!"

I was writhing now, churning downward against his hand. His fingers were buried deep, his tongue fluttering over my clit. My body was hot, my skin on fire. I could feel my orgasm rushing out of me, beyond the point of being possible to passing the threshold of inevitability.

"Oh God, oh God, oh... oh... *FUCKKKK...*"

A third finger joined the party, and suddenly I was coming — no, gushing — all over Brody's lovely face. I screwed down into him, crying out as the euphoria crashed over me in waves, one after the other. Each was somehow better than the last, delivering me to all new levels of screaming satisfaction.

I was left heaving and spent, tears of pure joy streaming down both sides of my face. My naked ass was still being supported by Brody's two strong hands. Only now he was kissing me gently, his lips planting a series of soft kisses along the insides of my warm, wet thighs.

"Seems like you needed that," he grinned, sliding up alongside me. I could only nod as he lowered his mouth over mine. He kissed me hotly, and I could taste myself on him. Somehow it made me even hotter, causing me to whimper, breathlessly, into his mouth.

"My turn."

I expected him to spread my legs. To just push between

them and sink himself deep, all the way to the hilt, burying himself in my sopping wet pussy. Instead, I found Brody rolling sideways, onto his back. He lifted me by the waist with two strong hands, pulling me onto him, and I helped him by throwing slick thigh over his body.

It was just like mounting his motorcycle... only a thousand times better.

"*Ahhhhhhhh...*"

His cock was hard and thick as he guided it to my entrance, pausing only to drag the bulbous head through my molten furrow. A moment later I was sinking down on it. Our eyes met again, burning the moment into our brains as I took him completely. Sheathing him all the way to the balls in my swollen, satiated center.

Oh my God Holly, you're fucking him.

The realization was obvious, but no less real for me. I was two weeks out of a two year relationship. Screwing some total stranger, at the end of a first date.

No, not a total stranger.

Brody arms flexed as he lifted me up and down on his cock, reawakening places deep inside of me. His hands felt like magic on my hips.

And not just any first date, either.

No, it had been the mother of all first dates. The kind of romantic date you only saw in those Matthew McConaughey and Kate Hudson movies, or the ones with—

"Damn Holly, you feel *amazing...*"

I smiled down at my new lover, splaying the fingers of

both hands out across his hard chest. I tested an old trick, squeezing my innermost muscles tightly around him. When his eyes flared, I rolled my palms over his nipples and winked.

"Fuck..."

I wanted to make it good for him. As good as he'd made it for me, and then some. For the first time in a long while, I wanted to *impress*. Not just bring the guy off, as I did with Malcolm, but *really* make things special.

I leaned down, pressing my breasts against Brody's warm flesh. My long hair cascaded over us, tickling his chest and shoulders as I lowered my face until our lips were barely brushing.

"Where do you want it?" I breathed huskily.

Brody responded by leaning up to kiss me, but I pulled back. His look of complete surprise caused me to smirk proudly.

"W—What?"

"Your come," I whispered, putting a dirty emphasis on the second word. I stared down sultrily, looking him square in the eyes. "Where do you want to *put* it?"

His hands squeezed, Brody's fingers digging into the flesh of my hips. It felt so good, so masculine. So unlike Malcolm it was actually scary.

"In me?" I continued teasing him. "On me?"

I took one strong hand, and he gave it to me. Bringing it to my face, I sucked one long finger into my mouth.

"You can put it anywhere you know," I whispered, leaning even further so that my lips were against his ear. "I'm on the pill..."

Oh my God, Holly!

It was insane, what I was doing. Totally crazy, to be speaking and talking like this! And yet somehow the words flowed. Somehow the dirty talk had always been there, just beneath the surface. Hidden away by a tedious sex life and a mundane ex-boyfriend and—

But Holly! You don't even—

I knew what the voice in my head was trying to say. That I didn't know this guy. That I should be taking precautions, that I should be careful, that I was a lunatic for just letting him inside me like this. And yet...

And yet I *trusted* him. The same things that endeared Brody to me were the same things I'd seen all night: a guy who took dozens of wonderful photos for the benefit of his sick grandmother. Who even stopped at the gift shop, to bring her home a trinket to mark the memory.

They were the very same things that somehow made him... safe.

"You can come *inside* me," I murmured, rolling my hips to take him deeper. I opened my mouth, showing him how I could slide his finger along the flat of my tongue. "Or you could come right here if you wanted. Right here in my mouth, where it's *so* hot..." I closed my lips and sucked hard. "So hot, and so very, very wet..."

It happened in an instant. An abrupt, unexpected shift of weight and muscle preceded Brody's hands clamping down on the tops of my thighs. He pulled me downward, so hard it nearly hurt, and then suddenly his jaw clenched and he was coming inside me.

"*Ohhhhh...*"

Seeing his eyes glaze over to stare at nothing was the most satisfying thing in the world.

"FUCK YESSSSS..."

His cock jumped and pulsed, delivering jet after jet of white-hot sperm into my willing womb. It was like being impaled and filled all at once. Pounded deep, but with the warmest, wonderful feeling of fullness and contentment.

Brody held me against him throughout his orgasm, while I gently kissed his face, his neck, his mouth. His eyes had been long ago screwed shut, but I still got a distinct sense of the euphoria swirling around his endorphin-addled brain.

"Jesus Holly..."

He came to, as if waking from unconsciousness, his hands and arms and body once again stirring with life. Brody fucked me slowly through the rest of his orgasm, holding me tightly and kissing me deeply while his come ran out around the base of his shaft.

"*Now* who's the one who apparently needed something?" I laughed into his mouth.

My lover blinked dreamily and smiled. "Touché."

Eight

HOLLY

I woke sometime later in the darkness, to a warm mouth closing over one stiff nipple. I was already soaking wet. Still leaking from what we'd done, and still excited beyond words with the thrill of having been taken by my handsome new lover.

I had no clue what time it was, and for once I didn't care. Brody nudged my thighs apart and I spread for him willingly, taking him balls deep in a single glorious stroke. He was hard again somehow, or maybe he'd been hard the whole time just pressing against me. Either way the sensation was incredible, being pinned into my bed beneath the weight of his hard, muscular frame.

We screwed slowly this time, kissing groggily beneath the comforting warmth of my winter blankets. I clutched Brody tightly as he glided in and out of me, relishing in the feel of my body as it was overcome with a deep, radiating comfort. It was an odd mixture of satisfaction and serenity I hadn't felt with anyone else, and definitely never with

Malcolm.

God, he fits so perfectly, too.

He did, really. Putting aside how well he filled the void between my legs, it was like our bodies were the front and back halves of the same, sexy mold.

After what seemed like an eternity of soft, lingering kisses, Brody rolled me over and buried himself inside me from behind. I remember rocking back and forth on my stomach, screwing my ass back against him. Moaning softly into my pillow while gripping the sheets, as the tingles of another incredible orgasm rolled my eyes back into my head.

By the time dawn's light filtered in through my window I was still warm but alone. I'd been tucked in at my sides and feet. Wrapped snugly in a cocoon of blankets and fond memories, all happy and sleepy and secure.

Did I dream all that?

I knew the answer of course, even before I saw the little pewter figurine jutting up from my nightstand. It was an armored knight, standing proudly over his sword. The same figurine we'd laughed about in the gift shop last night, while Brody was buying a memento — an enameled unicorn pin — for his grandmother.

I yawned and propped myself up on one elbow. The knight stood on a piece of paper that had been taken from my desk, guarding a handwritten note in black, masculine cursive:

Morning princess!

> If the knight seems a little cliche, too bad.
> Think of him as me, riding in to rescue
> you from a boring sex life
> (you're welcome by the way).
>
> Sorry for the stealth-exit. Would've woken
> you, but you looked way too cute sleeping.
> Off to slay dragons.
>
> - B

I couldn't help but laugh out loud. Saving *my* sex life? Sure, maybe that part was true. But if I remembered last night correctly, my sexy classmate seemed to have an equal amount of fun.

I rolled out of bed, my body screaming in protest. For

a moment I debated climbing back beneath the covers. Delaying the inevitable shower just long enough to—

Oh shit! WORK!

My heart-rate doubled as I scrambled into the bathroom, spinning the hot water spigot. How could I forget it was Saturday! I had to be at the office!

Brody. That's how.

My mind spun wildly with thoughts of last night; our perfect date, the quiet museum, our cozy talk in the little cafe. The comfort of hugging my body against his on the motorcycle. The thrill of kissing so wantonly in the park...

All of it was so fresh, so new for me. So much fun that it had completely taken the place in my brain occupied by work, or school, or my ex-boyfriend...

I arrived at the office a half-hour late, which all things considered wasn't that bad. The good part about Saturdays was the place was mostly empty. On weekdays, it was filled with leering bosses and frenzied deadlines. People walking like zombies, stumbling their way through the cubicle hedge-maze wearing an alternating combination of long faces or plastic smiles.

No, the office wasn't my favorite place to be, and it was certainly not the reason I came to New York. Even as I took the CPA courses the company paid for, I saw it for the long con it really was. It was a trap that crushed dreams. A place of good intentions, mediocre aspirations, and really bad coffee.

I now liked Saturdays because I wouldn't have to worry about running into Malcolm, either. It was my day to catch up on work, and then slack off if I wanted to. Only in this case, because of finals, I had too much to do. Too much work I'd set already aside during my pity parties.

But last night...

Last night was an extremely pleasant distraction. I replayed it again and again, savoring it for the shiny new experience it was. It made the day go fast, and by the time five-thirty rolled around it felt like I'd cheated the gods of work. I could go home now. Kick back and relax. Maybe take a hot bath, or pick up the book I was reading, or think of something clever to text Brody, or—

DING.

Grinning broadly, I grabbed for my phone. The little red '1' next to my text message icon was like an unopened gift. An exciting little mystery that I could I solve just by pressing the—

Oh my God...

Still need your address, hon.

Unless you want me to guess.

I stared at the message for a moment. It made absolutely no sense, until I realized who it was from.

Donovan!

Holy shit!

A cold realization stole over me. In the wake of Brody, I'd completely forgotten about my date with my personal trainer. A date I'd been looking *very* forward to, at least until...

How could you just forget something like this?

I didn't know. It made no sense! Getting asked out by my personal trainer had been like a dream. And yet somehow...

I glanced over at the clock. There was still time to get home, get cleaned up, get changed. Get ready to go out, all over again.

But Brody...

Yeah, so what? What about him?

It didn't seem right, did it? Going out after last night. After what happened between—

You made this date before Brody even asked you out, the little voice in my head reminded me. *And you* can *go out on two dates in a weekend, Holly. You are single after all.*

Damn, that was true also. I couldn't really argue. Even so...

Oh, stop over-analyzing everything. Just go out and have fun.

I thought about it as I gathered my things. It was date, that's all. A date I already had.

Maybe the thing with Donovan is nothing. Or maybe it's just another great date. Shit, we both know you could use the practice. Enjoy it.

I laughed at the fact that I was arguing with myself. And I couldn't *believe* I had to talk myself into going out with someone as amazingly hot as Donovan.

Grabbing my phone, I hammered out a quick response. I gave Donovan my address, and told him I looked forward to seeing him tonight.

There you go.

I hurried on my way to the bank of elevators, taking long strides through the empty halls. For some reason the butterflies were all back in my stomach.

Yeah, I thought to myself. *There I go.*

Nine

HOLLY

"A *cooking* class?"

Donovan smiled as he slipped his hand into mine. It was big and warm. His palms were calloused, from hour after hour of daily weightlifting.

God he looked good. Casual but cool, in dark jeans that accentuated his amazing bubble-shaped ass and a button down shirt with the sleeves rolled up to mid-forearm.

"I— I thought you said dinner?" I asked again.

"We're *eating* dinner," he smiled. "We've just gotta cook it first."

He examined me, and his smile faded amidst my confusion.

"Did you not want to do this" he asked genuinely. "Because we could just as easily—"

"No, no," I smiled back. "It's not like that at all! I just, well, I wasn't sure what to expect. I've never been to a cooking class."

He smiled as he led me into the room. A dozen or so other couples were standing together at various cooking stations. Colorful bowls of ingredients lines the counter-tops in the well-lit cooking area.

"What are we making?" I asked, suddenly excited.

"Cajun, I think," he replied. "The class sounded good when I signed us up: 'Date Night in the French Quarter'."

Spicy food, I thought to myself. That might be good, actually. But I couldn't let him know that.

"So you basically invited me out to cook dinner for you," I teased. "Is that it?"

"Yup."

"Well... shit."

"Hey," Donovan protested. He put up his hands. "I'm cooking for you too. So it's not *all* bad news."

The instructor walked in — a middle-aged woman with short blonde hair — and things quickly started up. She went over the cooking process, the ingredients, and how we'd prepare the meal and eat it in stages. The whole thing seemed like it could be a lot of fun, if not for the fact I was utterly *starving*.

Either way, I was determined to make the best of it. We started off with the first course: a chicken and andouille sausage gumbo. The blend of meats and spices simmered for a tantalizingly long time before we could actually taste it, at which point I nearly took off Donovan's hand at the fingers.

"I should've taken you out to dinner first," he laughed, dropping the fork. "Before I took you to dinner."

"Sorry," I apologized. "I missed breakfast, and my lunch literally dropped out of a vending machine."

"Ugh."

'Yeah, totally."

As it turned out, cooking together was a lot more romantic than I ever thought it could be. Not surprisingly, I was enjoying myself immensely. Especially with Donovan standing behind me, laying his hand over mine, helping me chop and mince things. We were flirting like mad. Feeding each other random ingredients, and generally goofing off... much to the dismay of the instructor, Jenny.

"You're going to burn your grits," Jenny warned. "If you're not—"

"Can you actually *burn* grits?" someone asked from the other cooking station.

Half the class laughed, while the other went on stirring. Eventually we were left with two steaming plates of creamy white grits, topped with plump, tender shrimp. Donovan shook his head in disbelief as I handed him a clean fork.

"You've never had grits before, have you?"

"No ma'am," he admitted.

"They taste like whatever you put on them," I explained. "Sort of like pasta."

"Is that your genuine Texan opinion?"

"That's just plain old fact," I replied.

We fed each other some more, like the bride and groom at a wedding. And although Jenny wasn't all that amused, our behavior did elicit a few nods and smiles. It was obvious to just about everyone that we were on a first date.

"Dessert," Jenny exclaimed, "is dangerous. So we need to treat it seriously."

Donovan burst out laughing. His laughter triggered mine, and soon we were clutching each other... like two high school kids in the back of a class, about to get in trouble.

"You're gonna get us *detention!*" I warned. "Cut it out!"

"No, *you* cut it out," Donovan smirked. Pulling his fork back, he flicked grits on me.

Jenny gave us the death stare. The one that said "*seriously?*" without her having to say anything at all, and so we eventually calmed down.

Humorously enough dessert actually *was* dangerous: New Orleans' style Bananas Foster prepared with two types of flaming liqueur. Ours was a controlled burn though, and it turned out the real culprit was the couple on the other side of the room. As they sent flames a good five feet into the air, Jenny abandoned all interest in us and rushed over.

A shiver ran down one side of my body as Donovan leaned in, taking my hand in his. He helped me dribble the melted, caramelized mixture into the serving dish, where is sizzled and bubbled and created a frothy white cream.

"Are you really gonna eat this?" I asked incredulously. "I mean, butter, brown sugar, vanilla ice cream... the whole thing must be about a zillion calories."

Donovan lifted the first spoonful of melty, sugary goodness to his mouth. "It's my cheat day," he explained.

"For six days I'm meticulous about everything I put into my body, down to the last calorie. But on Saturdays?" he shrugged. "I'd eat a whole box of donuts if I wanted to."

While eating a whole box of donuts didn't sound too appealing, I had to admire his discipline. I guess it was easier to starve yourself all week when there was a really bright light at the end of the tunnel.

"What about you?" Donovan asked. He swung a fresh spoon of deliciousness my way. "Are you going to eat this in front of your personal trainer?" He smirked and raised an eyebrow. "Knowing that he's going to *ask* you if you were good when you come to your workout on Monday?"

I locked eyes with him. A thousand thoughts passed between us, wordlessly, as I parted my lips and accepted his offering.

"It better be worth it," Donovan sighed, still holding my gaze.

"Oh it *is*," I smirked back, not sure we were talking about Bananas Foster anymore. The distraction of his handsome face, sexy stubble and all, prevented me from fully enjoying the decadent dessert.

But as long as he held me with those crystal blue eyes, I didn't care.

As the cooking class drew to a close, I was a little bit sad. I'd had so much fun with him in the casual yet intimate environment. We'd seemed to click so easily, so *naturally*, I didn't want our time to end.

"Where do you wanna spend the remainder of your cheat day?" I asked, leaving the question open-ended.

Donovan took my hand and led me down a narrow staircase, into the bustling City streets. "I'll show you."

The anomaly of yesterday was over, and it was much colder now. For a brief, fleeting instant I thought of Brody... of his motorcycle, and how warm and powerful it felt vibrating between my legs.

Then I glanced back at Donovan and pushed those thoughts away.

We walked for several blocks, holding hands, laughing and flirting and enjoying more conversation. Donovan was like a different person now. Gone was his stern expression, the unforgiving demeanor I always saw at the gym. He was happy now. Smiling constantly, and listening attentively to everything I had to say.

"You're a lot more friendly," I finally chuckled. "While we're out on a... you know..."

"A date?"

"Yeah," I smiled. "That."

"Maybe I'm just trying to impress you," he said. "Would you rather I give you the scowl?"

I looked up and there it was — the face of utter seriousness. The drill-sergeant expression that always came whenever I missed a set, or phoned in a rep, or showed up after a canceled appointment.

He squeezed my hand and he was smiling again. "This is my natural look," he grinned. "I save the scowl for when I need it."

"Well I like this Donovan a lot better," I said,

squeezing back. "In fact—"

My sentence died as he pulled me in and planted his lips against mine.

Ten

HOLLY

I melted into him willingly, my body going to putty in his big, strong arms.

Oh God...

The kiss was intense! Hot and passionate and so, so amazing. Every nerve ending in my body tingled as I reached up to slide my arms over his shoulders. I was left standing on my toes, kissing him back, my tongue exploring his sweet mouth as my nostrils flared with the most incredible scent of aftershave or cologne...

Everything disappeared. The City, the streets, the people walking along the sidewalks — nothing else mattered but the feeling of Donovan's arms around my body and his lips against mine. The kiss could've gone on for ten seconds or ten years, I really couldn't say. All I knew was that by the time it was over, I was left woozy and jelly-legged.

"I've been wanting to do that," he said, "for a very long time."

I tried to swallow but couldn't get past the lump in my throat.

"W—Why *didn't* you?"

"Partly because of Eddie," he said, still holding me close. "Ever since I started working at Crunch Time, he's been watching me like a hawk. But also partly because of... well, other things."

We were face to face, pelvis to pelvis. The idea that the only thing separating us below the waist were a couple of layers of clothing was wholly distracting.

"What other things?" I asked breathlessly.

"I'll tell you about it sometime," smiled Donovan. "Not tonight though."

We walked some more, our body language much more intimate now. I was leaning into my sexy trainer. Locking arms with him as well as holding his hand.

Is this really a good idea?

The voice I'd identified as 'cautious Holly' nagged in the back of my mind. She whispered about the potential pitfalls of dating my personal trainer. Of how I was already avoiding Malcolm at the workplace... and how if things went south in this case, I'd be avoiding someone at the gym as well.

Donovan slid one corded arm around my waist. It felt so good, so *right*, I promptly told cautious Holly to fuck off.

Eventually we were wandering through Soho, into a part of the lower City I didn't really know. Everything was decked out for the holidays. I saw reds and greens and golds — twinkling Christmas lights, strung out along beautiful railings.

Garland draped over window sills and doorways.

"We're here," said Donovan.

I looked up, and we were standing beneath a pretty orange awning. Through the windows before us I could see a beautiful array of cookies, cakes, pastries, and quaint little tables filled with excited, chattering people.

"Sant Ambroeus?" I read aloud.

"Ever been here?"

"No."

Donovan laughed. "You're in for it."

Apparently my date had planned the whole night, because he actually had a reservation. After taking the place in for ten minutes, through our nostrils as well as with our eyes, we were seated at cozy table and given menus. Not long after that, we were drinking the richest, most amazing coffee... paired with shots of sweet liqueur in dark chocolate shot glasses.

"Boy, when you cheat you *really* cheat," I observed.

"Yeah, I guess so."

Our waiter arrived again, bringing a large mug of steaming hot liquid to the table. Donovan pushed it my way with a not-so-secret smile.

"Try that."

I shrugged and brought it carefully to my lips. The deep brown liquid smelled absolutely delicious as I tipped it back.

Holy shit...

It tasted even better.

"Is this..."

"Yup."

I laughed as I set the beverage down, licking a thick brown mustache from my upper lip. "It's a mug of pure, melted chocolate, isn't it?"

"The most decadent thing on the menu," Donovan affirmed.

I stared back at him, losing myself in how good-looking he really was. His face was as amazing as his body; strong and masculine, with angular features. His black hair was streaked with brown, perfectly offset by his stunning blue eyes. Even his sexy jawline had just the right amount of stubble.

I took a second sip of the melted chocolate, rolling my eyes as it flowed easily down my throat. With two painted fingernails I pushed it back his way.

"You know my personal trainer is going to kick your ass, right?"

Donovan laughed. "He sounds like a dick."

"He *is* a dick," I shot back. "In the gym, anyway. Outside the gym he's really sweet and thoughtful. And he makes great first date plans, to boot."

"First date huh?" He shifted closer from across the table. "Does that infer there's going to be a *second* date?"

"If you keep feeding me stuff like this?" I pointed down at the mug, "I can't see what would possible stop it."

Our faces were drawing close again, and memories of our kiss came flooding back. I could feel the blood rushing to my cheeks.

"Maybe I'll just keep feeding you so you show up for your sessions," said Donovan.

"With stuff like this?" I countered. "You're gonna need to up my workouts."

Donovan's nose brushed mine. I wanted his lips — wanted to taste them again — but there were just too many people, too much around.

"*I'll* work you out," he purred seductively. The way he phrased it left very little to the imagination. "All you have to do is say the word."

The waiter dropped our check on the table without asking. He'd asked three times already, but we'd just been having too much fun.

"Word," I said, without even blinking.

Eleven

DONOVAN

The cab ride to my apartment was a steaming hot mess. A frenzied tangle of arms and legs — and of mouths and tongues — as we made out frantically in the short, six-minute trip.

Once inside I slammed the door behind us, divorcing us from the millions of people below. It was finally just she and I. Me and the beautiful brunette I'd been training off and on for the better part of the last year, waiting and hoping and praying for her to be single.

The best part was she didn't even know it.

Holly kissed me hotly, her lips traveling down my neck as she pulled clumsily at the buttons of my shirt. I wanted to help her. Wanted to get undressed as quickly as possible so I could help *her* get undressed, but something in the back of my mind told me to savor the moment.

Slow. Down.

I had to slow down. *Willed* myself to slow down. It

was just too exciting — too overwhelmingly amazing — to finally have arrived at this point. To not only have Holly here, in my shitty little apartment, but to have landed this beautiful woman after one of the greatest dates of my life.

"God, you smell incredible," she mumbled into my neck.

I reached down with both hands, cupping her ass. Finally getting my hand on those tender globes of firm, unyielding flesh I'd watched and ogled and fantasized about for so long. How many times had I put her on leg curls? Laying her flat on her belly just so I could watch her ass?

Too many to count, I chuckled to myself. And although it seemed almost inappropriate at the time, I'd always been careful when I stole my glances. Throughout every single workout, I'd always been the consummate gentleman.

But now...

Now I had that ass *in my hands*. That very ass I'd molded and shaped and firmed through my own strict regiment of training. From that perspective, I was merely reaping my own rewards. And when you looked at it that way...

"Oh *wow!*"

Holly finally had my shirt off. Her palm smoothed down on its own, sliding over my abdominals, feeling the firm, washboard ridges I'd worked so hard and dieted so stringently to earn and maintain. A second hand joined the first, and then she was sinking... kneeling to the floor before me. Rubbing her warm cheek against my belly before planting a line of soft, slow kisses across my lower stomach.

All guilt flew out the window as my head lolled back.

It seemed Holly was having just as much fun with my body as I was with hers.

"I— I've always wanted this..." she admitted humbly.

I glanced down just as she looked up. Another understanding passed between us.

"I've always wanted *you*," I said. "I... I just never thought..."

I let my voice trail off as Holly's fingers fumbled with my fly. She undid the button. Took down the zipper...

And the entire time, her eyes never left mine.

Awww, fuck yes.

My cute little date looked like a goddess on her knees. A beautiful, long-haired vixen batting her eyelashes at me while her mouth curled into a sexy smile.

Should you really be doing this?

Holly pulled down hard on my boxers, freeing my cock. It swung her way, looking magnificent against the side of her face.

Eddie would kill you.

Yes, but Eddie wasn't here. And Eddie would kill me just for taking her out, or even looking her way. It was all hypocritical of course: Eddie would date just about anyone at the gym, and had tried on several occasions. If he could see me right now, he'd only hate me more than he already does.

Oh... oh man...

Blinking dreamily, Holly turned her full attention to my rapidly swelling manhood. It jumped electrically as she wrapped one little hand around the base. Her lips parted and her mouth went wide.

My eyes screwed shut as she took me in.

Oh fuck...

It was like reaching nirvana. Holly's mouth was a warm, wet heaven, especially with her hand working me from the base. I reveled in the sensations for a good half minute. Just concentrated on the exquisite feel of her lips dragging tightly up and down the full length of my smooth erection.

Then I opened my eyes and looked down... to find her staring up at me.

Damn.

There was an instant connection between us — one that superseded our sex act. It was an understanding, a mutual respect. An intimacy that came with knowing each other for an entire year before doing this, even though we'd never gone out until tonight.

My hands dropped to her head, sifting through soft layers of fragrant hair. I guided her up and down on my cock, enjoying how beautiful she was. How perfect she looked on her knees, blowing me, her blue-green eyes filled with abject lust. It felt unbelievable. Like a long-awaited dream, finally realized.

But it was her body I wanted most.

"Get up here."

Holly sucked me tip to base two or three more times in defiance, pumping me with her fist like she wanted to bring me off. If I'd let her go on, she would've. It would've been easy to just let go, right in her sweet little mouth.

"*OH!*"

She gasped as I lifted her, and abruptly spun her around. The bed was too far. The couch would have to do. I stripped her in seconds, sliding my hands around her waist and then yanking her clothes down, the same way she'd done to me.

Then she was bending over the arm of the couch... half obediently, half because my hand was pushing down on her back.

"*Ohhhhhhh...*"

Her pussy was soaking wet. It drenched my palm as I rubbed it up and down, coating my hand and making my fingers nice and slick. I slipped two of them inside her, carefully probing her depths. I pushed them in firmly and deliberately, smiling in satisfaction as Holly shoved back against my hand.

"You need to be fucked."

I saw her hair move as she nodded, her face obscured against the smooth leather seat cushion. The height was perfect. My cock was jutting straight out from my body, harder and more throbbing than I'd ever been in my life...

"OH *FUCK!*"

She wiggled her ass as I rubbed it along her entrance, getting it all slick and wet with her juices. Then I pushed the head inside. Holly's legs quivered, her whole body shaking with pleasure.

"*Yessssss...*"

She felt like warm butter as I sank into her.

An image flashed to mind of our Bananas foster, all that hot butter, melting in the pan. Holly feeding me slowly, sensually. Smiling as she licked caramelized sugar off tips of her fingers...

"*Fuck fuck fuck fuck...*"

She was grunting the word breathlessly as I sank into her. Inch by inch I slid in, stretching her around me, my cock bigger and thicker than I ever remembered. I kept pushing until the softness of her ass was pressed tightly against my abdomen, my hands having gone to her hips mechanically. And then I was finally there: *buried* inside her. Buried so deep, so wonderfully, achingly deep, that the whole rest of the world just melted away.

"Holy fucking *shit*, Holly..."

She giggled, and her cute little laughter caused her body to bounce around me. I felt like I could come at any moment. As if all she had to do was *squeeze...* and everything would be irrevocably lost.

"Are you going to fuck me?" she asked innocently. Her hair had parted a little, and I could see one turquoise eye.

"In a minute, yeah," I smirked back. "I just... you're just so..."

She arched an eyebrow.

"Wow..." I breathed.

Twelve

HOLLY

It took another half-minute before Donovan moved again. I spent that time studying his expression, enjoying the dream-like look of ecstasy on his face as he held my ass against his perfect, washboard stomach. We were lovers now. He was *inside* me! And through the many fantasies, all the times I'd thought about doing this with him, I never could've imagined it would start with a one-stroke timeout.

I guess I should be flattered.

Donovan's hands flexed as he regained control. His fingers dug in, dimpling the supple flesh as his hands slid down to my ass. Then he began fucking me, for real this time, and I felt a wave of goosebumps spread over my entire body.

Ohhhhh...

Two strokes turned into three, then three dozen. We were screwing, now. Actually doing it. Our relationship up until this point had been friendly but professional. But now... now there was no going back.

Thank God!

I wanted to bury my face in the couch. Just squint my eyes shut and enjoy the raw feel of being so filled by him. Instead, I kept glancing back over my shoulder. I needed the visual — needed to see every ripple of his flawless stomach, every quiver and flex of muscle as he continued pounding himself into me, again and again.

"Fuck!"

Cursing wasn't something I did often. In my conservative Texan upbringing, I'd always been chastised for it. But right here, right now, anything went. I was thousands of miles from home, surrounded by millions of people... screaming anything I fucking wanted while being drilled by the most perfect specimen of a man I'd ever allowed inside me.

God... just look at him!

His body was beyond amazing with his shirt off. Even more incredible as it moved behind me, pumping me like a machine. I could only imagine the discipline it took for him to maintain such a physique. And here I was, benefiting from all his hard work. Stretching my arms high overhead on the couch so I could shove back against him, taking every last inch of him inside my body.

"Oh my God..."

My trainer's hands slid up my body. They'd touched me before of course, but never like *this*. He pushed up my bra, exposing my nipples. Two firm hands closed over my swaying breasts as he continued laying into me...

Donovan's gaze traveled everywhere, like he was taking some kind of inventory of his own. Probably taking mental pictures, for his own gratification. Either that, I laughed to myself, or he was locating problem areas that he'd have me work on, when I saw him again on Monday...

Monday...

It occurred to me that we'd crossed a line. That nothing could be the same between us after this.

"Mmmmm..."

I realized, as he rolled me over, that I didn't care. That everything that came afterward could be handled afterward... and that right now, all that mattered was fucking him *good.*

I found myself sitting on the arm of the couch, facing my new lover as he guided himself back inside me. My legs spread wide for him. Our lips came together so fast our teeth clicked, and we laughed into each other's mouths.

"To the bed?"

"Yes please," I grinned.

Donovan lifted me up, staying inside me the whole time. I wrapped my legs around him, locking my hands behind his neck as he carried me into his bedroom.

From there, things got *crazy.*

The initial lack of control my love experienced when he first entered me was totally gone now. As if to prove it, Donovan spread me open on his queen-sized mattress and began hammering me with long, deep strokes of his magnificent cock.

Holy shit....

He pushed my legs high overhead, stretching me to the limits of my flexibility. His assault was merciless, his erection a steel piston driving in and out of me as I cried his name and clutched his incredible arms and rolled my eyes back into my head.

There was no pause on his end, no stopping to even catch his breath. In no time at all I was clawing his back, raking my nails down the hard muscles along his two ribbed flanks as I was gripped in the throes of a powerful orgasm.

"*Unnggghhh...*"

And that was just the beginning.

Donovan dropped back onto the bed, pulling me on top of him once again without breaking our union. I rode him hard, grinding my ass on the downstroke, rolling my hips which were now firmly being grasped by his two strong hands. He felt almost unbearable at this angle. So thick and full and impossibly deep inside me, it skirted the border between pleasure and pain.

Ohhhhhh...

It didn't take long to get off this way, and this time my orgasm was an explosion from within. I felt that familiar surge rise up inside me. That welcome series of contractions as wave after wave of pleasure crashed over my brain.

My breathing was rapid now, from all the bucking and screwing and riding. Smirking down at him through my tangled cascade of hair, I couldn't believe his wasn't.

"This is... fucking... insane..."

My trainer grinned wickedly and pulled me down on top of him. Our lips met again and we kissed like true lovers, hotly and passionately, my tits pressed warmly against his hard, ripped body. I remained thankfully motionless while he continued fucking me from beneath, clenching and unclenching his ass in strong, controlled strokes that drove upward and into me like a reverse pile-driver.

I should've known...

It was funny, thinking about it that way. I'd always figured Donovan would be good in bed, but I never considered how his strict regimen of strength training and cardio might translate into him being a complete sexual dynamo.

"You tapping out?"

It was a challenge, I knew. One he'd put to me numerous times before in the weight room, but only when it came to completing my sets.

Now his words had a wholly different meaning, of course.

"Never."

I jumped up and spun around, whirling to face his legs. Shifting my body backward and downward, I dropped my mouth over Donovan's glistening cock. At the same time, I lowered my dripping sex to his wonderfully stubbled chin...

OHHHH...

His tongue went inside me, and I jumped for joy. Two hands closed over the globes of my ass, spreading me even wider so he could utterly consume me.

My heart was racing! My skin prickled all over, like it was on fire. Grateful for the breather, I swallowed my new lover all the way down to the hilt. He moaned into my pussy — more of a vibration than a sound, really — and I responded by grinding even harder into his face.

I sensed movement off to my left. I whirled, startled, and found myself staring into a full-length mirror.

Whoa...

In the reflection I could see absolutely everything: our two bodies stacked together, sixty-nining hotly. Pleasuring each other in the dim bedroom light. It was all so crazy to watch — so incredible and sensual. So wantonly hedonistic. I stared back at myself as I went down on him, watching as Donovan's cock disappeared into some brunette's wet, willing mouth.

Only that brunette was *me*.

Holy shit.

"MmmMmmmmm..."

Donovan groaned again, and I focused on bringing him off. I worked harder with my hand, moving my mouth in a tight circle as I took him again and again, deep into my throat.

I knew he was close when he stopped tonguing me. He lay back on his pillow, still working me with his fingertips but only half-heartedly. He was distracted now. I had him.

"Fuck, Holly..."

The final surge came with little warning; my lover's ass lifted from the bed and suddenly he was shooting off, straight into my mouth. I squeezed his balls when he came — a little trick I'd learned in a magazine — and simultaneously pushed with my thumb on the area of skin and muscle just below that. The added pressure against his perineum had him crying out loud, exploding ever harder and more forcefully, filling my mouth with thick jets of his hot, sticky come.

That little trick I'd learned from a particularly dirty ex-boyfriend.

"Oh *FUUUCK!*"

I couldn't contain it all, and it was foolish to try. I swallowed the bulk of it, allowing the rest of his seed to spill from the sides of my mouth. They ran down my lover's cock, over his balls, disappearing into the soft, jersey-knit sheets beneath his magnificent ass. I watched it go, then looked up into the mirror to stare back at myself... my lips all plump and sticky, my expression satisfied.

Donovan's head lolled back and forth on his pillow as I climbed off of him. He was still moaning, still lost in the final throes of his climactic release.

"What the fuck..."

I laughed and slid up next to him. I felt perfectly at home in the crook of one big arm.

"You like?"

"*Like?*" He blinked at me several times. "What in the world *was* that?"

"That's for me to know..." I teased, kissing the curve of his beautiful chest. "And you to enjoy..."

Thirteen

HOLLY

This time around it was I who performed the stealth-exit. I was the one who woke before the crack of dawn, gathering my things to silently slip from Donovan's apartment.

He'd promised me breakfast. In the fashion of a true gentleman, he'd promised me a ride home as well. Still, as temping as it was to stick around for an inevitable *third* round of love-making, I wanted to be home, stretching out in my own shower. Letting the heated water run over me, maybe even cleansing me of last night's sins.

Yeah... right.

Besides, I wanted to get going while the going was good. And it was Sunday. I had things to do. Lists to fulfill. Clients, whose shopping needs had to be satisfied...

Oh shit! Lincoln!

The thought didn't hit me until I was halfway home, checking the text messages on my phone. One had been from Brody, and my stomach tightened as I read it. It was short.

Sweet. Flirtatious. It made me fell insanely guilty at what I'd done with Donovan, as if somehow I'd "cheated" on the cute classmate who took me out on Friday night.

The next *four* messages were from Jocelyn, asking how my date went. Three of them demanded updates, politely at first, and then with an increasing sense of annoyed urgency. In the fourth one she flat out scolded me for being a terrible friend, ending it by blowing me a kiss and calling me a 'hussy.'

I smiled at that, but my smile quickly faded as I realized who the next message was from. I pressed the button, and read the early morning text from Lincoln:

Still on for tomorrow?
Pick you up at noon if that's good.

Noon was actually perfect. It gave me time for a good rally: two cups of coffee and a scalding hot shower. I texted him back, apologizing for the delay and letting him know I'd be out in front of my building. Ready to be picked up... for the third time in three days.

When it rains it pours, right?

To say it had been a crazy weekend would be an understatement. And yet I was, about to go shopping with Lincoln Wallace. The man I'd been excited about seeing in the first place, before Donovan had even asked me out and before Brody had rescued me in the park.

Just treat it like a date...

Jocelyn's words were still tattooed on my brain. Did I

really *want* another date? Lincoln was heartbreakingly good looking. Incredibly successful. The CEO of his own marketing firm, and wonderfully single.

I thought about these things in the shower, and while I got dressed. I found myself putting on a cute outfit. A black skirt and knee-high boots, with a white cashmere sweater I'd treated myself to during one of last year's after-holiday sales.

That said, maybe shopping was just shopping. And lunch was just lunch. Maybe I was reading too much into a client who barely had time for anything other than work, one who'd hired me to remember two dozen birthdays and anniversaries. Not to mention mother's day, father's day, and now Christmas shopping, gift-wrapping, and—

"Holly!"

The sleek black Lexus was parked on the corner, as close to my building as the holiday traffic would allow. The City was nuts this time of year. Just a few weeks before Christmas, everyone was doing what we were about to.

"Hi Lincoln!"

I made my way across the sidewalk, through the swirl of light snow flurries that had popped up overnight. It was amazing, how fast the weather could change here. How it could be so unseasonably beautiful one day, and then freezing cold the next.

My client greeted me with a warm hug, ushering me into the back of the beautiful, four-door sedan. The doors closed. The noise of the City disappeared instantly, like someone had flipped a switch.

"Temperature good?" he asked, shaking out his coat.

"Perfect," I smiled. It really was. Between the soft leather seats the warm flow of invisible air, it was bordering on the most comfortable ride I'd ever been in.

"Thanks for doing this by the way," Lincoln said. "I realize you're probably mega-busy this time of year, especially on the weekend."

If only you knew... the little voice in my head chuckled.

"Nonsense," I grinned. "I *always* have time for my favorite client."

Lincoln smirked. "I'll bet you say that to *all* the boys."

"Maybe."

"Yes, well it's appreciated," said Lincoln. "And I'm sorry I couldn't pick you up earlier. I'd planned on the morning, but something came up at the office and—"

"Lincoln it's *okay*," I smiled pleasantly. "This is better actually. I had, uh... a busy morning."

I looked down, and realized I'd laid my hand over his. It was pretty forward of me. Or rather, it was forward of *old* Holly. Maybe not the new one.

"Well you have me all day," he said with a wink. "All night too, if you need it."

I studied his expression, looking for the slightest hint of suggestion. Did his smile turn into a smirk? Just a little bit maybe, at the very corner of his mouth?

Leaving my hand where it was, I took stock of him. Lincoln always knew how to dress, and today was no exception. He was business casual, and like me, decked out in black and white. Sharp, pleated slacks. Beautiful, Italian leather shoes. A white button-down shirt with a tab collar that screamed for a tie, only he wasn't wearing a tie. Probably to break some kind of business-dictated mold. He was always a little bit of a rebel like that.

The car pulled away from the curb, smoothly entering the City traffic. I almost hadn't noticed the driver in the front seat, separated by a small partition.

"So, I wanted to give you some ideas this year," said Lincoln. Reaching into his coat pocket, he pulled out a folded, printed list. "You did amazing last year of course," he said quickly, "but my nieces and nephews are getting old enough to have specific interests now."

I took the list from him and scanned it quickly. "So Brandon's off dinosaurs?"

Lincoln smiled. It was the kind of smile that lit up his face, and made him even more handsome, if possible.

"He loves superheroes now," he said. "He's been stealing his brother's. And Laura loves science all of a sudden, which is awesome. I dropped off some of those chemistry and biology sets, but my sister threw out the grasshopper and frog before Laura could dissect them, and—"

I giggled, picturing the whole thing. "Wanna drive your sister crazy? Maybe we'll get her an ant farm. One of those really good light-up ones, with the gel."

My favorite client laughed, and his laugh was even better than his smile. "That's *perfect!*"

"Or an easy-bake oven. Imagine your sister's face when she's forced to eat burnt cookies and sloppily-iced cakes the size of a silver dollar."

Lincoln looked at me and raised an eyebrow. "You're diabolical, you know that?"

"Oh yeah."

My hand was still on his. I hadn't moved it, and he hadn't moved either. The realization struck me that I was enjoying the warm, masculine feel of it beneath my palm...

Uh oh.

I glanced excitedly out through my tinted window. The city sped by in silence, looking beautiful in the tiny flakes of swirling snow.

"So where are we going?" Lincoln asked.

"Where *aren't* we going," I grinned back.

Fourteen

HOLLY

The whole ordeal was beautiful and breathtaking, exhausting and chaotic. All great things as far as shopping trips went, or at least they were in my book.

Lincoln was a trooper throughout. He kept pace with me as we sawed through the crowds, holding bags and pushing carts and never once uttering a single word of complaint. Money was never an object with him, and he paid handsomely for everything. Especially when it came to his nieces and nephews, where he was generous to a fault.

It was adorable, how much he loved them. He was constantly treating them as his own children, giving them the Christmas he always remembered. Or maybe, I realized as the day wore on, the Christmas he always wished he'd had.

We paid for delivery where possible, sending everything to his uptown office. Where it wasn't possible, we carried them out. Hour by hour, the car was filled with bags and boxes. Gifts wrapped in colorful red and green paper, presents topped with shimmering gold ribbon.

We started at the Shops at Columbus Circle, the two of us wandering the beautiful, glass-enclosed mall with a child-like sense of wonder. From there we dove into the sea of people jamming the Manhattan Mall, laughing that we were somehow able to come out the other side unscathed.

The City was alive with shoppers, with tourists, with all manner of people buzzing excitedly through its glowing streets. Between each stop we caught our breath in the back of the car, red-faced and rosy-cheeked. Our heads leaned close together as we examined Lincoln's list, checking off family and friends one by one like we were on some top-secret, highly-expensive scavenger hunt.

We hit the gleaming white cathedrals of the Westfield World Trade Center, then shot uptown to Macy's to ogle the magic of their Christmas window display. We crossed off a few more names here as well, but for the most part I just wanted to witness the amazing show they put on each year.

"Nothing like this in Texas, huh?" Lincoln asked, after we'd fought our way to the front of the crowd.

"Not in my town no," I said. "But I've been known to shoot up to San Antonio or even Houston for the holiday. They do some good stuff there. But of course..." I held my hands up toward the sky. "No snow."

Lincoln's brown eyes shimmered with the reflection of a thousand twinkling lights. He looked awestruck staring through the picture window, and for a second I could see the excited little boy he must've been on Christmas mornings.

"Overwhelmed yet?" I asked.

"No," he said quickly. "Maybe. Okay, a little."

"That's because you're never out this much," I chided him. "Every time I talk to you you're always working. Always in your office."

He shrugged. "Someone's gotta pay the bills."

I bumped him playfully with my hip. "And with *these* bills we've been racking up today?" I teased. "You're not getting out of that office again until *next* year."

Five minutes later we were back in the car, warming up again. Our driver — Ulrich — smiled over his shoulder before whisking us off to one last destination.

"You don't *sound* like you're from Texas, you know," Lincoln said. "Very little use of the word *Y'all*, which I understand is a staple."

I nodded. "I dropped that pretty fast when I first came up here. Also popular is the plural, *Y'alls*. And the ever-important plural possessive, *All Y'alls'.*"

"Holy shit."

"Yeah," I laughed. "It can get complicated."

I glanced up, and Lincoln was grinning back at me through his perfectly-manicured goatee. In all the fun, we'd both gotten a little messy. He had an adorable cowlick going on, and without thinking I reached up and smoothed it back for him.

The gesture was small, but intimate. Maybe because we were looking at each other. Also maybe, because we'd inexplicably found ourselves holding hands throughout most of the day.

"Why'd you leave Texas anyway?" he asked. "You never

told me."

I shrugged with one shoulder. "You never asked."

"I'm asking now."

I opened my mouth, hesitated, then stopped. When I closed it again, Lincoln was staring back at me curiously.

I let out a long, resigned sigh.

"What?"

"I'd tell you," I said sheepishly. "But I'm afraid it would sound too stupid."

He stroked his chin for a moment before snapping his fingers. "Sex in the City?"

I laughed so hard I ended up squeezing his hand. I didn't let go, however.

"No. Great guess, though."

"Hmmm..." he said. "So what then?"

"Promise you won't laugh?"

Lincoln grinned wickedly. "Can't do that."

"Fine. Just promise you won't hold it against me."

He nodded and held up his free hand. "Scouts honor."

I eyed him shrewdly. "Were you a scout?"

"No," he admitted. "But I'm told they have honor."

"Fine then," I sighed again. "There's this really cheesy rom-com."

Lincoln rolled his eyes over-dramatically.

"And it takes place here, in the City. And... I don't know. It got me thinking about where I was. And where I *could* be. And Manhattan was so damned *beautiful* in the movie, so totally unlike—"

"We're here," announced Ulrich over his shoulder.

Lincoln glanced out the window and did a double take. "The heart of the *diamond* district?"

I poked him in the ribs before pulling him out the door.

"Trust me," I chuckled. "Your mother will thank you."

Fifteen

HOLLY

The IGT Jewelry Shopping mall was a glass-framed masterpiece centered in the middle of West 47th street. I'd only been there once before, and the sprawling, multi-level showcase of shops and vendors had overwhelmed even *me*.

"Earrings," I said, dragging Lincoln along.

"*Earrings?*"

I nodded. "In every photo you've ever shown me, your mother is wearing the same dated pair of earrings. She needs new ones. *Diamond* ones."

"But how do I know which—"

"You leave that to me," I said. I glanced back and delivered my most reassuring smile. "I'm your personal shopper, remember?"

"Oh, I remember."

"Then it's settled."

We took our time here, examining a variety of different

options. Hoops, studs, hinged clasps... I had it narrowed down to a few choices in under an hour. I showed Lincoln how to haggle too, despite his embarrassment and protests. How pulling ourselves intentionally away from vendors caused them to suddenly lower their prices as we left, trying to entice us with an on-the-spot sale.

Ultimately we emerged dizzy but victorious, with the absolute perfect pair of earrings in all of New York City. By now though, it was getting dark. Our feet hurt, our energy was running low, and for once in my life, I was actually shopped-out.

"Dinner," Lincoln said, matter-of-factly. "Me and you."

I nodded mechanically.

"Got a preference?"

"Anywhere they serve food," I breathed.

My hunky new shopping-buddy murmured something into his driver's ear. The blond man in the front seat nodded, made a quick phone call, and the car sped off again. Though I'd been in and out of the vehicle all afternoon, I still couldn't help marveling at how smooth the ride was.

Wish I still had my car...

For the first time all day, my thoughts strayed back to my dick of an ex-boyfriend. I wondered absently what Malcolm had done with my car. Probably turned the lease in early, if I knew him. He'd never use it, and there's was no way in hell he'd pay for garage space.

I glanced around jealously. My car was nothing like *this,* but I loved it just the same. Silently I hoped Malcolm had to pay some kind of a termination penalty.

"Holly, I wanted to say thanks again," Lincoln said, leaning back. He actually undid the top button of his shirt. "You're a champion."

I was pressed against him now, hip to hip, leg to leg. Partly because of all the presents jammed in the back seat with us. Partly because it was what I wanted.

"So what are we having?" I sighed dreamily. "Italian? Chinese?" The mention of each made my mouth water. I would've eaten anything at this point.

"Well on our *next* date," Lincoln said slyly, "I plan on taking you to a *real* restaurant."

Next date...

The phrase ended all speculation in my head. So we *were* on a date. Of sorts, anyway. And apparently, at least as far as he was concerned, there was going to be another.

"*Next* date huh?" I chided him. "Real restaurant?"

He nodded amicably.

"But for now?" I asked, my stomach growling on cue.

The luxury sedan rolled to a flawless stop. I turned my head to one side and there it was.

"Oh shit!" I laughed. "You're *kidding,* right?"

"Good guess?"

The strange windowed doors and little black awning looked exactly as they did in the movie! A thrill surged through me.

"YES!" I screamed. "Yes, amazing guess!"

Lincoln folded his arms in triumph. "Thought so."

The line streaming out of *Serendipity 3* was a few dozen people long. It stretched out into the street and down the sidewalk a good long ways. At this rate, we wouldn't be eating for another two to three hours. The idea caused my stomach to rumble again.

"C'mon," said Lincoln. He jumped out, skirted the back of the car, and arrived in time to open the door for me.

"But the line—"

"Screw the line," my date smirked. "We already have a table waiting."

Sixteen

HOLLY

Lincoln spoke briefly with the maître d' before pulling me into the restaurant, where I gasped at the eclectic mix of odd yet beautiful furnishings that seemed to explode from everywhere. Dozens of Tiffany glass lamps hung from the ceiling. Ornate vases sat on Corinthian pedestals. Mirrors of all shapes and sizes lay scattered across the walls: round mirrors, funhouse mirrors — all of them adorned for the holiday with twinkling Christmas lights. The whole thing reeked of insanity, like something out of *Alice in Wonderland.* Yet even the chaos was just as cozy, just as romantic, as it was in the movie.

We were led past crowds of laughing, merry people sitting at round tables until finally I knew where we were. When the hostess pointed downward at our two empty seats, I was too stunned for words.

"The Star Table," the slender man announced proudly. He laid down two comically oversized menus. "Enjoy!"

Lincoln held my chair out for me, but I wasn't sitting

down. I was still standing there, hands over my mouth, taking the whole thing in.

"This... this is..."

"The table they sat at in the movie," Lincoln smiled. "Yes."

I glanced down at the little round table set against a tiny, unlit fireplace. The positioning was the same. The chairs were same. It was unreal.

"H—How did you—"

"I do work for the owner," Lincoln explained. "Three different campaigns so far — other restaurants, not this one. I've also played racquetball with him on certain weekends." He sighed. "Not for a while though. Too busy."

A patron bumped into my date from behind, jostling him. He was still holding my chair out.

"Oh! Sorry!"

I slid into the same seat Kate Beckinsale sat in. Lincoln slid into John Cusack's. The movie was my favorite of all time, and yes, I'd come here before to see the place from the outside. But there had always been a line. I'd never even tried to get inside.

"This is unreal," I breathed. "Like living out a fantasy, or..."

"Or a romantic movie!" Lincoln laughed, handing me a menu. "Congratulations. You're starring in your own rom-com."

I beamed at him as I took the giant piece of laminated plastic. "You're starring in it too, you know."

"Oh, I know."

As far as food went, the restaurant was limited. It was more of a coffeehouse and dessert shop, really. Luckily we were hungry enough that it didn't matter. It wasn't long before we were diving into hot soup and blue corn nachos, greedily devouring everything down to the porcelain white plates. I glanced up at Lincoln and laughed.

"You have a little bit of... on the corner of your..." I reached out and wiped the edge of his goatee. "There you go."

He grinned back and caught my hand in his. It was warm and strong. Our eyes met, and for a moment he held my fingers against his face.

"Thanks."

It was a long moment, and full of meaning. Somewhere under the table, I felt my stomach do a sexy backflip.

"I can't believe you're eating New England clam chowder here in Manhattan," I teased.

"Why?"

"I dunno. It seems sacrilegious."

I was distracting myself. Trying to break the tension. But Lincoln's eyes held me prisoner, even as he shrugged one big shoulder.

"I'm originally from Maine," he said with a smirk. "Besides, our chowder's way better."

Our entrees arrived: shepherd's pie and some kind of barbecued chicken. We split everything, spoons and forks rising and diving, until virtually nothing remained.

"So how in the world did you guess the movie?" I asked finally.

"*Serendipity?* It's a New York classic."

"I wouldn't think you'd be a romance fan."

"I'm a John Cusack fan," Lincoln acknowledged. "*Better off Dead. Con Air...*"

"*Say Anything*," I smiled.

"That one too."

"I would've thought you were more of a Kate Beckinsale fan."

Lincoln's grin spread even wider. He let out a low whistle. "Who isn't?"

I kicked him under the table. Not hard, just enough to be flirtatious. I no longer felt the least bit tired. I felt alive, in fact. Charged with energy.

"Ah," Lincoln said as our waiter approached. "Here we go."

Two very large, very familiar mugs were set in front of us. They were topped with a mountain of whipped cream and chocolate shavings... just like in the movie.

"The infamous *Serendipity 3* frozen hot chocolate," I sighed happily. "We're never going to finish these, you know."

"Speak for yourself," said Lincoln, leaning in the direction of his straw.

It turned out Lincoln's sweet tooth was significantly longer than mine. While he finished his dessert, I barely made a dent in mine. The way I'd been eating all weekend, I'd have to go the gym twice a day next week.

The gym...

I fought hard to keep my mind from wandering, but then my date's phone buzzed. Lincoln excused himself and checked the screen. His face went blank.

"Uhhh..."

"What is it?"

He looked troubled all of a sudden. There were lines his forehead that weren't there a moment ago.

"Do you mind if we stop by my office before I take you back? There's something I need to get."

"No," I said. "Of course not."

His smile returned as he called for the check. "Have I told you you're a champion?"

"Not in the last hour or so," I laughed. "But go ahead. I'm all ears."

Seventeen

LINCOLN

She looked amazing wandering my office, spinning in every direction to admire the open-glass view. In turn, my eyes wandered her legs. They crawled up from her sexy black boots to where her skirt bounced merrily around the backs of her thighs.

"This is incredible!"

The folders spread out across my desk weren't the right ones. Or maybe they were, and I was just too distracted.

"This is all yours?" asked Holly. "The entire floor?"

"We shared it with another firm for a while," I said. "But yes. It's ours since last year, when we expanded."

The place really *was* impressive. Twenty-fifth floor, southern-facing exposure. Floor to ceiling windows on most of the walls, bringing in blue skies and sunlight for most of the year. And I was proud of the expansion. Proud at having taken on so many new clients in such a short amount of time.

I sighed as I reached the last folder. With the perks of having this many clients came the perils of being this disorganized.

"I can't believe you started this place from scratch," said Holly. "This is amazing, Lincoln. It really is."

I smiled at her from behind my big mahogany desk. The entire office was illuminated solely by computer screens and nighttime lighting. It only made the City lights look that much more spectacular.

Holly strode through the door and into my office, crossing one sexy leg in front of the other. I glanced up once more, totally lost in how pretty she was. What the hell was I looking for, anyway?

"Can I help you find anything?"

"I– Uhh..." I blinked a few times to focus. "I need last month's financial records," I said. "I have the income and cash flow statements, and part of the financial position. But I'm missing something."

"The statement of changes in equity?" Holly asked.

I blinked at her in disbelief. "Yes, actually. That's the one. How in the world did you—"

"I work in accounting," she smiled. "Remember?"

Actually I did remember, it just slipped my mind. There was a lot I already knew about my beautiful personal shopper. And a lot more I *wanted* to know.

"It's probably up there," I said, pointing to a high cabinet. "Should be in a folder, I just forgot what color."

Without missing a beat, Holly dragged one of my guest

chairs away from my desk. She slipped out of her boots, leapt up, and began thumbing through the files.

"Let me see..."

The chair had wheels on it. I cringed and ran over, to make sure she didn't fall.

"Looks like purple," Holly said. "Which month did you need?"

"October and November."

She pushed up onto her tiptoes. The chair shifted.

"Hold me for a sec."

My hands went automatically to her waist, and she felt wonderful beneath my fingertips. Her legs looked fantastic like this, especially her calves.

"Ah, here we are. Hang on..."

She stretched higher, and suddenly I found myself hoping she'd fall. I'd catch her, and sweep her into my arms. Then we'd kiss... hotly, passionately. It would be romantic, like something out of a movie.

"Is this it?" she asked, stepping down from the chair. "I think—"

I swept her into my arms and kissed her anyway.

Holly stiffened against me for a split-second, but it was only out of sheer surprise. A moment later she was kissing me back. Sighing softly as her arms slid over my shoulders, the rest of her body going limp in my arms.

Her lips were sweet and magnificent — and every bit the experience I'd imagined they would be. Holly's soft tongue probed mine as our passion grew, our mouths rolling hotly and hungrily as if we'd waited all night for this.

We had of course, only for me it had been much longer than that. I'd had my eye on Holly since she took over the job. I'd been crushed to learn she had a boyfriend, and recently elated to find out they'd finally broken up. She was so cute, so smart and funny, I knew she'd have another boyfriend sooner rather than later.

If I was going to take action, it was now or never.

Holly cooed into my mouth as we continued kissing, my hands sliding down her waist to cup her lovely ass. She pulled me tighter against her. In the process, she dropped the records to the floor.

"Oh!"

The folders landed upside down, papers and spreadsheets sliding in every direction. She knelt immediately to gather them, but I cupped her face in my hands and stopped her.

"Fuck that."

She gasped again as I lifted her, spinning around to push her backward on my desk. Holly's ass shoved my keyboard backward. She spread her legs to bring me closer and I pushed between them. I continued kissing her madly, even as our hands began fumbling with each other's clothes.

Holy shit...

I almost couldn't believe how hot we were for each other. Though it was our first and only date, what we were about to do felt like the explosive culmination of a long, agonizing courtship.

"Lincoln..."

She murmured the word, looking up at me innocently. Staring at me with those doe-like eyes, even as her sinful fingers fumbled to unclasp my belt.

The sensations on my end were indescribable. I could feel heat, passion, lust. An intense thirst and longing for something I'd obviously wanted for so, so long. Holly's arms went up, and her sweater slipped over her head. She wore the sexiest black bra with criss-crossing straps. The tops of her silken breasts looked so amazing in it, I almost didn't want it off.

"Oh... *yes...*"

My zipper came down, and a slender hand made its way through the front of my boxer-briefs. Holly's fingers closed over my stiffening manhood as she drew a sharp intake of air. Probably because at the same time, I was burying my face between her luscious breasts.

"*YES...*"

It was astounding, how quickly I'd been overcome with the irresistible need to have her. I suddenly wanted her physically, mentally, emotionally — I desired her in every possible way. I was becoming drunk with the smell of her body, the sweet taste of her mouth. The warmth of her skin as my palms slid beneath her skirt, and the feel of her lips brushing against mine, gasping together as we breathed the same breath...

Her hand stroked me openly now. It moved with knowledge and practice, but also with the slightest and most adorable hesitation. I helped her pull the rest of my clothes down and shifted her towards me, at the edge of my desk.

"Do you want this?"

I had to ask. I had to be sure.

Holly chewed her lower lip. She nodded without looking away, the answer punctuated by a slight tug on my manhood.

God, yes.

I took another half step, and her thighs opened wider. My hand found the thin strip of fabric that served as her panties. I stretched it to one side, marveling at how wet it was...

Then she pulled me inside her, and my whole world was warmth and fire.

Eighteen

HOLLY

I stared open-mouthed as Lincoln slid into me, filling me with his thickness. It felt absolutely enormous, and not just in the physical way either, but in the mental and emotional sense too.

Oh my God, Holly...

Visually, I was lost in a haze. The man fucking me now was absolutely beautiful. Tall, dark and handsome, he was also successful beyond my wildest expectations. His strong, masculine face felt perfect in my hands, and his piercing brown eyes made kissing him an absolute dream.

And his body...

Lincoln's shoulders were impossibly broad, his arms firm and sinewed beneath my gripping hands. As hard as he worked on his business, I could tell he took time for himself too. And wherever he worked out, or whoever was training him, they deserved some sort of medal or award.

"MmmmMMmmmMMMmmm..."

The moans leaving my throat were low and gravelly, blending together like a purr of satisfaction. Down below, my lover's cock was thick and hard. I could feel it throbbing wildly inside me, even as he pumped it in and out of my body.

I leaned back on my elbows to watch him work me, and in the process bumped into his mouse. Lincoln smirked at me before sweeping everything on his desk back with one big arm, clearing the way to fuck me properly and without any further collisions.

"You feel... so fucking good..."

I nodded my acknowledgment, still whimpering. Still reeling from the giddy sensation of taking him so deep and long. My new lover's thrusts were slow and controlled, as if he were measuring the success of each one. He seemed almost surprised when I grabbed him by the back of his neck and pulled him to me again, kissing him hard while keeping buried inside me.

Jesus, Holly. Are you actually doing this?

I was. I was doing it, I was enjoying it, and I wasn't the least bit ashamed. In my heart, as well as within my fantasies, I'd always dreamed of enjoying him. And I knew by the way Lincoln treated his family he'd be a sweet, thoughtful, and wholly unselfish lover.

Or at least, so I'd hoped.

Maybe, the little voice in my head admitted reluctantly. *But should you really be fucking someone you work for?*

Technically, I worked for myself. Lincoln Wallace was only a client, and one of many. My biggest and most profitable client, sure. But still just a client.

That was the story I was going with, anyway.

"Oh fuck, Holly..."

A little devil on my shoulder laughed. I'd been hearing a lot of that phrase recently.

This isn't you. This isn't—

One last time I shoved away the voice of reason, or guilt, or whatever the hell it was. I wanted to *enjoy* this. Lincoln was an associate, a friend, a client. Now he was a fantastic date, and a lover as well. He'd asked me out before any of the others. I was doing nothing wrong.

"Ohhhh..."

On the contrary, judging by the lost look in his eyes? I was doing everything *right.*

We were screwing harder now, my body bouncing in rhythm with his long, deep thrusts. The desk itself didn't budge a single inch — a testament to its construction. It was heavy and well-built. Expensive.

Kind of like Lincoln, I laughed inwardly.

My lover lifted my legs over his shoulders to take me deeper. His hands went to my breasts and pulled down the top of my bra. Then he began rubbing my nipples in slow, arousing circles that made my eyes roll.

Mmmmmmmm...

I could feel the familiar ache rising up inside me. My body began making greedy adjustments, independent of my brain. I found myself rocking back against him on the longer thrusts, screwing my pussy hard against his pelvis. My hands began pulling at his arms, urging him into me.

"I need to see it," Lincoln said, his breathing growing rapid.

"See what?"

"Your ass."

His hands went to my waist, and suddenly I was sliding back to my feet. Lincoln spun me around and bent me over his desk, so quickly and commandingly I felt myself gush a little. Then he was lifting my skirt... and sinking back into me from behind.

"*FUCK.*"

It was more a grunt than a word, but I loved it. I also loved the feel of his hand on my back, pressing me downward, into his desk.

"That better?" I chuckled huskily.

Lincoln was already busy fucking me. His strong hands roamed the curve of my ass, stopping now and then to cup my cheeks and squeeze them in his warm palms.

"Much," he groaned.

I laid my face down on the smooth wooden surface, all cool against my cheek. As my body bounced, my mind wandered. I was being bent over a handsome CEO's desk, screwed deeply from behind. Pumped hard in the leather-scented shadows of some high-rise office, with only the spectral glow of LED lights and computer screens to illuminate our act.

It was dirty. Filthy, even. That this was our first date only made the whole thing even more taboo, but also, somehow more special.

Lincoln's fingers were digging into my ass now, curling downward with his rising arousal. He was close, but I was already closer. I took one of the hands I was using to brace myself and slid it between my legs, only to find his fingers already there.

"Ohhhh..."

His hand closed over mine, dwarfing it, applying pressure against my favorite three fingers. I shifted them downward, showing him where to go. Soon we were pushing and pulling together, the delicious friction against my swollen clit triggering a violent, screaming orgasm... all while he continued shoving his cock in and out of me, doggie-style.

In the end I returned to earth with my knees buckled, my body collapsed forward across the surface his desk, all spent and sated. I was a rag doll now. His own personal plaything. It turned me on to think of Lincoln using my body any way he wanted to, as long as it got him off...

He came in a rush of heat, pulling himself from my body and showering me with his hot sperm. I felt it splash warmly across my naked back: long, thick, ropes of sticky, runny seed.

Lincoln cried out during his own orgasm, his teeth clenched so tightly I thought his jaw would shatter like glass. When he was finished he wiped himself clean against my ass, smearing his come all around. I could tell the whole thing was visual for him. He wanted to *see* everything as much as experience it.

"That... that was..."

"Really fucking hot?" I suggested.

He nodded, only now he looked slightly embarrassed. "Yes."

Still bent over his desk, resting on my elbows, I laughed. "A little help please?"

"Oh... sorry."

It was cute how quickly he moved, rushing to a nearby set of drawers and emerging with a soft white T-shirt. My lover cleaned me dutifully then discarded the shirt in what looked to be a nearby hamper with a hidden lid.

"I sleep here a lot," he said by way of explanation. He nodding toward a comfortable-looking leather couch. "Too much to do, not enough hours to do it — that sort of thing."

My eyes were fully adjusted to the darkness now. I glanced around.

"You had a couch... and you fucked me on your *desk?*"

It took a second or two before he realized I was teasing. When he did, he smiled smugly.

"The desk was more memorable anyway," I winked. "Next time though..."

I let the words trail off suggestively, without finishing the sentence. Here I was, having had sex with the man on our first date... and I was already inviting myself back to screw on his couch.

Who in the hell are you?

Shit, at this point I wasn't even sure anymore.

Lincoln handed me my sweater and looked away chivalrously. It was adorable, the way he gave me time to readjust myself and smooth down my skirt.

"Next time — if you're still interested — I'll show you my bed," he said.

I considered mouthing the words 'still interested', but I didn't want to scare him. As it was, I was already scaring myself. Then I looked down.

"Oh shit."

Quickly I began scooping up the reports and placing them back in the folder. "I'm so sorry," I told him. "I have no idea what order they—"

"Me neither," he laughed. "Just leave it for now. I'll have my assistant arrange them tomorrow."

Tomorrow. Monday.

Ugh.

"You sure? I could probably figure it out. In fact, if you ever needed any help looking at this stuff…"

Lincoln raised an eyebrow. "Really?"

"Sure."

"Because I might take you up on that," he said. "I was going to do it myself because I… well, I kinda need someone impartial."

I knew what that meant. His expression confirmed it.

"You having trouble with someone here?"

"Sort of."

"The books not adding up, or—"

"Another time," he said with a sigh. "Right now? It's getting late, and I should probably get you home."

"Home..." I repeated blankly. I grinned at him. "Before I turn into a pumpkin?"

Lincoln scooped me back into his arms and kissed me.

"You're turning into *something*, that's for sure."

Nineteen

HOLLY

It was an interesting Monday. Possibly the most interesting one in Holly history.

I'd returned home the night before walking on air, dancing happily through my little apartment after a jubilant cab ride. My date with Lincoln had been the stuff of legends. He'd wined me, dined me, and all but sixty-nined me, before paying and tipping the taxi driver to get me home safe.

Once there, I charged my phone enough to turn it back on and check my text messages... and that's where things got complicated.

The first one was from Brody. Attached was the selfie he'd taken of the two of us, cheek to cheek, looking absolutely amazing together. And the message:

Princess —
My Grandmother wants to know where

> I 'found such a beautiful young woman'.
> I told her you landed in my lap. :)

Sweet, cute, adorable. Sexy, even. We'd had an amazing time together on Friday, even if by now our date seemed so very far away.

I'd scrolled through three other messages from Jocelyn, and almost even answered one. She'd have to wait, though. The second I texted her back my phone would ring, and I'd be required to answer. Girl code.

The next message was from Donovan, sent the morning after our date:

> Well... it's official: Your (ex)boyfriend
> is biggest idiot in the universe!
> See you Monday, sexy. And don't think
> for a second I'm going easy on you.

My body went flush with heat. God... I'd *loved* our time together! Especially the sex. Donovan's ridiculously-chiseled physique had gone way beyond fulfilling the simple fantasy of screwing my sexy personal trainer. Yet instead of feeling satisfied with that little notch in my bedpost, the memory of him sawing away between my legs only made me want more.

And Lincoln...

Lincoln had apparently texted me before I even arrived home. With any other guy that might've seemed a bit stalkerish. But with him it was the sweetest, most gentlemanly of gestures:

> Just so you know, it took me fifteen minutes to put my desk back together again! (It was well worth it though) Couch or bed next time for sure.
> Be ready...

Each of the messages had made me smile in equal but different ways. Confidence level soaring, I'd showered and slipped quickly into bed... still reeling from the most eventful weekend in my life — sexual or otherwise.

Monday morning found me sleepy, happy, and sore. It was a strange and delirious combo, but one that delivered me over the two bus routes and five extra blocks to arrive at my office.

Once there I took the garage entrance, not caring who I'd run into. My brain argued that it was the shortest possible route, overruling my heart so I could arrive at my desk just *that* much sooner.

I was still waiting for the elevators when my car drove by.

At first, I didn't recognize it. At least not without me in it. But then I did a double-take, just in time to see the long blonde ponytail streaming out from behind the silhouette of the driver's head.

What the fuck?

My car — my beloved little car! — raced up the ramp and disappeared into the next level. The elevator doors opened and closed without me taking a single step forward, *that's* how miffed I was to see my own vehicle speed past.

That bastard!

I stood there shaking with rage, still clenching my yellow Metro card. Then the doors opened again, and this time I punched the eighteenth floor.

Up until now I'd been riding high — filled with a giddy, welcome energy that was sailing me through the day. Right now however, my mood had been spoiled.

Malcolm...

I'd been avoiding him for too long. Making things too *easy* for him. But not now. Not after—

"Oh! Hey..."

He was staring me in the face, five steps after the elevator doors opened. The expression he wore was slack-jawed surprise.

"Holly..."

It wasn't a good look, especially on him. Malcolm looked somehow smaller than I remembered him. Paler and more uncertain, too.

"Wh—What are you—"

"Where is she?"

His eye twitched — one of his more annoying tells. It happened whenever he was trying to think up a lie, or make up an excuse. Come to think of it, all of his excuses were cataclysmically lame.

"Malcolm, what the fuck?" I demanded. "My car just drove past me in the parking garage."

He swallowed dryly. "So?"

"So I've been taking the *bus*, Malcolm! The bus and the subway! Sometimes even a cab or an Uber, when I'm running late." I put one hand on my hip. "I've been huffing it all the way here on foot each morning, and *my car is still on the fucking road?*"

His eyes narrowed — another lame tell. He pulled *this* one whenever he was about to lecture me or correct me on something.

"Technically," Malcolm said matter-of-factly, "it's not *your* car. It's a lea—"

"I know what it is!" I yelled... and then suddenly stopped. No less than ten people were staring back at us now. I knew most of them just from hanging out on Malcolm's floor. Back when we were dating, I'd come here a lot.

"What?" I sneered at Glenn. "You need something?"

Glenn shook his head silently, all at once looking very uncomfortable as he sat back down in his cubicle. I had to keep myself from bursting out laughing, it really was that comical.

"You *know* I would've paid out the lease," I explained to Malcolm... and the rest of the eighteenth floor. "You *know* I would never have screwed you on that. But I at *least* thought you took it back to turn it in. In your own strange, militant little way, I figured it would bug the shit out of you until it was back at the dealership. But now—"

I was scanning the room, going from person to person, head to head. My gaze stopped dead on a young blonde girl in a very tight pony-tail.

All the color drained from her face.

"*Her?*" I swore in utter disbelief. "*She* has my car?"

"Like I said, it's not your car," said Malcolm. He reached out for me, as if to usher me back toward the elevators. "Come with me Holly, I can explain."

"Fuck your explanation," I seethed. My eyes stared daggers at the girl in the ponytail. The only thing keeping me from charging like a bull was the fact she looked utterly terrified. There was zero challenge in her eyes. Hell, she could barely keep from looking at the floor.

"You have any *idea* how cold it gets waiting for the bus, Malcolm?"

My voice broke. Suddenly there was a lump forming in my throat.

Uh oh.

"The wind *stings,* Malcolm. No matter how much you bundle up, one cold snap and you're standing there shivering, your hands in your pockets and—"

I felt it coming on fast. The choking up with emotion, the crying, the eventual red eyes. I didn't want any of it. Especially not now, not in front of *these* people.

"You know what? Fuck it."

I pulled out my keychain and slid the little Volkswagen fob off it — the one Malcolm had given me on my birthday, along with the lease. It shined cold and silver in my hand.

"Here..."

I tossed it through the air, thinking the blonde with the ponytail would catch it. Instead she ducked. It flashed brightly beneath the fluorescents, sailing past her head, clattering loudly on the desk behind her.

God, I looked like such an asshole.

Malcolm opened his mouth to say something else, but I turned away. I was back at the elevators, choking back tears. Pressing the down button frantically, as if the more I pushed it the faster the car would arrive.

My car. He gave away my fucking car!

The glowing button went double as my eyes glassed with tears.

To a perfect stranger!

I shuddered, feeling the icy stare of a hundred judgmental eyes against my back.

To some girl...

Somehow I held it together until the doors closed behind me.

Twenty

HOLLY

I spent the rest of the morning alternating between crying over my hatchback and telling myself I really didn't care. But it wasn't the loss of my beloved car that bothered me. It wasn't even Malcolm.

It was the *betrayal* of having it given so freely to someone else.

It took less than an hour for word to spread about what I'd done. They didn't say anything, but I could see their looks. Feel their stares. Old Holly would've been utterly humiliated, to the point of curling up into a ball.

New Holly — the one who'd just confronted her ex on the eighteen floor — couldn't give a rat's ass.

"Holly, could you come see me when you get a second?"

My blood ran cold. James had already walked away, sipping his coffee, without waiting for an answer. I couldn't tell if he was angry or disappointed or any of those things.

But it was never a good thing to be called into your bosses office.

I waited five minutes, to give the illusion I'd been in the middle of something important. Then I went, slipping inside and closing the door behind me.

"Hey..."

James was behind his desk, typing away. He finished the sentence he was working on, then folded his hands in front of him before looking up at me.

"How's your day going, Holly?"

I smiled weakly. "Busy Monday. It's going okay, I guess."

He cocked his head. He wasn't buying it.

My gaze dropped. My shoulders slumped. There was no use in lying.

"Alright," I sighed. "My day sucks."

"That's more like it."

I glanced up again and James was smiling. It was a warm, genuine smile. The kind that would instantly put you ease.

"Listen, I know you've had a rough day," he said. "Why don't you take the rest of the afternoon off?"

I swallowed glumly. "Are you mad?"

"Not at all," he said. "These things happen. I get much more drama than you realize, and usually from repeat offenders. I'm not allowed to give you names," he chuckled, "but you already know them."

Oh, I knew them. It was funny to think he knew them too.

"You're one of our best people, Holly. And you *know* I'm not just saying that. If anyone deserves a break, it's you."

I felt my heart swell with gratitude. The tears threatened to come again, but this time they'd be good tears. "T—Thank you."

"No thanks needed," said James. "And between you and me? You *should've* gotten that promotion." He sighed wistfully. "I still don't know why you didn't. But I want you to know I gave the people upstairs a glowing recommendation."

My boss leaned forward and pushed a box of tissues my way. It was covered in one of those crazy-colored yarn things, probably some heartfelt craft done by one of his kids.

"I appreciate that," I said miserably. "I—I just want to..."

"Slip out of here Holly," James smiled, "while everyone's at lunch. I'm ordering you to do something happy with the rest of your day. Get some Christmas shopping done. See a movie. Have fun."

Christmas shopping...

With the exception of Lincoln, I'd been neglecting my second job. I still had so many clients to fulfill, so many people left to buy for.

"Thanks again," I grinned back through glassy eyes. "I — I could really just hug you right now."

James stood, rising to his full height of just five-foot

seven inches. He was big, round, grey-bearded. Smiling beneath his mustache, he looked like Santa Claus with his arms held out.

"If anyone needs one it's you," he grinned merrily. "Hug away."

Twenty-One

HOLLY

I spent the rest of Monday shopping... and avoiding Donovan's text messages. I'd called the front desk at *Crunch Time* to cancel my training appointment, which was pretty cowardly all things considered.

Between my whirlwind weekend and what had happened at work, I really just wanted time for myself. Shopping was twice as hard without a car. I'd had to lug everything home on the bus with me, or in the case of bigger items, arrange for them to be shipped. My better clients would probably reimburse me for the cost. But some, I knew, would question why I was suddenly charging shipping when I never had before.

And it wasn't just Donovan I was ignoring... it was Brody and Lincoln too. After responding sweetly to their initial messages, I'd gone totally cold when it came to answering subsequent texts.

"Meet me," Jocelyn's voicemail had warned sternly. "Or DIE."

It was the one part of my day that made me laugh. I'd listened to the message twice already, chuckling each time, before texting her to invite her over for dinner.

Dinner consisted of Chinese take-out. I'd always thought the #1 Best Kitchen was a hilariously redundant name, but considering how good their shrimp fried rice was, maybe not.

In the comfort of my little apartment, we unpacked everything together. Jocelyn waited until our drinks were poured, and the sleeves were off our eggrolls. I was surprised she even gave me that long.

"Alright," she said flatly. "OUT with it!"

I smiled back at her innocently from my end of the couch. "Out with *what?*"

"You know Goddamn well what I'm talking about!" she said. "Your *date* on Saturday. Your meeting with Lincoln yesterday. What the hell happened to you *today* that you somehow got out of work early. All of it."

"So you wanna know about my date, huh?" I asked.

"Hell yes."

I grinned evilly as she took the bait. "Which one?"

It took a few seconds for my words to sink in. When they finally did, Jocelyn threw a packet of duck sauce at me.

"Bitch, you'd better start talking!"

She reached for the mustard. I laughed and held up my hand defensively. "Okay, okay..." I said. "I'll start the from beginning."

"With Donovan," she said.

"With *Brody*," I shot back.

My friend's eyes went ridiculously wide. She dropped her eggroll onto her plate.

"*Brody?*" she repeated. "Who the hell is Brody?"

"The super-cute guy from my psych class who took me out Friday."

I had to admit, I was enjoying this. Usually *I* was the one living vicariously through her. It was nice to have the tables turned for once.

"*Now* do you understand why I didn't call you back?"

Jocelyn nodded like a robot, her mouth still slightly open.

"Good," I grinned, picking up my plastic fork. "Now, I'll start from the beginning..."

I told her *everything,* from the moment my bag was snatched on Friday afternoon, to the minute the cab dropped me off Sunday night. Jocelyn listened intently as I went over every date, every kiss, every dripping detail. By the time I'd finished, neither one of us had even touched our food.

"Holly..." was all she said when I finally stopped talking. "Oh my God!"

"I know."

"You went out on three dates?" she swore incredulously. "In three days?"

"I know."

"With three different guys?"

"Yes."

"And you... you slept with..."

"I *know!*"

My friend wasn't trying to make me feel guilty. If anything, the half-smile plastered across her face was one of pure admiration. Jocelyn had been trying to get me to see the anti-Malcolm light for quite some time now. She was my head cheerleader, begging me to come out of my shell.

And well... here I was.

"I've always said you should get back in the game," Jocelyn swore. "But *Holly!* You went and played three different sports at once?"

"That's a shitty analogy."

"No it's not! Look at you, you're a legend! A rock star! Donovan *and* Lincoln? And this other guy..."

"Brody."

"And you said he's cute too?"

"Beautiful," I confirmed. "A green-eyed hunk."

I punched a few buttons on my phone and brought up the photo of us together, the one taken at the Cloisters. Brody's boyishly handsome face and bright white teeth made him look like a male model.

"You're an asshole," Jocelyn swore, grabbing the phone and staring into it. "You know that?"

"Why?"

"Juggling three guys at a *time*, Holly? I can barely keep up with one!"

"I'm *not* juggling three guys..."

"Oh no?" she said. "Then give me one."

"Wha—"

"Him," she said, taking the phone. "He's *cute!* I'll take him. Brandon."

"Brody," I corrected her. "Jeez, you can't even get his name right!"

Jocelyn laughed and squirmed back into the cushions. "Fine, I'll take Donovan then. Holy shit, I can't believe you *slept* with him! Look at his body! He must've been amazing..."

He was, I thought to myself fondly. *So was I, come to think of it.*

"You don't want any of these guys anyway," I chided her. "I already had sex with them."

"So?"

"So?" I repeated. "That's like... it's... wouldn't it be weird to—"

"Not at all," she shrugged.

I shook my head. Leave it to Jocelyn to take something that would've bothered any other girlfriend in the world, and just shrug her shoulders at it.

"You're not getting *anyone,*" I said. "I'm not even getting them."

Jocelyn stared at me like I'd grown seven more heads. "Why the hell not?"

"Because I have a very big problem!" I cried. "I have to *pick* one, Jocelyn! And they're all so incredible, I have no idea which one I—"

"Wait. Why do you have to pick just one?" my friend countered.

"Because that's what people *do*."

"Not all people," she winked.

We stopped talking only because we both ran out of breath at the same time. Jocelyn spoke first, one side of her mouth curling into a wicked smile.

"So you're saying you don't know which one to choose, right?"

"No clue," I admitted helplessly.

"Then why decide now?"

I blinked in confusion. "What?"

"You could date all three," she pointed out, "for a little while at least. See which ones you like or don't like..."

"That's just... it's..."

"Hey, you already slept with them right?" Jocelyn pointed out. "So it's not like sex would be a factor. The damage is already done."

I sighed. She actually had a point, there.

"Go out with them each again. And again after that. If you find yourself attracted to one in particular, you can break it off with the other two — no hard feelings."

She made it sound so simple. So easy. Like juggling three boyfriends at once was something women did every day.

"And what if I like them all?" I found myself asking.

Jocelyn popped a wanton into her mouth and bit down. Juice flowed down her chin, into her napkin.

"Then you're screwed," she smiled, wiping her lips. "*Literally.*"

Twenty-Two

HOLLY

It took the better part of a week — several long days of avoiding and not answering. A week of running from the three most amazing guys I'd met, dated, and yes, screwed, in my entire life.

And for no real reason.

I'd stopped going to the gym altogether. I'd even skipped the review class for my psych final, to avoid seeing Brody. It was amazingly stupid, and childish too. But it seemed the longer I went without making a decision, the bigger a mess I was making of the whole thing.

Just date them all, Jocelyn's voice sang in my head. *See which one you like, already!*

I'd almost taken my friend's advice. In fact, I'd come painfully close to making dates with each of them. It would've been easy, just picking different days. At least in the beginning, while things were still casual.

In the end though, I did the only thing I could do.

The only thing that made any sense to the old Holly, or even the crazy new one:

I made the same date with *all* of them.

Standing outside the coffee shop, I was more nervous than I'd ever been in my life. One by one I saw them go in. Through the window I watched as they sat down alone, picking their own little spots, completely obvious to one another.

My stomach was doing barrel rolls the whole time. I felt like throwing up.

You could leave now, you know.

I supposed I could. None of them had even seen me yet. I could concoct an emergency. In just three little text messages, no one would be the wiser.

But as much as I wanted to...

Summoning every ounce of courage, I forced myself to walk through the door. Lincoln saw me first. He stood up with a smile, and I greeted him by taking his hand and pulling him along.

"Come with me."

I reached Brody next. His back was to me. I tapped him on the shoulder and nodded in the direction of an empty table. He followed grinning, but his grin faded as he saw Lincoln coming along too.

This is it...

My heart was thundering inside my chest! I sat them down next to each other, the both of them wholly confused. Then I held up a single finger as I left.

"Wait here. Just one sec..."

Donovan was clear on the other side of the room. It took another minute to grab him. By the time I'd gotten him back to the table, Brody and Lincoln were already discussing something. They still looked confused though.

"Brody, Lincoln, meet Donovan."

I motioned my personal trainer into a third chair. He went reluctantly, totally bewildered. But he still went.

"Donovan, this is Brody and Lincoln."

All three men sat in a circle now, sizing each other up like gunfighters. Only Brody made a half-hearted effort to shake hands. He quickly stopped himself though.

"I know this is weird," I said, taking the fourth seat. "And I know you're all here expecting to meet up with me. But please, hear me out. Let me just say everything I have to say, because God knows I've practiced it enough times."

I had their attention, all three of them. For one strange and wondrous moment, an electric thrill shot through me.

Just do it already!

One deep breath later... I did it. I told them everything, just as I had with Jocelyn, only this time I left out all the more heated details.

It was crazy, telling the story to all three of them, each one knowing a third of it already. I talked about my impromptu date with Brody. My date with Donovan. My shopping trip-turned-romance with Lincoln, too. All three of them listened intently, as if I were telling the most interesting story in the world rather than an account of my very busy weekend. I left nothing out, but I also left certain things to the imagination. I wanted to be honest, not raunchy.

By the time it was over all three of them were staring at me. From time to time, they'd stare at each other, too.

An uncomfortable silence blanketed the table. It was as if each one of them was waiting for someone else to make the first move.

"So?" I said finally, prompting them. "Now you all know the story, and you all know each other." I sighed and sank back in my chair, my shoulders slumped. "Let the fun begin."

The last part came off intentionally sardonic. Or at least I hoped it had.

"What fun?" asked Brody.

"The fun of calling me a complete asshole?" I said, totally exasperated. "I mean... look at what I did. I played with your feelings. I went out with three of you in three days."

"So?" Donovan asked.

"So nothing! I broke rules. I betrayed all three of you."

Lincoln shrugged. "Seems to me you didn't really betray anybody."

"Are you even *listening* to me?" I practically shouted. "I can't decide! I just can't make a decision, so I called you all down here to make it for me. *That's* how shitty a person I am. That's how cowardly I—"

"You could've dated us all," said Donovan. "We wouldn't have known. *That* would've been the act of a shitty person. But rather than hurt us, you brought us here to explain."

Brody and Lincoln nodded. "Hey, at least you were honest about it," my classmate said. "I mean, you could've easily—"

"But I'm being *selfish*," I tried to explain. "I'm not strong enough to reject anyone, so I'm making *you* do it."

"More like you're putting it all out in the open," Lincoln disagreed. "This is total transparency, Holly. You're laying everything bare."

I sat back in my chair, totally stunned. *Are they crazy?*

"Look," said Donovan. "You obviously brought us here with an end goal in mind. Or at least an idea of how this should go."

"Yeah," Brody jumped in. "What exactly did you expect *us* to do?"

"I— I don't know!" I practically shouted. "Get mad? Get pissed? I—I figured someone would drop out. Or walk out. And maybe someone else would back away."

The guys looked at each other and laughed. I couldn't believe it.

"Maybe I expected one of you to fight the other," I said. "Shit, I don't know. Maybe I expected to lose you all."

"Is that what you wanted?" Lincoln asked.

"No, not at all!"

"Then what?"

I was suddenly upset. I'd pictured this going a thousand different ways, but this definitely wasn't one of them.

"I—I don't know *what* the hell I wanted," I admitted. "Maybe this whole thing was a terrible idea. I just know I wanted to be honest. I never intended on hurting anyone..."

Lincoln folded his arms across his chest. "That sounds kind of admirable, actually."

My eyes went to Brody, then Donovan, then back to Lincoln. I was at a loss.

"He's right," said Brody. "This was sweet of you. It was the best case scenario really, considering how your weekend went." He winked at me and my heart melted a little. "You came clean."

Twenty-Three

HOLLY

A waitress finally arrived, asking if we needed anything. Somehow it broke the tension for me. One by one the guys took turns ordering; a surreal little circle of my suitors and lovers, all talking casually. Ordering coffees and lattes as if none of what was happening here was a very big deal.

I'd expected outrage. Anger. Jealousy. Instead, there were none of those things. I felt like the whole world had gone opposite day.

"Well I'm here to stay," said Brody, breaking the silence with a smile. "It's up to you of course, but *I* still want to date you."

The other guys looked at each other for a moment, then turned back to me.

"I want to date you too," said Donovan simply. "I'm not going anywhere."

My stomach twisted, like I was riding the first drop from the highest roller coaster.

Now what?

"Well shit," Lincoln added, "I'm not going to step aside and let these guys just *have* you." He leaned back in his chair and began stroking his goatee. "I'm all in. I want you too."

I sat there awkwardly, just staring back at them. As far as men went they were beyond beautiful. I fixated on Brody's flowing blond hair. On Lincoln's incredible shoulders. On Donovan's powerful, muscular physique...

"Well I can't date you all!" I blurted helplessly.

Another span of silence followed. Then Donovan cleared his throat.

"Why not?"

My breath caught in my chest. *What?*

"Yeah, what he said," added Brody. "Why not? There are seven days in the week. Maybe we each take a couple."

My throat was a field of dust. I could barely swallow.

"B—But..."

"Hell," Lincoln said, cracking his knuckles. "I'm so busy at the office, maybe this works out best for me anyway. I get all the fun of spoiling a girlfriend, without feeling guilty and constantly pressured about time."

I looked up, and my gaze found his. "W—What?"

"Every relationship I've ever had has ended in a battle over the clock," he admitted. "Her getting mad that I'm working late, or staying at the office, or whatever else. This way would actually be different. With the other guys taking you out, you'd never get lonely. And we'd only be seeing each other one-third of the time, so..."

"So every date would be three times as special," Donovan finished for him. The grin on his face was slowly growing wider. "I work long hours too, actually. And absence makes the heart grow fonder, right?"

"Speak for yourself," laughed Brody. "Any days you guys don't want, I'll take em'."

Lincoln and Donovan both threw sour faces his way. "Easy there, chief."

By this point I was dumbstruck. Totally speechless. I sat there like a zombie as the waitress dropped off our coffees, listening to them talk among themselves.

"Holly, you're not saying anything," Lincoln pointed out.

I shook my head slowly. "I... I don't know what to say."

"Say you'll try it," said Brody. "Obviously, we're interested in seeing you. We all want a second date, at the very least."

Donovan cradled his mug in both hands. Of course he'd ordered his coffee black, no sugar.

"You've been honest with us and we're saying we're okay with it," he said. "So sure, date all three of us. Maybe sometime down the line you make a choice. Or maybe you don't. Or maybe one of *us* does," he shrugged. "Who knows?"

Just like Jocelyn, he was making it all seem so simple. When in reality...

"What about sex?"

The question tumbled from my lips before I even had a chance to consider it. All three of my lovers glanced at each other.

"What about it?" asked Brody.

"I mean... obviously you'll get jealous if I'm sleeping with all three of you," I said. "How's that going to work?"

"You've slept with all three of us already, right?"

Another pause. I nodded, numbly.

"Then what's the difference?" asked Donovan. "If you're only dating *us*, it's not really cheating. Not if you're staying within our own little triangle."

"Quadrangle," Lincoln corrected him.

"Wait," said Brody. "Wouldn't it be a square?"

"A square *is* a quadrangle."

"Whatever."

I couldn't believe the way the conversation was going. My mind was blown.

"Anyway," Lincoln went on, "you know what we mean. None of us should be jealous of the other," he said, gazing pointedly at Brody and Donovan, "because we all sort of happened simultaneously. We all got together with you at basically the same time."

They were looking at me differently now. Staring at me the way each of them had before... on our date.

"So... you *really* won't be jealous?" I still couldn't believe it.

"Not if you're honest," said Donovan. "Besides, we'll

each be taking you out on different dates. We won't even need to talk to each other, unless we need to switch days or something."

"What happens on Monday stays on Monday," Brody joked. "What happens on Tuesday—"

"She gets it," sighed Lincoln.

It was all so surreal. In my wildest dreams, I would've never imagined the scenario they were suggesting. It didn't make any sense! And yet... it also did.

"Of course if this is too much for you we'd understand," said Donovan. "It's a little unorthodox. It might not be something you—"

"I want to try it."

My heart skipped three beats. My brain couldn't believe the sentence my mouth had just formed.

"Yeah?" Brody grinned.

"Yeah," I said. "Sure. Why not?"

"No reason why not," Donovan smiled.

"I mean, I loved my dates with all three of you," I said truthfully. "You're all so amazing. So fun and funny and romantic. And you're all so... well, you know." I blushed. "I came here reluctantly, not wanting to lose *any* of you. But I thought I might lose you all."

"And yet here we still are," quipped Brody.

I sat there in stunned silence, until someone laid a hand over mine. It was Lincoln. He looked at me reassuringly from across the table.

"You can take this at your own speed, Holly. Move as fast or slow as you want. We're not here to rush you, or make you feel any pressure."

"Good point," said Donovan. "Feel free to turn us down when you need to. Take time for yourself and all that."

"Also feel free to date me two or three nights in a row," added Brody. "These older guys might need a rest, but I'm always up for—"

Brody ducked as Donovan threw a sugar packet at him. "Older? I'm only twenty-five, you jackhole."

"Oh yeah? Well I'm twenty-one."

I sat up straight at that news. "Really? Holy shit, I'm two years older than you."

"So?"

"I... I just figured..."

"And I'm twenty-nine," added Lincoln, setting down his mug. "Which makes me the oldest, so I get first pick."

"Bullshit," laughed Brody. "I was the first date, so *I* get first dibs on which—"

"Guys, stop."

They stopped instantly, all three of them. Once again they were looking at me.

"I... I need some time to process this whole thing," I said. "So for now, give me tonight. Let me wrap my head around this, and I'll... I'll be in touch?"

Donovan and Brody nodded. Lincoln smirked. "Sounds fair."

"You'll stop ducking me at the gym though, right?" Donovan asked. "It's hard to train you when you're—"

"Yes," I interrupted with a grin. "I promise I'll be at my sessions. Effective immediately."

"Good."

"And the offer to look over my financial statements still stands?" Lincoln asked. "I have to admit, I've scoured them three times already and I don't know what the hell I'm—"

"*Definitely*," I smiled. "Bring them on our next date. I'd be happy to."

Our next date...

Holy shit.

Lincoln squeezed my hand before returning to his side of the table. All three of them were leaning back now, arms crossed, shooting sideways glances at each other. Their body language was, in a word, competitive.

"Thanks for... understanding," I said awkwardly, rising from my chair. "And again, sorry for—"

"Holly," said Donovan. "You have nothing to apologize for."

"I know, but—"

"It's alright," said Lincoln. "Really."

I managed a smile, but it seemed contrived. When I opened my mouth to say something else, Brody shushed me by placing a finger against his own lips.

"The old men are right," he grinned diabolically. "Better get the hell out of here now, before we all end up taking you out *together.*"

Twenty-Four

HOLLY

The treadmill beeped again. I felt the belt rising beneath me as it went into another incline, this time five-percent. The muscles in my ass and lower back threatened to cramp up in response.

"How's it lookin'?"

I was sweating bullets. Hot and sticky. Whatever hair wasn't bouncing around behind me in my ponytail was now plastered to the sides of my face. I used to hate him seeing me like this — in fact, I was very self-conscious of it. But over the last week and a half, Donovan had seen me a *lot* more sticky.

"Looking... like this program... might be bullshit..." I gasped.

My trainer broke into his familiar sadistic grin. "Does it hurt?"

"All over," I said. "And... I'm sweating... like a..."

Whore in church?

"Sweat is just fat crying," Donovan interjected. It was one of his more corny sayings, but I think he particularly liked this one. "Your body's going to thank you for this later."

"Yeah... if it doesn't kill me now."

I was waiting for the next statement: something about 'what doesn't kill you makes you stronger'. Instead, Donovan crossed his arms and looked up at me with a smile.

"You gonna be ready for tonight?"

The treadmill beeped again. The hill steepened.

"Not if you... tire me out... right here and now..."

His smile faded, as if suddenly realizing I had a point. Reaching out, he pressed a few buttons and the belt I was running on slowed considerably.

"Thanks..."

The treadmill went into its two-minute cool-down cycle. I reached for my towel and began mopping up.

"You can thank me later," Donovan winked. "When I pick you up for our date."

Pick me up for our...

Dating. The word had taken on a whole new meaning over the past week. My love life had gone from zero to a million miles an hour, in all the time it took to say 'three boyfriends.'

Of course, I wasn't complaining. Not even the tiniest bit. What I had worried might be strange and awkward had somehow become uncannily natural. I'd gone out with Brody, with Lincoln, with Donovan too — one by one, day by day. I'd reaped the benefits of three distinct personalities; three uncannily strong, beautiful men with their own particular interests and hobbies and dreams.

And I'd been the center of their focus each time.

I'd been taken to some of the most romantic places in the City. Wooed with flowers. Showered with attention. Any initial nervousness I'd felt was long gone, leaving me free to enjoy Brody's infectious energy, Lincoln's unfailing confidence, and my tough personal trainer's softer, sweeter side.

And the sex...

Between the sheets, not one of my lovers had missed a beat. They took me hotly, devouring me with all new passion and hunger. Each date ended with one of them pleasuring my body, as if trying to win a contest. Which I realized, after a few straight nights of getting my doors blown off, they probably were.

In all, it had been an amazing, intoxicating experience.

"So where'd you go last night?"

By the tone in his voice, I could tell it was the second time Donovan had asked the question. I stepped off the treadmill.

"Out."

"I know *that*. But where'd he take you?"

My eyes narrowed. "You sure you want to know? I thought one of our rules was that you guys didn't want to hear about details."

"Oh please," Donovan said dismissively. "That was the young gun's rule, not mine."

The young gun was Brody. Lincoln — not even thirty

— was somehow the old man. I didn't even want to tell Donovan what *his* nickname was.

"I *know* I'm sharing you," he went on, "and I'm fine with it. Last night was Lincoln's night. It's not like it was a secret, I'm just making conversation."

"Fine," I said. "We went out to a steakhouse."

"Which one?"

"Insignia."

Donovan let out a low whistle. "Wow. Nice."

"Yes," I said, fondly remembering the 8oz fillet that had, quite literally, melted in my mouth. "It was."

"I should put you back on that treadmill," he joked.

"Not a chance."

"Maybe one day I'll save up and take you someplace that fancy."

Without thinking, I reached out and placed my hand lightly on his arm. "The places you take me to are already amazing," I smiled sweetly. "You don't have to—"

"Hey BURKE!"

We whirled, and there was Eddie again. He looked redder than usual. Like he'd already been furious, way before he screamed Donovan's last name.

"I don't pay you to flirt with the members!" Eddie yelled. "I—"

"You don't pay me at *all*," Donovan shot back angrily. "I make commission based on the clients I bring into this dump! In fact, I pay *you* a percentage of—"

"One more word," Eddie broke in. His voice had gone low, but his tone was no less menacing. "Say one more word and you're out of here, clients or no clients."

His teeth were clenched. They had a yellowish hue to them. The tension in the room was palpable, even to the innocent people working out nearby.

"You could just be *nice* you know," I said carefully. "Connecting with the people you train is an important part of building relationships. Donovan's only being friendly."

Eddie laughed. "Yeah. Sure he is."

I shrugged. "He's an amazing trainer," I finished. "You're lucky to have him."

The gym owner's gaze shifted back and forth between us a few times. He waited just long enough to enforce his point before finally turning away.

"Friendly is one thing," said Eddie. "Touching is another."

He growled — actually growled — before finally stomping off.

"If I see this shit again," he said over his shoulder, "You'll be training your people in the alley outside."

Twenty-Five

DONOVAN

It was raining *buckets*. The kind of rain that made it seem like you just emerged from a pool, rather than walked from your car parked at the curb to your girlfriend's front door.

"Oh my God, get in! You're drenched!"

Holly pulled me up the stairs to her third-floor apartment, her tiny hand unreasonably strong. I lagged intentionally behind, just enough to catch a glimpse of her smooth thighs sliding beneath her bouncing skirt. Thighs that had been recently developing some very nice definition... thanks to me.

She pushed me inside and slammed the door closed, stripping me out of my coat. As an afterthought she stripped off my shirt too, then crossed to the little laundry area at the back of her kitchen to shove it into the dryer.

"This is the fastest you've ever gotten me naked," I quipped.

"Half naked," she smiled back, looking me up and down. "And are you complaining?"

"No ma'am."

She threw me a clean towel. "Then shush!"

I spent the next few minutes taking her place in, staring out through the windows and enjoying the feeling of being warm and cozy and dry. The place was clean and comfortable, plush and soft. A scented candle burned someplace — coconut, or maybe cinnamon. The lights were dim but not dark, giving the whole place a calm, snuggly feel.

"This is nice," I said, spreading my arms out as I fell into her couch. "Very homey."

"Thanks," she said from the kitchen. "Beer?"

"Yes, please."

I stretched out as she twisted the cap off two bottles and handed me one. She did it without wincing or making a face, too. It raised her stock another couple of points... and her stock was already high.

"So what movie are we seeing?"

"Whatever's not sold out," I laughed. "Sorry, I really should've bought us seats already. This is the busiest time of the year for—"

BEEEEEP.

Holly's eyes suddenly narrowed. She walked over to her intercom and pushed the button.

"Uh... hi?"

"Hey it's me!" a voice called up from the street. It was

hard to hear it over the sound of the pouring rain. "Could you unlock the door? I'm getting soaked!"

Holly glanced back at me hesitantly as we both recognized the voice.

"Brody?"

"Yeah! C'mon, I'm swimming out here!"

Quickly she buzzed him in. I rose from the couch, looking back at her quizzically.

"Did you know he was coming?"

"No, not at all."

I paused. "Was he supposed to—"

"Not until Tuesday."

We heard the sound of footfalls on the steps outside, and Holly opened the door. Brody pushed his way in, dripping water everywhere.

"Oh man!" he said, peeling off his jacket. "It's NUTS out there! Have you ever seen so much—"

He suddenly stopped cold. Holly took his jacket as his eyes locked on mine.

"What's *he* doing here?"

"I invited him."

Brody stared back at her, totally bewildered.

"I mean... it's not your date," she said quickly. "Not tonight. We're not supposed to see each other until—" She halted long enough to push him backwards, onto the welcome mat. "Stand there a second, you're dripping."

He stood where he was told, dripping away. While he did that I tilted my beer back and took a long, casual pull.

"This is *my* night, young gun," I said with half a smirk. He looked to Holly, who nodded her silent agreement. "Seems like you fucked up."

Brody returned my look with one of his own. "Not according to the text she sent me."

He slipped his phone out of a very wet pocket and pulled up a message. "Right here," he said. "You sent me a message two hours ago. *You're coming at six, right?* To which I replied: *Sure.*"

All eyes fell on Holly. She was shaking her head. "I– I sent that message to Donovan. I wanted to be sure of the time." She glanced at me. "Did you get it?"

I shook my head slowly back and forth. Brody's smile grew wider.

"Shit," Holly gasped. "Then this is on me. *I'm* the one who fucked up. I– I must've..."

"Sent the message to the wrong boyfriend?" asked Brody.

Her chin sank to her chest. "Yeah. Sorry."

Brody sighed in disappointment. He was a good-looking kid, I'd give him that. Lithe yet strong. Scrappy. He seemed to be in good shape, like he could take care of business if it came down to it.

He sort of reminded me of myself.

"Well shit, that sucks," Brody sighed, reaching for his coat. "I just figured you were inviting me over last minute. I thought I was getting an extra date."

He slipped an arm through his sleeve, dripping more water on the floor. Holly looked crushed.

"You just *got* here," she said apologetically. "Did you want to warm up a bit first? Dry off before—"

"Before I go back out into *that*," the kid laughed, pointing out the window. "What's the difference?"

"I guess there is none."

She looked utterly miserable. Like someone was sending her dog away. I realized it wasn't because she wanted to be with Brody, it was because she felt responsible for him. She was looking out for him, even though what happened had been her mistake.

"Gonna hit the bathroom first if you don't mind," he said, heading down the hall. "When it rains like this the subway men's rooms get disgusting."

He wandered away, leaving Holly staring back at me. She looked gorgeous, even with pity in her eyes. I let out a long, resigned sigh.

"Want me to tell him to stay?"

Her whole face lit up. She bit her lower lip and clapped her hands together happily.

"Fine."

I said it with such overacted disdain, such sarcastic resignation, I thought it would be funny. Instead of laughing she hugged me, pulling me tightly against her body. Bare-chested, beer in hand, it felt incredibly, immeasurably good.

"Hey young gun," I said as Brody emerged from the

bathroom. "As tempted as I am to send you back out into the rain, that's not the type of guy I am." I walked over to the fridge and pulled out another beer. "You okay with a double date?"

His whole body language changed. For a second, I thought he was going to run over and hug me.

"*Really?*"

"Relax," I told him, "it's nothing spectacular. We were going to grab a little food, maybe shoot over and see a movie..." I paused to glance outside. "Although the way this storm is going, maybe we'll just make something here and *rent* a movie."

Holly leaned in excitedly and kissed me on the cheek. "We could totally do that!"

Before I knew it she was scrambling through cabinets, diving into her fridge and freezer. Everything she pulled out looked incredibly unhealthy. I know that whatever she'd make, I probably wouldn't eat it. But I'd still make a good show of telling her it smelled delicious.

Across the little apartment, Brody grinned and removed his coat again.

"I'm in," he said cheerily. "But on one condition."

"Oh yeah? And what's that?"

"You gotta put your shirt back on."

Twenty-Six

HOLLY

It was a strange, wet, extremely fun night.

We abandoned plans to make dinner, after Donovan turned his nose up at every last one of our choices. Part of me wanted to be insulted. The other part couldn't blame him.

"Well there's a Thai-fusion place across the street," I offered. "That is, if there's anything you'll eat from there."

He pulled his mouth tight as he considered it. "Maybe some steamed shrimp. Brown rice."

"Water?" offered Brody. "An air sandwich?"

"Laugh it up," sneered Donovan, poking Brody in the chest. "In another four years, let's see what you—"

"Easy boys," I smiled. "Want me to pull up a menu on my phone, or..."

After a short debate, we decided to go down there. The rain was *crazy*, but it was a fun dash across the flooded streets. We pulled hoods over our heads as we splashed our way to the opposite side, Brody stepping up to his ankle in a pothole filled with freezing water.

The lights of the City were even brighter in the rain. They shined and reflected back from every rain-slick surface, making the inside of the Thai-fusion restaurant look as bright as a hospital operating room.

We stood in line, trying not to slip on the watery, dirt-smeared floor. After ordering, I pulled my dates into the bar next door for a couple of drinks to celebrate the weekend.

Like the restaurant, it was absolutely packed. Donovan muscled his way to the bar, parting the chattering throngs of holiday shoppers like a modern version of Moses. He came back with three beers and three shots of something that tasted like cough syrup but felt warm and smooth going down our throats. It was so good, Brody went back for another round.

We stayed for the better part of an hour, just laughing and talking and working on our appetites. By the time we picked up our food and splashed our way back home, all three of us were having a wonderful time.

"Think the city will ever fill up?" Brody asked, staring back out my window. "Look at all these people!"

Donovan stood next to him, his arms braced on the sill. He glanced down and nodded. "It's worse every year."

"I dunno... I like it."

They turned to stare at me. I could only shrug.

"Texas is big," I said, "but the people are spread out. This kind of life is fun. There's always something to do, always something going on."

"Always someone stepping on your foot," Donovan said.

"Or robbing your purse," Brody smirked.

I stuck my tongue out and unpacked our food. It didn't take long for my apartment to fill with the pungent scent of spiced noodles, lime, and peanut sauce.

We ate ravenously, using the chopsticks provided. Brody was having a tough time with them. Donovan took a moment to give him a crash course on how to hold them properly, and I leaned back for a second to admire my two lovers.

"Look at that," I laughed. "You *can* get along!"

Each of them smirked back at me, but couldn't help turning one shade redder. "Yeah," said Donovan. "After a few drinks, maybe."

"Bullshit," I said, crunching down on a spring roll. "Admit it. You actually *like* each other."

We finished, and the guys graciously cleaned up while I found some music to put on. It was soft, background music. Christmas music. The kind you only heard once a year, but always reminded you of friends, or home, or family.

Donovan's ears pricked up. "This is that Snoopy song, isn't it?"

"The Red Baron song," I laughed. "Yes."

"I love this fucking song," Brody admitted.

I stopped everything for a moment, just to soak it in. My quiet little apartment suddenly wasn't so lonely. It wasn't so quiet either. It was pleasantly spicy — filled with people, and music, and warmth. On a night where I should've been alone under a blanket against the cold rain outside, I was enjoying the sights and sounds and smells of *life*.

"What movie are we watching?" asked Donovan.

"*The Notebook*."

The guys both rolled their eyes in tandem. "No fucking way."

Try as I might, I couldn't hold it any longer. I burst out laughing.

"Okay, okay, I'm kidding." I flipped Donovan the remote. "Here. I don't care, really. You pick something."

Donovan's eyes lit up? "Really? So I can pick *Predator?*"

Brody jumped onto the couch, landing in Jocelyn's usual spot. "Ohhh..." he sighed happily. "I could *totally* go for some *Predator!*"

It was my first real mistake of the evening. I wasn't even counting my mistaken text to Brody, because that happy little accident had resulted in a really fun night.

In the end we settled on *Die Hard*, which the guys argued technically *was* a Christmas movie. Nestled comfortably on the couch between them in my favorite sweat-shorts, I quickly found that I didn't care. I was happy just to be with them. Just glad to have them here with me, enjoying my place, smoothing out the rough edges of our imperfect little perfect date.

One of them turned the lights low. Donovan fixed us some drinks while I microwaved some popcorn, and soon

Brody and I were munching away while Donovan went over the laundry list of synthetic chemicals we really shouldn't be putting into our bodies.

It could've been the music, the drink, the warmth of the big blanket I'd pulled over us — maybe a combination of all three. Soon however, my attention was drifting away from the movie. I began stretching out, laying my head in Brody's lap. Resting my legs over Donovan's, groaning with pleasure as he began rubbing my feet through my fuzzy socks.

At some point they began tickling me, and I rolled off onto the floor. I was a giggling mess, ready to fight back, when Brody announced he had to use the bathroom.

I felt a gentle hand beneath my chin, and suddenly Donovan was kissing me. All the flirtatiousness, all the passion and longing — an entire night's worth of buildup — had led to this one, singular moment.

Holy shit...

His kiss was rough and strong. Soulfully delicious. I found myself melting into him, rising up onto my knees to grind my body against his hard chest. We were already only half-clothed. We'd stripped off most of our stuff when we came in from the rain.

"I *need* you."

Donovan's voice was urgent, even desperate. Kneeling at his feet, I was shocked to see he was already fully hard. He dragged me between his legs, which were spread eagle from his seat on the couch. Then he took my hand and closed it over his manhood, which had somehow been drawn through the front of his boxers.

I gasped from my hands and knees, stopping to glance back at the darkened hallway. Slowly but commandingly, he guided my head downward.

"We *can't...*" I whispered. "Brody's still—"

He took over control, pressing his cock against my lips. Reflexively, I opened halfway.

Can we?

Our gazes met, his eyes soft but unflinching. I saw challenge in them. Like he was daring me to keep going.

"I... we..."

Donovan thrust his hips forward, and the head of his cock popped into my mouth. At the same time, he took one of my hands and placed it over his hard, rippled abdominals.

"That's a dirty trick," I mumbled around him.

"All's fair," he shrugged.

I sighed happily, my fingers moving on their own as they roamed his beautiful, flawless stomach. Somehow I was still blowing him. Still moving my head up and down in the semi-darkness, enjoying the power that came with bringing him all the way into my throat.

Down the hallway I was dimly aware of a sink running. It stopped, and I heard a door open. I tried to move...

Holly, get up!

But Donovan's two hands still rested gently on my head.

You have to—

Brody entered the room somewhere behind me... and

halted dead in his tracks. I only knew this because I heard his feet stop moving.

"Oh, hey," he said awkwardly.

His voice was thick, heavy. Like he was trying to talk, but also trying to concentrate on something else too.

"I uh... I guess I'll leave you two to the rest of your date..."

My head was still moving up and down. My eyes shot up to look at Donovan though. My pulse was racing.

"Or..." Donovan began casually, "you could stay."

It was as if my whole body been lit on fire. My heart felt like it might explode.

Stay?

Silence reigned. For three or four agonizing seconds, no one said anything.

"Yeah?" asked Brody.

"Yeah," Donovan replied with a fiendish grin. "You should *definitely* stay." He leaned forward with one long arm and spanked me firmly on one asscheek. "Right Holly?"

I was frozen on my hands and knees, blowing one boyfriend, listening to the other. Very slowly I popped Donovan from my mouth and glanced back over my shoulder, letting my eyes settle on Brody's.

"Yes," I smiled wickedly, wriggling my ass at him. "You should stay."

Twenty-Seven

HOLLY

My whole body turned to goosebumps as Brody knelt down behind me. His hands brushed my waist. Inch by inch they brought my sweat-shorts down, lifting one knee after the other to help me out of them entirely.

Holy shit holy shit holy shit!

I couldn't believe it was happening! I was actually *doing* this! And even more astonishing to me, that Brody and Donovan were really going through with it. Two romantic rivals calling a ceasefire, just long enough to team up together.

To team up on you...

Brody was on his back, sliding beneath me, and suddenly I felt his mouth close over my pussy. I let out a long moan, practically screaming around Donovan's cock. In the meantime, Brody's hands clamped firmly over my thighs. Gently he pulled me downward, to sit on his face.

Oh. My. GOD...

I was doing it — I was having sex with *both* of them. I was going down on the full length of Donovan's gorgeous, glistening shaft... while my other boyfriend devoured me expertly from beneath.

This... this is...

It was paradise, that's what it was. Pure nirvana, having two sets of strong, masculine hands roaming their way over my body.

Holly. Holy fucking shit, Holly...

Holy fucking shit was right. I wasn't just experiencing this, I was actually *thriving* on it. All at once I was sucking Donovan harder and faster. I found myself screwing down into Brody's mouth, driving his tongue deeper and more forcefully into my most secret of places.

This is... is like...

It wasn't like anything, really — not even in my wildest fantasies. I was moaning and grinding and licking and sucking, and then all of a sudden they were switching places. Brody was on the couch, and I was sliding his pants over his thighs. A moment later I was taking him deep into the back of my throat, while Donovan's clamped down on my hips.

Oh God.

He entered me from behind, completing the circuit. Making that final, lust-fueled connection between the three of us, with my warm, writhing body right in the middle.

"Fuck... that's *hot*."

Brody's voice was tight, like he was trying to hold it together. He smoothed a long lock of hair over my ear, freeing up my vision. Allowing me to shift my gaze backwards, so I could watch Donovan take me.

Look at yourself! The voice in my head sounded as stunned as I was. *Just look at what you're doing!*

Whatever I was doing, I was enjoying the hell of it. And it was way too late to turn back now.

"Oh my God, you're forcing me down her throat," Brody murmured. He had both hands buried in my hair now. His arms were locked to give himself leverage, to push me backward on the outstroke, impaling me against my other lover.

Instinct took over. I let my body go, lost in the wild, seedy abandon of being spitroasted between the two of them. It felt *soo fucking good!* So starkly empowering, to be both receiving and delivering pleasure to two men at the same time...

I took Brody from my mouth, lowering my head so I could enjoy getting fucked for a while. Donovan was drilling me with long, beautiful strokes. Sending me into a happy, almost delirious euphoria as Brody cradled my face in his hands.

"You okay?"

I nodded dreamily and smiled. I was much *better* than okay. He leaned down and planted his lips against mine, swirling his tongue into my mouth.

We kissed, sensuously, while Donovan and I fucked. And then, just as before, they switched off. Brody bounced me feverishly against his body, filling me wonderfully, while Donovan fed me his cock.

This wasn't supposed to happen...

It wasn't something I'd planned, that was for sure, but it was incredible nonetheless. And should it matter that I was being enjoyed by two lovers at once? They were both my boyfriends. They both knew they were sharing me with each other, even if it was on different nights.

But two of them at once!

"Let's get her on a bed," said Donovan abruptly. "That way we can *really* go to town on her."

I felt like a queen, being carried off in his arms. Stretching out across the softness of my own bed, while both lovers slid up on either side of me. They kissed me forever, touching me, feeling me, letting their hands and fingers roam. I sighed as they lowered their heads to my breasts simultaneously. I pulled them hard against me, feeling the tease of their teeth nibbling my sensitive nipples before they took turns, once again, between my legs.

It was always a fantasy, to be fucked like this. To entertain two lovers instead of one, the both of them focused on me and me alone. I'd always thought I'd be too chicken to try a threesome. I didn't want it to be awkward. I didn't want to be let down...

But right now they were exceeding even my hottest, craziest expectations.

They fucked me solo. They screwed me together. Donovan held my feet pinned back while Brody pounded into me... ultimately eliciting a screaming, blinding orgasm that left me shuddering with joy, my legs trembling.

"Do you need a break?"

I shook my head and kissed them some more. I

wanted every moment. Every shining, forbidden second of what was happening between the three of us. In the back of my mind, the looming fear that this might be it. That somehow this night was one in a million — a perfect alignment of all the right planets.

The selfish worry that it might never happen again.

Donovan finished first. It happened while Brody was kissing me; my eyes flared wide as I felt him go off, pumping my hot, silky channel full of his seed. My other lover watched, spellbound, as my personal trainer pushed all the way into me one final time. He held himself there, groaning with pleasure, his arms and chest shaking as he emptied himself completely.

"My turn," Brody smiled, planting one last kiss on my forehead.

He flipped me over, planting his hands on my lower back. Then he pushed all the way inside in a single, well-lubricated stroke.

"Jesus Christ."

All the air left my lungs as Brody pushed me into the bed. The weight of his body was delicious as he crushed me from above, sliding in and out of me, my asscheeks clenched tightly beneath his roaming hands.

Wow...

My brain flooded again, this time with the sweet, nectar-like exhilaration of being so thoroughly dominated. Donovan had moved to the other side of the bed. He was holding my arms out, pinning both my wrists beneath one strong hand. Holding me in place as Brody pistoned in and out of me...

I'm... I'm going to come again...

I squeezed down hard, fighting it for as long as I could. Trying to ride out that penultimate moment, that frenzied few seconds just before release when everything was lust and heat and fire...

"Ohhhhhhhh..."

I screamed into the bed, my own breath hot against my face. Then I heard it as well as felt it — the wet, frothy sounds of my pussy being pumped with a second load of cream. Brody cried out as he came, growling something that sounded like a stream of semi-coherent curse words. His cock thumped and pulsed inside me. His hands curled into claws, digging deeply into the two supple globes of my ass.

"Easy bro..."

My sexy classmate's fingers relaxed a bit at Donovan's warning. He kept on coming though. Kept pushing and grinding and shooting the last of himself, somewhere deep in my womb.

By the time he collapsed beside me, my own orgasm was winding down. I was breathless, desperate for oxygen. I rolled onto my side like a wounded athlete, gasping with euphoria instead of pain. I was hot. Sweaty. Totally satiated.

The entire room *reeked* like sex...

"Well shit," Donovan laughed, sinking back to the bed. "We just broke about half of our rules."

Brody was still catching his breath. He mopped his dirty-blond hair back with a smirk. "Hey, you started it."

"*She* started it," Donovan countered, jabbing a thumb

my way. "Inviting us both over at once."

"Not on purpose..." I breathed. "But I don't mind telling you right now," I smiled at the ceiling. "I don't regret it."

We sat together for a moment, recovering as one. Reflecting on what we'd just done with a long but enjoyable span of silence.

"So who's gonna do it?" asked Brody.

Donovan and I turned to him simultaneously. "Do what?"

"Well *somebody's* gotta tell Lincoln," my classmate grinned, "that the rules have changed."

Twenty-Eight

HOLLY

"See this right here?" I pointed. "These are dividend payments. They're made directly to three different accounts, here, here, and here..."

Lincoln adjusted his glasses as he stared down at the financial statement. He was one of those guys who looked *good* in glasses. Like really, really good.

"The highlighted ones?" he asked. "What are they for?"

"Good question."

The anomalies I'd highlighted in yellow had come from a balance sheet summary. It had taken me three hours of digging through his files to find the document, which was in the wrong place to begin with. Three hours and just as many cups of coffee.

"So... does this explain the missing money?"

"Part of it," I replied. "Maybe all of it, if we go back

far enough. This should be accounted for on your statement of changes in equity, though. Only right now, that's the one piece that's still missing."

Lincoln's mouth twisted strangely. He looked thoughtful, confused... and maybe something else, too. All at once.

"When does she come in?" I asked.

"Eight thirty."

"Then I'd better get out of here now," I said, glancing at an expensive-looking wall clock. "If you don't want her to see me."

It had been Lincoln's idea, to come in early and scour the records. He didn't want to alarm Kathy though, or upset her needlessly. His CFO was very sensitive about the way she kept the books. And she'd been working for him ever since he'd started the company.

"I owe you one, you know," he smiled. Reaching out, he pulled me against his body.

"I know," I smirked. "And I'll see that you pay up."

His hands slid to my ass. He gave it a firm squeeze. "I bet you will."

I sighed into his mouth as he kissed me, feeling my resolve melt away. I'd wanted to talk to him. I'd spent all morning trying to figure out how to word things, how to say exactly what I needed to say. But it was too late now. His office would be filling with people soon – project managers, sales associates, executive assistants... and of course, Kathy.

"Listen," I said, breaking our kiss. "I need to talk to

you about something."

"Is is it something good?"

Oh boy. Is it ever.

"Sort of. Maybe." I hooked a finger into my mouth and chewed on it — my one big nervous habit. "I... I don't know."

"Then just say it," Lincoln smiled. "You *can* tell me anything, you know. We have personal shopper-client privilege."

It was a funny joke. On any other day I would've laughed musically.

"Holly, just tell me."

I swallowed, the bitter taste of bad coffee still in my mouth. He needed better coffee, that was for sure. And a better coffee maker. I added a mental note to my Christmas list, as Lincoln stood there staring back at me.

But now I was fucked.

"I..." Shit, how to tell him? How exactly do you break like this? "I.. Uh..."

"Holly, the guys told me."

It was a splash of freezing water to the face. I felt as if I'd been knocked back six feet.

"W—What?" I stammered. "How..."

"I grabbed lunch with them yesterday. They said they wanted to come clean about something, to talk about the rules. Then they told me what happened at your apartment. How things... progressed."

My heart was in my throat as I studied his expression. *Is he angry?* He sure didn't seem like it. *Is he jealous? Disappointed?*

"Are you upset?"

Lincoln folded his arms. He took his glasses off. "Want me to be honest?"

"Of course I do."

His hand slid upward, then back down again. It was inside my jeans now. Cupping the bare flesh of my thong-covered ass.

"I thought it sounded pretty fucking *hot*."

I lost my breath for a moment as he squeezed gently. I could feel his long fingers, curling their way between my legs. Inching into the snug warmth of my thigh gap.

"They told me everything, Holly," said Lincoln. "*Everything.*"

His expression was one I'd seen before, but only in the bedroom. Only when he was buried inside me, or when I was blowing him. His look was... rapturous.

"I—It didn't make you jealous?"

"If it made me jealous at all, it's only because I wish I'd been there." Lincoln leaned in, his breath suddenly hot on my shoulder. His hands were moving, curling, slowly manipulating me. I could feel myself getting wetter by the second.

Oh... oh wow...

"Did you enjoy it?" he whispered into my ear.

I stood there backed up against his desk, totally speechless. The desk where he'd taken me for the first time. The desk where he'd *fucked* me. Where he'd put his come all over my body...

Ever so slowly, I nodded.

"Good," Lincoln murmured, nuzzling my neck. "I'm glad to hear you say that."

Holy shit...

"Because next time, Holly? When we're all together?"

He pulled back from me. Just enough to look directly into my eyes.

"Next time it might be all *four of us*."

Twenty-Nine

HOLLY

I walked into work on shaky legs, and not because I'd been up since four o'clock looking at financial statements. Even after Lincoln had his driver graciously drop me off, I was still trembling from our conversation in his office.

'Thanks, Ulrich."

The driver smiled and tipped his hat as I emerged from the car. He waved a friendly goodbye before climbing back into the vehicle and speeding off.

Somehow I was able to make it to the elevators on my own.

All four of us together...

Lincoln's words had spiked all new levels of adrenaline in my body. I felt like I did as a teenager, waiting in line for a thrill ride. Feeling my stomach drop out from under me as I glanced upward and saw what I was about to do.

It was still insane to me, how Lincoln's reaction had

been the complete opposite of what I expected. He'd been thrilled instead of angry. Actually turned on, instead of turned off. Any jealousy he felt was only the left out kind. And that could be easily remedied...

Damn, Holly. Is that what you want?

I'd thought about it a lot since it happened, and even more on the ride over. And yes, it was exactly what I wanted.

Holy shit...

I felt like the proverbial flood gates had been opened. As if, try as the four of us might, it was going to be impossible to put the genie back in the bottle.

And I didn't *want* the genie back in the bottle.

Before I left his office, Lincoln had pointed out a few logistics of his own, too. Setting aside the sexual benefits of sharing me as one, it opened up all new avenues as far as seeing each other was concerned. No longer did we need to pick and schedule individual days. My boyfriends could double-date me. Triple-date me, if they really wanted to.

The very thought made my stomach do another somersault.

"I have a little place," he'd said, "back in Maine. A vacation chalet I've wanted to take you away to, but school was always in the way." He kissed me hotly one last time, on the way out the door. "Now that your finals are over, maybe the two of us could go. Or maybe we could *all* go," he winked. "We'll have to see."

Right now I was standing before the garage elevators, still reeling from a thousand less-intrusive thoughts. Christmas was less than a week away, and though I was almost caught up with my shopping clients, I still had plenty to do. On a personal level, I'd been neglecting my family. My mother had called and left two messages. My brother had emailed me, asking my opinion on something.

Slow down, Holly!

I still had to RSVP for the company's holiday party. Jocelyn wanted to meet for drinks. And on top of everything, I had a date with Brody tonight. Suddenly I had to wonder if he'd actually come solo. Or if he'd bring Donovan. Or Lincoln. Or even—

My attention was diverted by my peripheral vision. Off to my left, my car drove by again. Same driver, same blonde hair, same ponytail. Patricia, I'd learned her name was. Hey, I didn't begrudge her. Except for the fact the bitch was driving my car, she actually seemed pretty nice.

This time my hand went over my mouth as I realized something was different.

"My car!"

The whole front of my cherished little hatchback was smashed in! One of the headlights was missing. Half the bumper was hanging off. The lower part of the hood was crumpled...

Patricia Ponytail sped up the ramp without even looking my way. My car disappeared once again from view, leaving me feeling sick and disappointed.

Awwww... My car...

I felt like I'd been kicked in the gut, seeing my treasured vehicle like that. We'd shared hundreds of City miles together! But in a strange sort of way, I also felt vindicated.

Malcolm!

I could only *imagine* my ex-boyfriend's face! The things he'd say! How high his voice would climb through the octaves when he saw what happened, if he hadn't already.

Then again, he could've turned in the lease by now. He *should've* turned in the lease by now...

"Eat shit Malcolm," I smiled, as the elevator doors opened behind me.

Thirty

BRODY

"Oh I'm telling you, it exists."

Holly was slapping me in the arm every time I teased her. Somehow, though I maintained my stoic expression. I'd kept from laughing, even in the face of grave, boyfriend-slapping danger.

"There is *not* a museum of sex," she admonished me.

"Really? Are you sure?"

"Pretty sure."

"And how long have you been here in New York?"

She rolled her eyes skyward for a moment, as if the answer were up there. "Two years. Going on three."

"Then you're lying," I said. "Or you're crazy. Or you're blind. But there's no *way* I believe you haven't gone there yet." I looked her up and down. "Especially someone as sexy as you."

I sipped at my straw, until there was nothing left in my

cup but ice. We were already full of pizza. *Joe's* pizza. The best pizza.

"Not only *is* there a museum of sex," I informed her, "but they have a bounce house made out of inflatable breasts."

Holly let out a short bust of mocking laughter. "The fuck they do."

I stopped walking mid-stride. The people on the sidewalk behind us were forced to adjust their course, moving around us on both sides.

"Wanna bet?"

Her blue-green eyes narrowed. She regarded me carefully. "Sure. I'll bet whatever you want."

"Whatever I *want?*" An instant smile split my face. "You sure about that?"

"Yup," she said. "You take me to a museum of sex — and I mean a *real* museum, not just your bedroom," she laughed, "and yes. I'll do anything you want."

She drew out the word 'anything', and even added a wink. But it was a wink of confidence. A wink that told me she knew I was kidding around.

Not that I actually was, of course.

"Alright then," I shrugged, extending my hand. "Let's go. But hey, just remember... you were the one who made the bet."

A few blocks later we stood on the corner of 5th Avenue and East 27th street. I pointed with one arm, and Holly's mouth dropped open comically wide.

"OH MY GOD."

The Museum of Sex took up the whole corner, its steel-cut sign stating exactly what it was. I had to pull Holly across the street as the pedestrian light blinked, she was that stunned.

"Remember," I smirked back at her. "*Anything*."

We approached the entrance, and I nodded toward sign. In black and white, behind frosted glass, a simple set of instructions has been written:

Please do not touch, lick, stroke, or mount the exhibits.

"Holy shit," Holly breathed. "What's *in* there?"

"Not sure. I've never been."

She turned to me incredulously. "So you were lying about the breast bounce house?"

I chuckled. "Sadly, no. I've seen photos of it."

I paid our admissions and we worked our way inside. For the next hour or more we were entertained by exhibits that ranged from informative, to fanciful, to outright raunchy. We read about the history of sex, the stigma attached to it. There were entire sections dedicated to all things taboo, including BDSM. I couldn't help but notice Holly taking a particular interest in that part.

"Ever been tied up like that?" I smiled over her shoulder. Some of the mannequins were *really* good.

She hesitated. "Not really," she said.

"Then I'm buying rope and handcuffs at the gift shop," I announced. When she raised an eyebrow, I shrugged. "Hey, you did say *anything*."

The last section went over the evolution of sexual toys and games. Holly turned a vibrant shade of red as we passed a long array of dildos and vibrators, but it might've just been the lighting.

"See anything familiar?" I teased. Rather than answer, she only smirked back at me.

It turned out, of course, that the gift shop really *did* carry handcuffs. I bought two pairs of padded ones, while Holly pretended like she wanted nothing to do with the cash register. For someone who'd done some incredibly sexual things in private, it was cute to see her publicly shy.

By the time the museum spit us back out into the street, it was dark outside. We huddled together for a walk to my apartment, which she'd been curious to the point of killing the cat about.

"My roommates are sort of weird," I warned.

"You said that already."

"I know. Just... preparing you."

My apartment was on Bleecker Street, on the outskirts of SoHo. I'd been sharing it with various students over the past two years; between that and the educational subsidies we received from the University, it was the only way I could afford to actually live in the City.

"I wish we could be alone," I told Holly as we stepped into the elevator. "But when you live with three other people, there's always someone ho—"

She stepped in and kissed me, causing my stomach to drop at the exact moment the elevator rose. The double-dose of vertigo sent my mind spinning. Her lips were soft and pliant as they churned slowly against mine. Her hair smelled delicious, like a watermelon jolly rancher.

"I fucking *want* you," she whispered huskily. A shockwave went through me as her hand closed over my crotch. "*Bad.*"

"Where was this not-so-shy girl back at the Museum of Sex?" I chuckled.

"Waiting to get you alone."

I would've done her right there in the elevator — just like in books and movies. But I knew for a fact that the elevator had an alarm. An ear-piercingly loud, ringing alarm that would be wholly distracting from what I wanted to do to her.

"I don't know who's home," I murmured, "but maybe I can get them to leave."

Holly kissed her way down, to nibble at my neck. As she dragged her wet tongue sensually over my most sensitive spots, the entire right side of my body had the shivers.

"Fuck it," I groaned. "I'll *pay* them to leave. I'll—"

The elevator stopped. I pushed Holly giggling down the hall, hands on her hips, fumbling for the keys in my front pocket. But as I reached the door to my shared loft, it opened automatically.

"Oh... hey!"

My smile faded quickly. Sayid's face told me instantly that something was wrong.

"Brody..."

"What is it?" I asked, shifting my eyes beyond him. The apartment's big common area looked empty. "Is she *here?*"

"No," my roommate said. "But she was."

I pushed past him, dragging Holly behind me. Sweeping through our living room and through the doorway to my bedroom, which for some reason was wide open.

The place was a total wreck. Broken glass littered the floor. Clothes were strewn everywhere. And my bed...

Shit.

"We tried to stop her," Sayid muttered apologetically. "But she was doing it before we got here."

My bed had several long gashes down the middle, like a tiger had raked its claws across it. Memory foam was all over the surface, pulled out and shredded.

"What the hell, Brody?" Holly gasped from behind me. Her voice was all shock and concern. "Who in the world would *do* this to you?"

I let go of her hand as my arms fell limply to my sides.

"Andrea," I sighed miserably.

Thirty-One

HOLLY

"Andrea..." I didn't know who the bitch was, but her name already made me angry. "Who's *Andrea?*"

"Our fourth roommate," Sayid offered. "And..." His eyes shifted expectantly to Brody.

"And my ex-girlfriend," Brody admitted.

I watched as he walked the tiny bedroom, picking up pieces of things and dropping them again. She'd broken furniture, punched holes in walls. Shattered anything that could be shattered. In a way, I almost admired her commitment.

"You still live with your ex girlfriend?" I asked.

Brody nodded. My heart sank.

"When exactly did you break up?"

I wasn't sure I wanted the answer to that question. It had happened before; guys picking me up during the tail end of a bad relationship. Even dating me while they were still technically dating their "ex" girlfriends, which was a lie of course, because they still hadn't let go of—

"Nine months ago," Brody answered solidly. "Sometime before the summer."

Whew.

"And she's still *this* angry?" I asked incredulously. My eyes narrowed. "Were you still, umm..."

Brody turned over his pillow bitterly. It was slashed too. "Was I still what?"

"Hooking up with her?"

The words left my mouth reluctantly. As painful as it was, I had to know.

"Shit no," Brody spat.

"Because maybe, you know, if you were leading her on..." I continued. "Gave her reason to think you two might get back together..."

It was another thing guys did: see you after the breakup. Sleep with you after the breakup, when you were lonely and vulnerable and looking for any reason to get your foot back in the door of your past relationship.

"Not even a little bit," Brody said.

"He's telling the truth," Sayid offered, coming to his roommate's defense. "Brody's been avoiding her like the plague. We've all been, really, but he'll basically leave the apartment whenever she comes home."

The look of pure disgust on Brody's face told me it was the truth. I began helping him pick up his room.

"Ask Darren if you need to," Sayid added. "He'll vouch."

We grabbed the garbage, and the three of us went about righting whatever we could. Sayid explained how he and their third roommate had come home earlier to find Andrea going berserk, breaking his room apart. It took the two of them to drag her out, but by then the damage had mostly been done.

"She saw the... photo," Sayid said meekly. "And she went nuts."

I followed his gaze, to where a dozen pieces of a photograph lay shredded next to a broken glass frame. Even torn to shreds I recognized it: the photo of Brody and I together, on our first date.

"You put up that picture of us?" I asked, my heart melting a little. "And *this* is what happened?"

Brody nodded.

"Then call the police," I said, suddenly more pissed than ever. "Get her arrested, or at least thrown out of here."

"No," he shook his head glumly. "No, I'm not calling the police."

"This is bullshit, Brody," I told him. "An ex-girlfriend from *nine months* ago? You don't need to stand for this."

"How did she get in here?" Brody asked his roommate. "What made her break into my bedroom, anyway?"

"I don't know man, she's psycho." Sayid shrugged. "Like I said, we weren't here. Maybe you left the door unlocked?"

Unfortunately, the room was a total loss. The only

thing left unshredded was a single picture of Brody and his grandmother, a smiling blue-haired woman with her arm draped happily around her grandson. I recognized her immediately from some of the other pictures he'd shown me on his phone.

But down at my feet...

"What's this?"

I was holding another photo, this one torn jaggedly in two. On one side was Brody, grinning from behind a pair of sunglasses. On the other, a raven-haired girl with wild eyes and dark, curly hair.

"This is her, isn't it?" I asked, holding up the Andrea side of the photo.

Brody was in the kitchen at the time, getting another garbage bag. But Sayid looked up and nodded. "Yes."

Wordlessly, I shoved the photo into my pocket.

It took another thirty minutes to put everything back the way it was. Or rather, whatever wasn't broken. The bed was the worst part. It was a complete and total loss.

"Looks like it's the floor for a while," Brody frowned. "Or I could stay with grandma in Bayside for a bit. School's done, so—"

"Screw that," I told him. Moving closer, I slipped my hand into his. "You're staying with me until you can fix all of this."

He smiled wanly, but still looked sad. "I don't have the money for another bed," he sighed. "And I can't flip this one over. I checked."

"We'll figure it out," I told him. "Right Sayid?"

Standing in the doorway, probably not sure if he should go or not, Sayid returned a weak but friendly smile. "Of course we will. Don't sweat it, bro."

Brody stared at his roommate as if seeing him for the first time. Finally he grinned. "Oh, Sayid?" He let out a short laugh that came out a bit maniacal. "I'd like you to meet my girlfriend Holly."

Girlfriend... The word surprised me, but not in an unpleasant way.

"Holly, meet Sayid."

Thirty-Two

HOLLY

The next few days were a whirlwind of getting shit done.

At the office I kicked unholy amounts of ass, finishing every last report and summary document due before the upcoming holiday weekend. I dotted every 'i' and crossed every 't', before cleaning and straightening my desk in preparation for what promised to be a *very* interesting new year.

I was just about ready for lunch when a text popped up on my phone. I smiled happily. All my recent text-messages had been the most interesting ones of my entire life. Especially the sexy little group text we'd started, between Lincoln, Donovan, Brody, and I.

My smile faded quickly however, as I realized this one was from Malcolm:

Coffee?

I must've gotten hundreds of single-word texts like this in the past — all from him. Coffee during lunch break was one of our things. Or it *had* been one of our things.

I considered ignoring the message altogether. But something — probably the OCD part of me that wouldn't let things remain open-ended — made me hammer out a response:

No, thanks.

Short, simple, to the point, my answer left no room for misinterpretation. Besides, it felt good to be on the other end of the rejection for once. *Really* good.

Five minutes later I was street-level, walking briskly in the direction of my last stop: a specialty gift boutique where I'd custom-ordered a laser-engraved cigar box. It was the final pickup for my final client, signaling the end of a very hectic — but also very lucrative — personal shopping season.

Somehow I'd completed it all — everything for everyone, Lincoln and Donovan included. I'd lost count of how many times I'd trained at *Crunch Time* for free, but I'd done more than enough shopping for Donovan's friends and family to make up for the lost time.

Besides... you can do things for each other. He's your boyfriend now. Or at least, one of them.

The thought made me giddy whenever it came to mind. I didn't just have a boyfriend, I had *three* of them. All of which were gorgeous. All of which were fun and funny, strong and confident. And yes, even a little bit cocky, too.

Best of all, every last one of them made me feel like a princess.

A princess? Is that how we're putting it?

I was looking very forward to the coming weekend. Lincoln was closing down for the week on Friday, and we'd finally made plans for a quick trip to Maine. Apparently he shared a lease on a plane, and that fact alone was astonishing to me. Then again I'd seen his books, so I knew how much money he was clearing.

Two days, three nights, tucked away somewhere in the snowy backwoods of Maine. A cabin in the middle of nowhere, with not a single soul for miles around. The exact opposite of New York City.

Holy shit. It sounded absolutely magical.

We'd be back just in time for Christmas Eve, which the four of us were planning on spending together. Donovan's relatives were still clear across the country. And Brody's grandmother was always picked up for the week, staying with her sister and her family in Bridgehampton.

All four of us....

Together.

A knot formed in my stomach whenever I thought

about it, and I thought about it often. Fantasized about it, to be more accurate. Hell, I'd even picked out a few outfits...

I was sitting in the coffee shop across from the office building when I felt the tap on my shoulder. It snapped me out of my daydream. Caused me turn and look over my shoulder... while Malcolm circled around the other side and slipped into the empty chair across from me.

"Hey," he grinned, trying to sound casual. "I thought you said you didn't want coffee?"

My face must've registered my extreme disappointment, because his smile faded almost instantly.

"No, I said I didn't want to get coffee with *you*."

Awkward silence followed. Awkward for him, anyway.

"Oh," he said. "I just... I thought, you know, I saw you sitting here drinking coffee, and I figured—"

"What is it you want, Malcolm?"

Oddly enough, he looked entirely different than he had only a few weeks ago. He'd lost weight, and on Malcolm's already-slender frame that wasn't necessarily a good thing. He seemed twitchy, too. Fidgety. And there were dark circles under his eyes — circles I knew he got whenever he missed sleep. Beneath the circles, there were bags there too.

That's new, I thought to myself absently.

"Well first I wanted to say I'm sorry," he began, "about how we broke up. About how quickly I was... well, how fast I was willing to just let it all go."

I nodded, looking bored. Hell, I was bored.

"That's it? You're sorry."

"Yes."

"Good, we've established that you're sorry. Is that all?"

Wow, I sounded like a complete bitch!

"Well... no."

"Then what else?"

Malcolm looked down at the table. He was struggling hard. His hands were moving in circles, for lack of anything to manipulate.

"Speak up," I said, checking the time on my phone. "I have to be back soon."

He swallowed, then cleared his throat before continuing. "Holly listen," he said. "I think I made a mistake."

A laugh tore its way from my throat. "A mistake?"

"Yeah."

"That's it, right? Just a little mistake?"

"Well, more like a big mistake. More like—"

I stood up and grabbed my stuff in one fluid motion, purse, bag and all.

"It was a mistake to come here," I said, before stomping off.

Thirty-Three

HOLLY

What started as a conundrum turned into a very easy decision. Because when it came down to the night of the company's holiday party? Both Lincoln and Donovan were indisposed.

That left Brody, who was staying with me anyway. Brody, my breathtakingly handsome classmate that not one of my co-workers knew. A date so young and fresh-faced he was carded every single time he went to the bar to fetch us drinks.

"Holly, who *is* he?"

The question came time and time again, from those who knew and liked me as well as the same assholes who couldn't normally stand me during the average workday. I laughed it all off, giving different answers to each. Sometimes Brody was a friend, or a boyfriend, or just a lover. Other times he was a second cousin. A friend of a girlfriend. Even, after several drinks, my brother.

It all made the party a lot more interesting, as we

danced cheek to cheek. Brody turned out to be an incredible dancer, possessing more natural rhythm and groove than my last five boyfriends combined, including Malcolm.

Malcolm. Ugh!

That was an introduction I'd been avoiding all night, although luckily, it seemed like my ex-boyfriend had the same idea. He watched me from afar though. More than once I caught him stealing sideways glances, always when he thought I wouldn't be looking, once even while Brody had both hands firmly planted on my dress-covered ass.

"These people are nice," he smiled at one point, pressing his face against mine.

"Yeah, well they're drunk."

"So?"

"So the drunker they get, the more tolerable they all are. That goes for any party, any wedding, any event."

The overly-decorated venue my company had picked was oddly dark, the music unreasonably loud. Either they were compensating for some run-down decor or they were just plain cheap with the lights. Either way, it made it all the more fun hiding off to the side as the party wound down. Brody and I stood with our arms around each other, watching my co-workers get drunker and bolder as they wandered off into their little cliques and groups.

"Wanna get the hell out of here?" I asked.

"If it means getting you out of that dress, yeah."

Ten minutes later were in the back of a cab, laughing and poking fun at my co-workers and generally fooling around.

Once back at my apartment, we kept the party going. Brody poured me some wine while I jacked the heat up to a comfortably naked level. Then I put on some Christmas music to maintain the mood.

In no time flat we were sitting on the couch face to face, kissing like lost lovers. It was soft and beautiful. Tantalizingly slow, yet full of pent-up passion and promise.

"Holly..."

Gradually I opened my mouth for him, moaning sexily as his tongue slid against mine. He held my face in his palms. I blinked dreamily, and found him staring back at me with those piercing, emerald eyes.

"I think I love you."

My heart felt like it weighed a metric ton! My whole body surged with adrenaline, as goosebumps took over every inch of my skin.

"I... I love you too," I murmured, realizing the truth. We never broke eye contact. It was like I was staring right through him, straight into his soul. "I do," I smiled. "I so toally do."

He kissed me harder, his hand sliding deftly through the slit in my dress. It was warm and insistent as it traveled up my thigh.

Oh Holly...

Brody reached his goal, and I spread wide for him. I whimpered as he probed me with his fingers. Chewed down on his lip, as I felt him touch me inside...

"Now..." I purred, sliding my arms over his shoulder.

"You said something about getting me out of this dress?"

My lover smiled and stood up, bringing me along with him. I spun around on my heels so he could unzip me. Seconds later I was stepping out of my shimmering green dress, leaving me naked except for a Santa-red bra and matching G-string panties.

"So you never really told me what you want for Christmas," I teased, biting one of my fingers.

Brody's hands went to my hips, gripping me with authority and possession. He pulled me against him, and my body overloaded with tingles of pleasure as his lips brushed my ear.

"I just got it," he whispered.

Thirty-Four

HOLLY

"Mmmmmm..."

I writhed warmly across the sheets, pulling my restraints tight. Feeling my wrists straining against the handcuffs... each one tied off to a different corner of my bed.

"You like that?"

I nodded, dreamily. Brody's tongue swirled again, ever-so-lightly tracing the outer edge of my nipple. He was barely touching it with the tip — just enough to make it stiff and hard. Enough to make my ache for him to end the torment, by closing his hot mouth over it.

"What about this?"

Now his mouth *did* close over it, his lips all flush and warm. But inside...

"OH!"

I felt a sudden cold sting on the tip of my nipple. A blast of icy numbness that could only be one of the cubes from my freezer.

"Awww... Holy shit..."

The combination of hot and cold was uniquely pleasurable. It caused me to writhe some more as he alternated between sucking and licking and teasing me with his ice-filled mouth.

"Now this."

His mouth disappeared, and I felt nothing but the ice cube. Brody was holding it pinched between his fingers. Rubbing it in slow, teasing circles around my areola.

God...

Or at least, that's what I *envisioned* he was doing. I couldn't be absolutely certain, because for the last twenty minutes I'd been totally blindfolded.

"More?"

My body jumped as my other breast was suddenly stimulated. A second ice cube joined in, overwhelming my senses. My nipples screamed! Pointing skyward, they begged for the heat of my lover's hot mouth.

"Brody..."

Around and around went the ice, melting against the heat of my skin. I could feel rivulets of cool water, running down my breasts and ribs. Seeping into the sheets beneath me, as I twisted against the handcuffs.

"You want out?" my lover teased.

I sucked in a deep breath and let it out slowly. The cold was being replaced by a pleasant numbness that was starting to feel good.

"No..."

"That's my girl."

I felt the bed shift as he dipped downward, and suddenly his mouth was over my breast again. Only now it was *hot!* So hot it felt like more than his mouth. Like he'd been sipping on warm liquid, or—

"Hot chocolate," he chuckled, lifting his chin. "Found it in your cabinet."

The bed moved again, and two fingers pressed insistently against my lips. I opened to accept them. The warm taste of milk and chocolate flowed into my mouth.

"Good?"

I nodded obediently. Licked my lips.

"And what should I do to you next?"

My feet were still free. I spread my thighs for him, giving him a perfect view of my growing wetness.

"You could fuck me."

Brody didn't answer right away. His hands roamed my breasts again, his fingers lightly pinching my nipples.

"I could," he theorized. "If I wanted to."

He was tormenting me now. I'd been juiced up, ready to go ever since the couch. But he hadn't touched me. And with my hands locked overhead, I couldn't even touch myself.

"I don't know..." he sighed playfully. "This is a tough one."

He bent again, to hover his face over mine. I could feel his presence, eye to eye, nose to nose. His lips brushed mine, and when I stretched to kiss him he pulled away.

"Maybe I'll just let you do me."

He shifted again, straddling my face. His manhood dropped heavily against my chin and cheek. I opened for him, trying to find the head. Trying desperately to fit him in my mouth.

"Taste it first."

My tongue emerged, and I made it flat for him. Brody took over, sliding his erection up and down through the open channel of my mouth. Bathing himself against my warm, wet tongue...

"There we go."

He reached back, and I moaned as a hand slid between my legs. I was so wet, so slippery. He teased me again for a few agonizing moments, but then I bucked my hips so his fingers slid right in.

"Oh man," he swore. "Only bad girls do that."

I nodded, nuzzling against his scrotum. Eventually my mouth found him, engulfing his cock. "Mmm-hmmm."

"Really bad girls," he said. "Dirty girls..."

He was fingering me beautifully now, scratching that incredible itch I'd had for so achingly long. I bucked in rhythm to his thrusts, terrified he'd pull away at any time. Instead, he added another finger.

Please...

I was horny as I'd even been. Beyond frustrated! I wanted so badly to just reach down and start touching my clit. To pull it on it gently, rub it in the way I knew would bring me off...

But there was an inherent thrill in being tied down, too. A strange excitement that came with *not* being able to do these things. My toes curled, my body bending and twisting to meet my lover's touch. Brody's free hand was entwined in my hair now, holding me by the back of my head. He was controlling me fully. Using my mouth, solely for his own pleasure.

And God, it was *so* fucking hot.

I found myself sucking harder and with more desperation, breathing heavily through my nose. The blindfold was absolutely amazing. Not being able to see had the direct effect of heightening my other senses; I could smell better, taste better, hear every delicious sound that our bodies made. And of course, it made everything a hundred times more tactile. Every time Brody touched me someplace new, my body jumped as if jolted with electricity.

"Should I come in your mouth?"

I thought about it, then shook my head. I wanted him to fuck me. God, I *needed* him to fuck me.

"Is that a yes?"

With his hand on my head I couldn't resist, couldn't even speak. I could only mumble around him. I tried shaking my head again...

"Yeah, I think that's probably best," he said, stroking my hair.

His cock was bigger now, harder in my mouth. And his arousal was growing too. I could hear it in the thickness of his voice. Sense it in the irregularity of his breathing...

Is he really going to?

Alarms flashed through my brain. I squirmed even harder into his hand, desperate to push myself over the edge.

"Maybe afterward I'll just leave you here, all tied up," he teased. "Come back again later, when I feel like *really* spreading those legs..."

I screwed down with all might... and his hand abruptly disappeared. I felt the rush of impending orgasm slipping away.

No! Please!

The bed shifted again, this time somewhere below me. I gasped out loud as two strong arms suddenly wrapped themselves around my thighs. I felt my body being manipulated. My legs being pushed apart...

And then the unmistakable pressure of a thick cock being pushed against my opening. Parting me like a glistening flower...

"Or maybe I'll just call for reinforcements," Brody chuckled. "So we can fuck you *properly.*"

Thirty-Five

HOLLY

My eyes rolled back in pure ecstasy as a second lover slid into me. He was wonderfully long. Deliciously thick. His hands felt like two steel clamps, holding my legs in place as he rocked into my body.

"Oh... *YESSSS*..."

I cried the words more than said them. Had I not been wearing a blindfold, they would've been accompanied by tears of joy streaming down the sides of both cheeks.

Thank God!

Brody's cock slid from my mouth. It laid there heavy against my cheek, sawing back and forth across my face as my new lover began *really* fucking me.

"You good now, baby?"

Brody asked the question lovingly, while caressing my face. I moaned greedily in response. The pleasure between my legs was total now. It scratched that unreachable itch, obliterated that unquenchable ache of longing. I hooked my legs behind my mystery paramour's back, realizing by the thickness of his torso and the rhythm of his strokes exactly who it was...

"Lincoln..."

The blindfold came off, and I was staring into Brody's grinning face. "How'd you know?"

"You all have your own style," I chuckled, looking down my body. Now that my eyesight was back, I wanted the visual. I needed to save it.

Lincoln winked at me from between my legs. He didn't stop fucking me though. "You also had a 50/50 shot," he pointed out. He shrugged his big shoulders. "Just sayin'."

"I know," I smiled in satisfaction. "But you're all just... different."

"Oh yeah?" asked Brody. "Who's style's the best?"

"Mine," I purred, rolling my head back.

Oh.. Oh fuck...

My climax hit me like a freight train, rocking my body with wave after wave of sweet, orgasmic release. Lincoln did the right thing by picking up the pace. He screwed me harder and faster, digging so deep it made me delirious with pleasure. My grunts became animalistic. I was moaning, groaning. Screaming...

"Ohhhh... Ohhh please.... Don't stop..."

It was a needless worry. As I floated back to reality, my extended climax spun itself out into another series of contractions — a second orgasm, even bigger than the last.

And Lincoln fucked me through that one, too.

My mind was a haze of sex-fueled euphoria. My body a piece of clay, to be molded and shaped and positioned in their hands.

"Let me take a shot at her for a while," I heard Brody say. "I've been dying to fuck her all night."

I lay supine and helpless, my arms starting to ache from being spread eagle for so long. Lincoln took pity on me... but only long enough to handcuff my wrists together, behind my back. He pushed me face-down, ass-up on the bed. Then he held me there, so Brody could slide into me from behind.

"Ohhhhhhhhhhhhhhhhhhhhhhhh..."

With my eyes screwed shut, I let out a long, contented groan. When I opened them again, Lincoln's cock was just inches from my face.

"I was right," he said, holding me by the chin. "This is every bit as hot as I thought it would be."

I swallowed him as Brody screwed me, grabbing my bound wrists in one big hand. It hurt, but only for a moment. Once I relaxed my shoulders, I ceded control.

Oh... my... fucking... God...

"Is this what you wanted?" growled Brody, leaning over my back. He was pulling hard enough to stay dominant, while still leaving enough room for me to be comfortable.

I answered with my eyes, staring back at him over my shoulder. Lincoln's cock was still filling my mouth.

"You feel so *deep* this way," he grunted lustfully.

The two of them switched again and again, trading off

between my mouth and pussy. The handcuffs came off and on too. I was bound in the front, my wrists at at belly-button level. Forced to ride each of them while sucking the other, and somehow maintaining my balance throughout.

I won't lie... I got good at it. Halfway through I was learning new tricks to keep myself in place. Soon I was grinding down hard, reaching all new depths. Taking one lover as far as I could inside me, while working the other with my hands and mouth.

They released me in the end, just in time to lay me back across the bed. Then they finished, both of them, simultaneously on my chest. Each of my lovers firing thick, heavy streams of their warm seed... all over my sweaty, writhing body.

I still reeled from the wine, from the exertion, from the wonderful orgasms they'd made sure to give me. So much that it barely registered as my lovers collapsed on either side of me.

"Sorry I missed your holiday office thing," said Lincoln, pulling my face to his. Side to side on the pillow, he kissed me tenderly. "But I'm glad Brody called me in for the after-party."

I shifted delightedly, and was immediately spooned from behind. My laughter was delirious.

"Is *that* what we're calling this?"

Thirty-Six

LINCOLN

Her apartment was every bit as adorable as she was, and that was saying a lot. Her refrigerator though...

"You have *three* eggs?"

Holly giggled from her corner of the kitchen table, where she cradled an oversized mug of delicious-smelling coffee. At least *that* was good. She had a solid machine, and a good grinder. Not every girl knew enough to buy whole beans.

Shit, some of them still used a godforsaken *Keurig*.

"Want me to knock on my neighbor's door to borrow some?" she teased. "Ask for some milk too?"

"Nah. I'll make do."

I wasn't the greatest cook in the world, but I could hold my own. I considered Breakfast my strong suit. It was also my favorite meal. But an omelet for three people? Using three eggs?

"Morning." yawned Brody, stumbling into the kitchen.

He scratched his head. "Shit, did I miss breakfast?"

"Not yet."

"Whew," he grinned. "Bacon and eggs?"

"Egg," I corrected him, smirking at Holly. "Bacon and *egg*."

She brought her coffee to her lips, her middle finger extending to flip me off in the process. I laughed so hard I almost dropped the mixing bowl.

"You should put milk in those eggs," Brody offered. "Makes em' thicker."

I shook my head. "Milk for density is a rookie mistake."

"And I like my bacon crispy," he added, without missing a beat. "And if you're up for making hash browns, I—"

Holly elbowed him silent and slid the coffee pot his way. She looked adorable, even bedraggled. She had that sexy, smudged-makeup, 'I just got some' look about her. Only she'd gotten about *twice* as much as she bargained for, and then some.

I still can't believe you're doing this.

Ah, the voice of reason. The voice of 'sanity'. It was a voice I'd told to fuck off several times over the past two weeks, and so far the results had been... interesting.

Is that really the word for it?

No, actually. The word was awesome. Because as incredible as taking Holly on my desk and in my bed had been, taking her with someone *else* had been amazingly, unspeakably hot.

The voyeuristic side of me was more than satiated, as I knew it would be. But as much as I'd loved watching? I'd loved *experiencing* it from my end, too. It was twice as fun being responsible for Holly's pleasure, knowing I had someone else on my team. And just seeing her on the bed last night, writhing in her restraints... responding to our every touch...

My God.

It was truly astonishing, just how much I'd gotten off on the whole thing: Sneaking into her apartment with Brody's help. Taking her totally by surprise. Watching her magnificent body stiffen from head to toe, as I slid myself all the way inside her...

It really was a like a dream. The fulfillment of a longtime fantasy. And as with any fantasy, the danger existed that in actual practice it wouldn't live up to my imagination.

Yet the more I examined the events of last night, the more I came to realize it wasn't even the least bit awkward. Brody had been surprisingly cool. Holly had been unbelievably receptive. And fucking her from both ends... taking her so fully and completely as she moaned and whimpered between us?

Holy fucking shit.

My favorite part had been the exact moment the blindfold came off. I'd loved just staring into Holly's eyes. Watching them try to adjust before she finally saw me, her pretty irises all hazy and unfocused and swimming with lust...

But can you really do this? As in relationship *do this?*

That was the million dollar question. I'd had girlfriends before with various commitment levels. Women who required very little attention, and women who needed so much of it that it hurt our overall romance.

But Holly was mature, driven, self-sufficient. Intelligent and sweet. On top of that she was drop-dead gorgeous — everything I'd always wanted in a woman. Losing her because I couldn't keep up my end of the relationship due to business obligations would be devastating, yet given my work ethic, it was almost inevitable.

But with two other guys? Working side by side with you to fulfill her needs?

It was still so incredibly strange, even after last night, to think of sharing her with another guy. And yet, Donovan was a lot like me. The more I talked to him, the more I realized we shared common interests and goals. We'd even worked out together at his gym a few times, something Holly wasn't even aware of. Shit, we'd actually become friends.

That left Brody, the young gun. The one I figured I might easily butt heads with. And yet, for someone his age? He was every bit as mature as the rest of us. Maybe even more so, considering his circumstances. Given the unfortunate childhood of growing up without parents, his grandmother had gone above and beyond to raise herself a smart, well-adjusted, down to earth grandson.

Last night had been the bigger test of whether or not I could go through with it all. Could I *physically* share a girlfriend? And not just on a scheduled basis either, but simultaneously? The idea had always intrigued me. Secretly, I'd always wanted to try it.

And it turned out to be even hotter than I ever thought it would be...

"You're burning the eggs."

Brody's voice broke me out of my trance. By the time I looked down, it was already too late. My would-be omelet had solidified into a single piece of fried, buttery plastic, and my bacon wasn't cooking at all. I had it on the wrong burner, actually. It was still raw.

"There's a diner around the block," Holly chuckled, before adding a sigh. "Which one of you is treating?"

Brody glanced up and pointed a finger my way. I smirked back at him and lowered my head.

"Alright," I said, dropping the pan in defeat. "Let's go."

Thirty-Seven

HOLLY

"So unfortunately you have a problem," I said from my side of the booth. "A very big problem. And here it is."

I slid the open folder across the table, to where Lincoln was still chopping into his omelet. He dropped the fork long enough to pick up the cash flow statements, which had multi-colored highlights all over them.

"The yellow highlighted areas are operating activities. The green ones are for investments."

Lincoln squinted through his glasses, looking so handsome I wanted to kiss him all over again. I still had last night in my blood. Adrenaline from what the two of them had done to me was still coursing through my veins.

"So what's the problem?" he asked.

"The investments," I replied. "The charities specifically. Look at how many there are."

Beside me, Brody was sipping his coffee. I was hyper-aware of his hand on my leg, resting in the middle of my thigh. But I had to stay focused.

Lincoln shrugged. "We give to a lot of charities," he said. "Sometimes we have to dump money for tax purposes. We need the write-offs. We need the—"

"I'm an accountant, remember?" I grinned. "I understand all that. But shit, Lincoln, all these charities? You need some outside business write-offs, too."

"Like what?"

"Buy something small and self-sufficient, without a lot of overhead or employees or supervision." I shrugged. "Open a coin-operated laundromat. Or one of those self-serve car washes. Hell, open three of them. The write-offs will help balance you out come tax time."

He stroked his chin and nodded slowly, really considering my words. The validation felt good. Especially from someone so successful, when it came to business.

"Alright, forget all that for the time being," I went on. "But now here, look at this."

I pulled out a second folder and pushed it his way. He squinted even harder, adjusting his glasses.

Next time we have sex, he's wearing those glasses, the little voice in my head demanded. In the interest of zero distractions, I pushed the voice away.

"These are your missing changes in equity statements," I said. "Once again they were misfiled. Intentionally hidden away." I paused to give him a chance to catch up. "Now, see those places I highlighted in orange?"

"Yes?"

"Those are monies paid as dividends," I explained, "to outside accounts."

Lincoln nodded. He was starting to see.

"Those accounts are going to belong to Kathy," I said apologetically. "Your CFO."

Lincoln swallowed. "I— I don't think I fully—"

"Your chief financial officer is stealing from you, Lincoln. She's paying herself under the guise of charitable donations, and hiding those payments as dividends."

I saw the change. His expression went from one of confusion to disbelief to extreme disappointment.

"But wouldn't we notice—"

"Not if she kept the payments small," I said. "That's why there are so many of these accounts. The payments are steady and constant too, so they add up." If he wasn't going to get angry, I would be angry for him. "They add up to a *lot*."

Brody, who'd been chewing through bacon like he was in some kind of a contest, was now peering over the top of the folder with all new interest. "Someone's ripping you off, bro?"

Lincoln let out a long sigh. "Looks like it."

"That sucks."

The waitress came by and refilled all three of our coffees, allowing a nice span of silence for the whole thing to sink in. By the time she left, Lincoln's dark brows had finally come together.

"Well *fuck*," he spat.

I reached out and laid my hand over his. Lincoln didn't even flinch.

"I'm sorry honey. I know she's a friend."

"A friend? She's also my oldest employee. Kathy was there in the beginning, when it was just the two of us," he sighed. "She's seen everything. *Been* with me through everything..."

Brody shook his head sympathetically. "That sucks man. It really does."

"I just gave out Christmas bonuses..."

By now Lincoln had lost all interest in his food. He looked down at the reports again, as if hoping they'd change. As if begging them to show him something else — something other than what they did.

"That's it then."

He slipped out of the booth and stood up, moving with reluctant slowness. Digging into his pocket, he dropped some cash on the table.

"I'm sorry," said Lincoln. "I'll catch up with you guys later."

Brody nodded and extended his hand. Lincoln shook it, then leaned down to kiss me goodbye.

"Thank you," he croaked. "Without you, I would've never known. This would've gone on and on. I would've kept on believing everything she said..."

He let the last sentence trail off. I could see the hurt in his eyes. The grave disappointment. I was getting all choked up, just watching him.

"Lincoln," I offered as he walked away. "Do you want me to—"

"No," he said sadly. "It has to be me."

Thirty-Eight

HOLLY

"Mind if I run a fast errand?" Donovan asked. "It's not far."

We were walking the beautifully lit streets of the East Village, huddling close to avoid the cold. There was a winter storm gathering. It wasn't quite here yet, but you could feel it in the air — actually taste it on your tongue if you opened your mouth long enough. It was something we didn't have in Texas, and I was jealous of it.

"Is it a good errand or a bad errand?" I smiled.

"Neither one, really. I just need to duck into someplace real quick."

Donovan pulled me through Cooper's Square. The apartments and condos here were decked out in shimmering white lights made to look like icicles. A cone of larger bulbs had been strung around a central pole, creating a makeshift Christmas tree with a colorful star on top.

"Are you kidnapping me, or..."

"I'm afraid it's not anything nearly that exciting," he laughed. "Or at least, not exciting to you. Exciting to me though."

Happily I squeezed his hand, ready for anything. I'd been looking forward to seeing Donovan all day. I hadn't heard from Lincoln since he left the diner this morning, and I had tried real hard not to pry. I was looking for a distraction.

"Here," he said, turning onto 5th street. "Almost there."

Work was over for me, thankfully. All that was left was to enjoy the upcoming weekend in Maine, and then Christmas with the boys. That is, if Lincoln still wanted to go...

"Ah, here it is!"

I watched as Donovan punched the code on a keysafe, then extracted a heavy-looking key. A minute later he had everything unlocked, and was rolling up the corrugated steel door of what looked to be some sort of an empty, garage area.

"What is this place?" I asked.

"Come see."

He pulled me inside and flipped on a set of overhead lights. The place was fairly large, as far as commercial spaces in Manhattan went. A grey cement floor stretched from wall to wall in a big, barren rectangle.

"Welcome to *Donovan's*," he announced, his voice echoing loudly.

"Donovan's?"

"My gym," he smiled. "Or rather, my future gym."

My eyes lit up. Out of pure shock, I punched him in

the chest.

"NO WAY!"

His smile went crooked, which was a little weird.

"Actually you're right," he admitted. "It's not my gym. Not yet. Not for a long while still, although I've been saving like crazy."

His expression was one of longing more than excitement now. I wasn't sure what the hell was going on.

"So you're *eventually* going to open your own gym here?" I asked. "They're like... holding this place for you?"

He shook his head. "No," he said. "No, definitely not."

"Then what are we doing here?"

Donovan closed his eyes and inhaled deeply, as if breathing the place in. Not that it smelled like anything but a garage to begin with, but he didn't seem to mind.

"This *could* be my gym," he said matter-of-factly. "Or my gym could be someplace else. Somewhere nearby though, I think. Somewhere in the Village."

I cocked my head and stared at him. "Once you have the money though, right?"

"Right."

I was still confused. "So what are we—"

"Every month or two I call a real estate agent," he explained, "to look at spaces. To get an idea of what's out there. To see what my gym *could* look like, if I were anywhere near what I actually need to open one."

"So you like to *torture* yourself," I asked, hoping it didn't come out wrong.

"Yes. Sort of."

"Because if I were in your shoes, every time I did this it would be... well... sort of depressing."

Donovan laughed and even his laugh echoed. His voice sounded deep and beautiful.

"Just the opposite," he said. "Holly, take a look around. This is motivational. This is my *future*. My distant future, sure, but my future nonetheless."

I stared around at the garage like a great empty canvas. Solid walls. High ceilings. Even the neighborhood was good. The place really *would be* perfect, as far as putting up a gym went.

"Believe you can," Donovan said loudly, "and you're halfway there."

I chuckled at yet another one of his motivational quotes. "So you have *half* a gym?"

"I have half the money needed to start one," he said. "Considering I go with all used equipment, I do all the interior construction myself, and I save every dime I make..."

I whistled low. "Not bad."

"Maybe a couple of other sacrifices too," he continued. "Not eating... Not sleeping..."

I started to feel sad. The place was amazing, but yet he couldn't have it. Even worse, he *knew* he couldn't have it... but he'd still come to see it anyway.

"So you're just gonna lock this place up?" I said.

"Turn the lights out, and that'll be that?"

"Yup," said Donovan. "But it'll still live in my mind. It'll still serve to motivate me in the months and years that follow, until one day I *can* get a place like this." He shrugged. "Besides, at least I'll get an idea of what I like and dislike. What's out there, how much the rent is... all that sort of knowledge is good to have."

I walked to the middle, trying to envision *Donovan's* gym. I could see the front desk, the locker rooms, the mirrored walls. The place where the dumbbell racks would sit, designating the free weight area.

"This is kinda cool," I admitted. "I guess it's a good... catalyst."

"Catalyst!" he roared, sweeping me between the two steel cables that were his arms. "That's a great way to put it!"

He kissed me hard and forcefully, and I went limp as an overcooked noodle. My mouth opened helplessly against his. Before I knew it I was kissing him back with a passion and longing that seemed suddenly infectious.

"*You're* my catalyst," he breathed, crushing me to his chest. "You know that, right?"

I sighed and nodded, whimpering softly that I did.

"Good. Now let's get out of here and end our date back at my place," said Donovan lustily. "If I'm not going to see you all weekend," he winked, "I can at least give you a proper send-off."

Thirty-Nine

HOLLY

Friday morning found me wrapping up at the office, in anticipation of being done by lunch. It was already a skeleton crew. We'd been a half staff for most of the week, and now only a handful of us were left.

Maine...

I smiled happily, setting everything in its proper place for after the new year. Lincoln hadn't told me everything about how it went with Kathy, but I knew he'd fired her. I also knew that by now he was looking forward to getting out of the City, about as much as I was.

A cabin in the woods...

It sounded almost like a movie when I put it that way. One of those horror flicks that always started off so scenic and beautiful, and by the end everyone was dead. The once-idealistic cabin would be covered in blood. Ditto for the car which, of course, wouldn't start; the trees surrounding it...

"You have some imagination Holly," I laughed out

loud.

I was startled when a voice behind me actually answered. "What?"

I whirled, and there was Malcolm again. This time he had his hand up apologetically.

"Sorry, didn't mean to scare you."

I frowned as I spun back around in my chair. My ex had made the pilgrimage from the upper floors again, probably to wish me a merry Christmas or something equally stupid. Or maybe worse. I couldn't even *imagine* what he wanted now.

"What is it this time, Malcol—"

CLACK!

The sound was loud and obnoxious as his hand smacked onto my desk. When his palm moved away again, there was something shiny left behind.

I stared at it in disbelief.

"You're *kidding*, right?"

It was my Volkswagen key fob. The little silver one, he'd given to me once before.

"Here," said Malcolm. "I want you to have your car back." He paused awkwardly. "With my apologies."

I let out a harsh, bitter laugh. "Why, is Patricia finally done with it?"

"Patricia," he said, "is no longer a part of my life. And she's no longer welcome to my car. I mean... *your* car."

I whirled on him without warning. My expression could best be described as a sneer of contempt.

"*I'm* no longer in your life!" I snarled.

"I know, but—"

"You think I want my *car* back?" I laughed. "After you *took* it the way you did? After you just *gave it away* to your latest girlfriend?"

"I— I was only—"

"What happened Malcolm? She smashed it up?"

"Twice," he cried pleadingly. "Oh Holly, you have no *idea* what I've been through! It's been a nightmare! Not to mention how much this is going to cost me, when I have to turn in the lease."

I could see he was frazzled. Chewed up around the edges. Malcolm never did handle a crisis very well, and whatever was going on had been particularly rough on him.

"You've been taking the bus and the subway anyway, right?" he reasoned. "So just take the car. Finish out the lease. I'll even split the damages with you, when we finally—"

I picked up the keychain and threw it as hard as I could. It sailed across the mostly empty office, landing a good eight or ten cubicles away.

"Holly!" he cried, wagging a finger. "That's... that's immature."

"You're lucky I can't throw *you* across the office like that," I growled. "Very lucky."

But my boyfriends can...

Just the idea of it made me smile. I started to picture it in my mind's eye...

With characteristic sternness, Malcolm shook his head. "I should've known," he said sadly. "Actually, I *did* know. I knew you couldn't handle the responsibility of being promoted upstairs. I knew you were too hotheaded to even—"

"*WHAT* did you say?"

I was up now, out of my chair. Standing toe to toe with him, my fists clenched so hard I could feel my fingernails digging into my palms.

All of a sudden my ex-boyfriend looked very nervous. "Nothing."

"No, you said... you were going to..."

The full realization of what happened crashed over me in a giant wave. My mouth opened, my fists unclenched. All of a sudden I felt cataclysmically stupid.

"Ohhhhhh..." I swore. "I *get* it now..."

Malcolm swallowed and looked at me sideways. "G– Get what?"

"You talked your bosses out of promoting me," I swore. "You didn't *want* me up there on the eighteenth floor with you!"

"N–No," he stammered. "That's not true. Not entirely, anyway. I merely pointed out—"

"You put the word out with the higher-ups, didn't you?" I was livid now. Beyond livid. Malcolm actually began walking backwards, only with each step he took, I took a step forward.

"You *screwed me out of my promotion* Malcolm! Didn't you? Tell me, Malcolm! Tell me that's not the case."

He stared back at me without saying a single word. He didn't have to. His expression said everything.

"You wanted *her*," I swore. "Oh wow, this was over a *girl*, wasn't it? You wanted Patricia up there. You convinced your bosses to hire her instead of me, and then you swooped in."

His lips moved, but no sound came out. He looked terrified.

"You gave her my job, then you gave her my car, too." I took another step forward. "Holy *SHIT* Malcolm! You're a special breed of asshole, aren't you?"

By now a tiny crowd had gathered. It was only a small handful of people, but it was enough that word would spread through the office like wildfire. Not that I cared.

"Holly," Malcolm managed. "Holly, listen."

"Get the fuck out of here, Malcolm."

I took another step. He retreated, bumping into the partition behind him.

"Holly, I—"

"GET THE FUCK OUT!"

He turned and scrambled away, tripping over his own feet in the process. I watched with satisfaction as Malcolm sprawled to the floor of my little cubicle row, then got up and sprinted his way toward the elevators.

It was unreal. I couldn't believe I hadn't seen it before! And yet... I wondered who else had. I hurt to think about how many of my coworkers might be in the know, and how badly I'd been played.

I was shaking with rage, or adrenaline, or whatever it was. And all of a sudden, I had a massive headache.

"Merry Christmas," I said, whipping around to face to the little crowd. They scattered so quickly it was almost hilarious.

I would've laughed had my skull not been pounding.

Forty

HOLLY

The elevator took forever, but it was my last obstacle to being free. The last thing standing between me and a long weekend away. Between me and Christmas... and everything that came along with it.

Between me and the boys.

My body still shook with adrenaline, but now my mind raced too. I was looking just as forward to Christmas — with all three of my boyfriends — as I was to spending a few quiet nights out of the City. It was like having two vacations. Two very distinct, very enjoyable payoffs after a long month of working, shopping, and wrapping gifts for dozens of people I'd never even know or meet.

The parking garage was all but deserted — a byproduct of the last day of work. The higher-ups had all taken off early in the week, driving or flying out to their houses in the Hamptons or upstate New York to have beautiful holidays with big, happy families. That left the rest of us — the ones still doing the bulk of the work — to tie up loose ends.

I was walking down the elevator hallway when I heard it: a noise, somewhere behind me. It was a distinct shuffling. The rhythmic scuff of heels on cement.

The sound disappeared the second I stopped walking.

Was it an echo?

That made sense, although the hallway had never echoed before. Then again, I'd never seen the garage this empty.

Slowly I started again, listening intently. The noise still reached my ears. It was softer this time... but still there.

Don't turn around... don't turn around... don't turn—

I picked up the pace, until I was practically jogging rather than walking. And sure enough, the noise did too. Whoever was following me wasn't being careful, which meant either they weren't all that good at being quiet... or they just didn't care.

Both possibilities terrified me.

Holly, go!

I kept going, too scared to look back. Too frightened of what I might see, of losing even a few precious seconds of distance between us in the time it took to turn around. The mouth of the building yawned before me, and through it, filtered grey daylight. I focused on the doorway, until finally I was running...

I broke out into the street, looking like a madwoman as I sprinted across the sidewalk. With throngs of people milling around in every direction, I felt safe enough to whip my head around and risk a glance...

The shadows of the parking garage remained absolute. I could sense movement in them, though. A vague stirring.

I walked backwards for a good half block, making sure I wasn't being followed. Eventually I picked out a small cafe, ducked inside, and slipped into the first empty chair so I could watch the window. I sat there for a good five minutes, heart racing, just watching as dozens upon dozens of people walked by.

"Miss?"

When I glanced up, a shaggy-haired waiter was staring down at me pleasantly. His smile put me somewhat at ease.

"Did you need anything to drink?"

"N—No," I said, starting to get up. "I was just..."

A man walked by the window, tall and gruff and determined. His eyes were scanning in every direction, as if he were on a mission.

Was that him?

Then again, the next man looked pretty much the same. So did some of the women. Half of all these people, I knew, were tourists. Walking with that swiveled-headed gait, that skyscraper-gazing awe, you only saw in New York City.

Shit, I'd done the same thing for *weeks* after I first got here.

"On second thought, you know what?" I told the waiter, "I *will* have a drink."

The man's smile returned. He pulled out his little pad as I plopped back into my seat.

"Make it a double, actually."

Unwrapping Holly - Krista Wolf

Forty-One

HOLLY

It was already dark by the time Ulrich arrived to pick me up, which was unbelievable considering it was only four O'clock. That was the worst part about Christmas here for me. This time of year the sun in New York City went down a full hour before it did in San Antonio. The short days and scant sunlight seemed to cast everything in a premature gloom.

But I tried to look on the bright side. At least it meant longer *nights*.

As I packed, I forced myself to forget about the incident in the parking garage. I chalked it up to my imagination, or maybe just another employee getting off the same time I did. There was no reason to think otherwise, and I didn't want to ruin the weekend with needless worry. Besides, it was New York City! There were people literally everywhere.

But not in Maine...

As the shiny black Lexus turned onto my street, I was already in a much better mood. The excitement at going away with Lincoln drove away everything else, even my anger at Malcolm. I stood on my tiptoes so I could plant a Christmas kiss on Ulrich's cheek, then jumped into the front seat instead of the back to make chit-chat with him all the way to John F. Kennedy Airport.

In truth, I needed the company. I wanted to work out every last bit of anxiety before getting on the plane. When the car finally stopped at the private aviation center, Lincoln was there to open the door for me. He took my hand, pulled me to him, and greeted me with a smile and a kiss.

"You ready?"

It was absolutely *freezing* cold! Windy too. My lover's body was warm though, especially as I slid my hands around his waist to kiss him back.

"Let's go then," said Lincoln. "Pilot says we gotta beat the storm."

Ulrich handed my bag to someone else, and I saw the aircraft that would take us into the sky. It was a small but beautiful jet, the interior lights looking warm and inviting through its rounded windows.

We boarded, and the first thing I noticed were the plush leather seats on either side of the fuselage. There were tables to sit at. Places to kick back and actually stretch out.

"I've never been on a private plane before," I admitted.

"You're gonna like it," Lincoln chuckled. "But only for about two hours. In this thing, Maine isn't all that far."

I sat down, marveling at how comfortable and spacious everything was. The cabin *was* warm, and well-lit, with a fully-stocked bar off to one side. When Lincoln picked up an already-open champagne bottle and some glasses, I nodded happily.

Glancing up toward the nose, I could see into the cockpit. Lights and avionics blinked from every surface of the control console. One of the pilots saw me looking, smiled back at me, and tipped his hat.

"He's here," I heard him say, his eyes shifting to Lincoln.

"Good. Get him up here already, he's late. And feel free to call for clearance whenever you're ready."

I looked back at Lincoln a little confused. "Who's he talking abou—"

Halfway through my sentence, someone else came up the ramp. He literally jumped on board, wearing an oversized backpack and a big, shit-eating grin.

"Brody!"

Brody smiled back at me with a wink as he began looking upward, presumably for the overhead compartments.

"Drop it anywhere young gun," Lincoln instructed him, "and take a seat. We're gonna be taxiing in a moment."

"Roger that," said Brody.

Lincoln leaned into me and nuzzled my neck, sweeping my hair back to get at my bare skin. His lips brushed my ear and a whole flock of butterflies took off in my stomach.

"You don't mind that I invited him, do you?"

My mouth was dry. Almost too dry to speak.

"No," I practically choked. "Not at all."

"Good," Lincoln murmured. "He had no plans for the weekend, really. And after the other night the three of us had together... well..."

His tongue dragged its way along my the rim of my ear. His breath was hot. Steamy. Driving me absolutely wild.

"I invited Donovan too... but he couldn't make it. Too many clients, too many sessions. He just couldn't get out of work."

I was relieved by that and yet disappointed, all at the same time. Handling Lincoln *and* Brody for the weekend would be challenge enough! I didn't even know the logistics of how it would work, being away for a few days with the both of them...

But I was more than ready to try.

Brody sank into the couch on the other side of me, with a champagne flute of his own. I felt a flood of wetness between my legs. My body was exploding with heat.

"We're going to do all kinds of things to you, Holly," Lincoln breathed.

He had one hand on my thigh already. Brody dropped a hand on the other. They both squeezed.

"*All* kinds of things."

Forty-Two

HOLLY

The climb was quick and choppy, but the rest of the flight remained smooth and beautiful. I spent our two hours in the air basically unwinding. Lounging out across the laps of my two attentive boyfriends, letting go of Malcolm's bullshit, of the New York crowds, and whoever might've been following me in the parking garage.

Lincoln stared at his laptop, playing absently with my hair. He claimed he'd ditch it once we landed, but needed to get a few last minute things done first.

Brody on the other hand, was giving me what amounted to a professional foot massage. I wasn't sure where he learned his technique, but he soon had me moaning and groaning with delight. I was still twisting happily beneath his firm, experienced grip as the pilot announced we were already descending, ending my far-flung dreams of joining the mile-high club... at least for now.

Once down, the weather was even more brutally cold. The storm about to sweep New England would be something else; the pilots were talking about it on the radio and to each other, all the way to the hangar.

A car had been prepared for us, or rather, an old Ford Bronco. Someone flipped Lincoln the keys, and ten minutes later we were piling into the front bench seat, all loaded and ready to go.

"This was my first vehicle," Lincoln explained, starting the engine up. "Not sure why I keep her, but she's well maintained. Nostalgia, probably."

It took several minutes for the heat to kick on, but when it did things got cozy. I was nestled happily between my two men, staring through the windshield and into the darkness. Already it had begun to snow.

"Is your place far?" Brody asked.

"Not too bad. An hour maybe."

The heat from the vents washed over us as Lincoln navigated the pitch black highways. Personally I couldn't see *anything*. There weren't even any streetlights.

"This reminds me of Texas," I sighed contentedly. "But without the snow."

"Yeah, but you have cow-tipping," Brody offered.

I rolled my eyes theatrically. "Oh yeah. There's always that."

What started out as small ice crystals turned into heavy white flakes as the drive went on. Snow began accumulating on the roads. The wind was whipping it across our field of vision, creating almost whiteout conditions that forced Lincoln to slow down.

"I didn't realize the storm would be this bad," he said. "I haven't had much time to look at the weather."

"Got firewood at this cabin?" asked Brody.

"No, but I have an axe," Lincoln answered. When Brody looked at me and mouthed the words 'what the fuck' Lincoln let out a hearty laugh. "Yes there's firewood," he finally admitted. "But the place has *heat* too."

I snuggled into him on the driver's side. His arm felt firm and wonderful beneath my cheek. "I want a fire anyway," I said.

"Then you'll have one. And soon too, because we're here."

The Bronco swung right, and a long driveway spilled out before us. Lincoln drove on for what seemed like several hundred more feet before a large but cozy-looking cabin came into view.

"Welcome to Chalet Wallace," he announced, as we rolled to a stop. He yanked up on the parking brake.

Lights were on throughout the house. High above, I could see smoke rising from the chimney as well.

"Is there someone else here?"

"No," said Lincoln. "But I had the place prepped for us ahead of time. Lights... heat... the wood-burning stove..."

Brody shook his head in awe. "Man, you've got a lot of people doing a lot of things for you," he whistled low.

"I do," Lincoln admitted. "I've been very lucky."

"You've also worked very hard," I pointed out. "You took risks. Sacrificed long hours. You *built* something for yourself, Lincoln. That's why you have this. Not luck."

He slung my bag over one shoulder, and his bag over the other. The look he gave me though, was one of admiration.

"Door should be open," he said, jerking his head at Brody. "Go on in."

Brody sprinted happily up the walkway and pushed his way inside. As he did, Lincoln made his way over to me.

"I need to thank you again," he said, "for all the help you've given me." He looked down at the ground for a second. "You know, with the books. And with Kathy. And..."

"It's okay," I smiled, grasping his one free hand. "Anytime."

"No, I mean it Holly," he said. "You're really... well..."

I laughed into the wind. "I'm what?"

"You're special to me."

We stared at each other, and suddenly I couldn't feel the cold anymore. There was just the two of us — his eyes, finding mine. Locking onto them. Drawing me in.

Lincoln dropped both bags, and sifted his hands through my hair. He pulled me nose to nose with him.

"I love you, Holly."

I couldn't breathe — somehow my breath was lost on the wind. Rather than try to catch it I just stood there, absorbing the gravity of the moment.

"I love you too," I whispered finally. It was so cold, my words came out as little puffs of white smoke. "You're *amazing*, Lincoln. You're everything I've ever—"

Anything else I might've said was lost there in the gravel driveway, as he pulled my face to his and kissed me.

Forty-Three

BRODY

I'd been skiing with friends once or twice, and I'd even rented a cabin. But it was never anything this remote. And never anything *nearly* this beautiful, as Lincoln's chateau or chalet or whatever the fuck he was calling it.

Out here on the ass-end of Maine, everything was breathtakingly beautiful. From the towering pines to the snow-covered lakes, everything we passed looked like something out of a postcard or a Christmas painting.

We were back on the road again, after a short stint in the cabin. Apparently whoever stocked the place had neglected a few things, and Lincoln claimed there was a shopping center 'just up the road'.

Just up the road turned out to be ten miles away. And shopping center... well, that was even more laughable. It looked more like a convenience store with a liquor store patched onto the end of it. And not one of those good liquor stores either. The ones that only sold wine and beer.

We'd made the most of it, laughing together as we shopped for snacks and drinks and whatever else we'd need to get through the weekend. Holly and I dipped next door to pick up some wine. Lincoln bought chips and pretzels and about five pounds of 'premium' beef jerky in all different flavors. I never could understand why people ate such a thing in the first place, but I figured to each his own.

In the end we finished quickly, as the store was already shutting down for the storm. The roads were filling up with snow fast, and the plows could barely keep up with it. We huddled back into the front of Lincoln's bronco, feeling warmer and cozier than ever before.

Holly sat between us, wearing tight jeans and an even tighter sweater. I caught Lincoln looking at her more than once, and each time he only shrugged and smiled that knowing smile.

It was crazy, how much we both wanted and desired her. Even crazier, how much she flirted back with us. The entire evening had been filled with non-stop sexual innuendo; with groping and kissing and touching between us and Holly that seemingly had no actual limits.

On the way back it got even crazier, as Holly grew a bit more daring during the ride home. She had one hand in each of our laps. Her fingers worked deftly at our buttons and zippers, working hard between our legs to massage our growing erections.

There was a certain camaraderie that came with sharing a woman that I never knew I'd enjoy. And yet here I was, making out with this wonderful woman. Feeling her body writhe beneath my fingers as she turned her head to make out with Lincoln... and not even feeling the slightest bit of jealousy.

We stayed in the truck for another fifteen minutes after arriving back at the house, just kissing and touching and licking her. Somehow we'd gotten her shirt off, and we'd been taking turns making out with her hotly. Alternating between Holly's soft, moaning kisses and drowning within the supple flesh of her warm, beautiful breasts.

Chasing her back inside, we locked the door behind us. The chalet was warm, the fire still cozy. And though the wind howled like crazy outside, inside we'd created a nice little nest of pillows and blankets right before the roaring fireplace.

So you finally found the girl of your dreams...

I really had. Holly was perfect, inside and out. And most of all I knew it too, unlike all those movies where the guys never really knew what they had until the end.

But does she want you too?

I sure thought so. Or rather, it certainly seemed that way. When we'd decided to all date her at once we'd made a pact not to pressure her, or push her, or be jealous of one another. And so far I'd kept up my end of the bargain. Every minute of every day.

And what if she doesn't? The voice of doubt crept unbidden, into my head. *What if she picks one of the other two?*

I couldn't imagine it — not the way things were going so far. And yet, it was still a distinct possibility. The idea that Holly would grow tired of all the attention and drama of having three boyfriends, and somehow decide upon the one she loved most.

That couldn't happen... could it? I tried not to think about it. Especially not as we were having so much fun, deciding on a whim to play a little strip poker... right there in front of the fireplace.

"I'll get the cards," said Lincoln, bolting for the staircase. "Be right back."

I sat staring at the fire, enjoying the hypnotic dance of the flames. Letting its warmth seep into my body, until last of the outside chill was driven from my bones.

"Brody?"

I turned and she was staring at me, her eyes liquid fire. They shined with new life in the orange, flickering light.

"You okay?"

I nodded and smiled placatingly. I was on a weekend getaway, about to play strip poker in front of a roaring fire with my beautiful girlfriend. What could possibly *not* be okay?

"You look... far away."

"Sorry," I said. "I was thinking of stupid crap. Of the problems back at my apartment."

It was a lie, but I didn't want to tell her the truth: that I was scared. Worried that though she loved me, in the end she wouldn't be *in* love with me.

Frightened that maybe she wouldn't pick me.

"You're not thinking of Andrea, are you?"

I wasn't. God, how I wasn't!

"Look, I know it sucks, not having a place to go back to," said Holly. "This lunatic is making it so that you can't even feel comfortable in your own home."

That much was true. I *did* need to get out of there. Even without Andrea — who wasn't leaving anytime soon — I had three other roommates, all sharing the same space. It was okay, but it wasn't ideal.

"I still want you to stay with me," Holly smiled, cozying up to me. The wine on her breath smelled delicious. I could tell she was pleasantly tipsy. "I love having you in my place," she practically whispered. "I love having you inside me..."

Her hand went to my crotch, where she gave me a delightful squeeze. As I stiffened in her hand, Holly grinned wickedly.

"I love you Brody," she said, and then kissed me. "Every last bit of you."

Forty-Four

HOLLY

It was by far the hottest night of my life. Mentally... emotionally... physically. Layer upon layer, on every beautiful level, it was every girl's wildest dream come true.

Strip poker was fun, especially considering how lucky I was. For some strange reason, I just couldn't lose. Piece by piece, I stripped the guys of every article of clothing they had on. I exposed Lincoln's wonderful shoulders. Brody's perfect, bubble-shaped ass. From the tremendous biceps and triceps of their sexy arms, to their flat, rippled stomachs, I made them take it all off — each and every piece — until they were both sitting naked before me.

"Turn around," I laughed as Brody lost another hand. Somehow I was still in my underwear. "You don't have anything left, so you have to do what I say."

At one point I accused the guys of throwing the game to get themselves naked, but Lincoln quickly pointed out how such a thing made little sense. It was their common goal to get *me* naked, and since there were two of them, it should've been an easy job at that.

Instead, here we were.

Hour by hour, the cabin became ours. Brody poured the wine, at a speed that kept us flush and happy without getting drunk. Lincoln fed the fire, bathing us in a comfy, glowing warmth that made being naked preferable to wearing anything at all. The wind raged outside, screaming in protest as the cold was kept comfortably at bay. Eventually the cards flew over our shoulders and we went straight to it, stretching our eager bodies right out across the floor.

Brody dove between my legs, pulling my G-string aside as he buried his nose in my dripping wetness. He teased me mercilessly with his tongue, gliding all the way up and all the way down. Resisting me as I tried screwing myself against his face. Holding himself intentionally back, every time I begged him to go deeper.

"God..."

My head was spinning with Lincoln's kisses, which were loving and passionate and full of meaning. I gasped as his tongue traced its way down the hollow of my throat. Squirmed as his wet mouth found one achingly pert nipple, and then two.

"One..." I gasped, spreading even wider for Brody's tongue. "One of you..."

"One of us what?" Lincoln teased, kissing me again.

I sighed, running my fingers through Brody's thick, blond hair. My hand clenched as I rolled my knuckles, forcing his tongue inside me.

"One of you has *got* to fuck me..."

I was beyond lost now. Totally in heat. My hips writhed in circles, smashing myself against Brody's wet, willing mouth. And my eyes...

My eyes locked on Lincoln's. Deep in our hearts we connected on the most primal and fundamental of levels.

"Do it," I gasped. "Please..."

"Please what?" he laughed gently into my mouth. He kissed me again, then kissed me some more. He kept kissing me and kissing me until it felt like my head would explode.

"Fuck me," I gasped when I could breathe again. "Fuck me fuck me fuck me *FUCK ME*..."

His goatee curled into a grin as Lincoln looked down my body, to where Brody was still devouring me in front of the fire.

"Heads or tails, bro?"

Brody lifted his head and grinned, all glazed with my wetness from nose to chin.

"I'll take tails for now," he said, "since I'm down here already." He made a sideways motion with his head. "But help me turn her over."

A minute later I was on my stomach, hissing with satisfaction as Brody sank into me from behind. His cock drilled me deep, his hands pushing my asscheeks upward and apart to gain the deepest possible penetration.

Kneeling before me, Lincoln guided his own erection into my willing mouth.

Ohhhhh...

It was every bit as good as sinking into a warm bath.

The satisfyingly familiar feeling of pure, sensory overload.

I was made for this.

It was such an odd thing to say. A strange thing to just pop randomly into your head. And yet in reality, the observation wasn't all that random. I fell so quickly and easily into the familiar push-pull rhythm, it was as if being filled from both ends were some common daily occurrence.

It's sure getting to be...

"That's it baby," said Lincoln, gently stroking my face. His voice was already thick with lust. "Just like that."

I was throating him easily now. Screwing my ass back against Brody and adding that extra gyration I knew he liked at the end. And I was getting *off* on it. I was so incredibly hot for them, so dripping wet. Every stroke brought me that much closer...

"She's getting too good at this," Lincoln observed. "She must really love it."

He held my head in his hands now, helping guide it up and down along the length of his cock. When I popped it from my mouth to lick it all over, he smiled.

"Tell us you love it," he growled.

I licked and sucked, jerking him with my hand. Bracing myself with my other arm, while working my way toward his balls.

"Tell us you—"

"*I love it,*" I moaned, soft and low. I swore I could feel him grow harder, just at the words. "God, I so fucking *love* it..."

I felt Brody's hands digging in as he pumped me faster. He pushed into me hard, shoving his balls up against me as he drove himself deeper.

"Fuck..."

My breath grew quick. The wind left my lungs in short little bursts. A hand went into my hair, pulling my head back. Forcing me to adjust, my chin tilting upward, as Lincoln sank deeper into my throat.

I don't know how long they fucked me, passing me back and forth. Sometimes they'd spin me around or flip me over. Other times they'd just get up and switch places, taking me in any position, any way they wanted.

I loved it all, though. I lay there snug in the blankets, warmed by the fire. Crushed beneath the weight of their hard bodies, rocking, groaning, spreading myself wide for them.

It was like being in another world. A world of sheets and pillows, of flesh and flame. I was sitting on Lincoln, my hands on his shoulders, when my first release came. My breasts were in his hands, the weight of them held in his palms, as a monster orgasm rocked my body... even as Brody held me from behind.

"Good?"

I nodded, gasping. So good. So fucking *good!*

"Now lean forward."

I did, pressing my chest against Lincoln's. Not even caring as my hair flopped down like a waterfall, enveloping our faces on all sides in a little cocoon of shimmering auburn.

"Sit tight," said Lincoln. "We're gonna try something."

My eyes went wide. My body stiffened.

"Easy," he chuckled, his lips brushing mine. "This will go better if you relax."

I felt it now, Brody's hands clasped firm on my hips. His body squatting, adjusting, positioning himself behind me...

Oh God.

Then it happened; his cock probed its way forward. But not in the way I expected. Not in the *place* I expected.

Oh my God, they're going to—

"*OHHHHHH!*"

My whole body went weak as Brody pushed himself straight up inside me.

Forty-Five

HOLLY

It was *tight*. So incredibly tight and intense and a whole host of other adjectives I couldn't quite grasp. But at the same time, it was the most wonderful feeling in the world! The craziest, fullest, most incredible—

"That's it," Lincoln whispered, kissing me tenderly. "He's *in*."

He sure fucking is.

I groaned as Brody slid out slowly and then back in again. He was fucking me from behind now. Fucking my *pussy*. Fucking the same pussy that Lincoln was already fucking, already buried in, and yet somehow they both managed to fit.

You're fucking two guys... the little voice in my head screamed. *AT THE SAME TIME.*

I was. And not just from a tag-team or a spitroast perspective either, but actually *fucking them both* simultaneously.

"God it feels good," Brody murmured from behind me. His voice was lower and thicker than I'd ever heard it before.

"Holly you're so. Fucking. Tight."

I sure hope so, I wanted to gasp. And yet I couldn't say anything. All I could do was keep still while Lincoln held my ass spread in his two powerful hands. Keeping me open for my other lover, so he could gain more leverage as he glided in and out of me.

"Two cocks inside you..." Lincoln murmured. "How's it feel?"

I wanted to pound his chest with my fists. Bite down on his shoulder so hard my teeth would leave marks.

"It's... oh, it's fucking *amazing*," I said truthfully. "It's so *hot*. So tight and full with the both of you in there. You feel so *thick* together!" I gasped as Brody's thrusts became more confident. He was getting bolder. Going deeper...

"Oh my God... Oh my God..."

I wanted to screw back against them, as I always had. Only I was afraid. I was already walking the razor thin edge between ultimate pleasure and what could possibly be pain... I decided to trust in what Brody was doing and let him take full control.

"You're so fucking *sexy*," said Lincoln, kissing my face. "The expressions you're making right now. God... they're so beautiful. I've never seen anything—"

Suddenly there was a surge, and I felt Brody let go. It happened without warning, without anything other than a flare of pain as his fingers dug into my hips and a screaming war-cry from just behind me.

I bore down as he thrusted up, feeling his pulses, squeezing every drop from my lover's throbbing cock as I milked him into my pussy. Everything was explosive: the heat, the wetness, the pressure of having two men in a place only one had ever been... it all combined to bring Lincoln off just seconds later, physically lifting us as his ass thrusted upward from the floor.

"UNNNGGHHHH!"

He hissed his orgasm into my face, every muscle in his body going utterly rigid. Then I felt him go off as well, in a searing, molten rush. Throbbing, exploding, pumping my impossibly tight channel full of his cream.

I collapsed forward onto his chest as he gripped me, still in the throes of ultimate pleasure. Still shooting, firing, filling me up... my pussy contracting around him, as if greedy for every last thing he could possibly give.

It was a full minute later before Brody slipped out of me, creating a giant, gooey mess. I could feel their combined seed come boiling out of me, running down my thighs, pooling on the floor between Lincoln's muscular thighs even as he kept himself buried in my sweltering core.

"We have *got* to do that again!" Brody cried, falling backwards into some pillows.

I was hugging my lover, totally spent. Unable to say anything. Unable to even move, until he wanted to move me.

"Yeah..." breathed Lincoln. "Definitely. And next time you need to last longer!"

"Are you kidding?" Brody protested. "I just couldn't. It was too hot, too tight. To fucking crazy in there."

"I know, I know," chuckled Lincoln. "I was in there too."

In time we slid apart, all of us on our backs with our feet to the fire. Feeling the warmth of the flames against our bare toes as we stared at the vaulted cabin ceiling.

"Merry Christmas," I laughed, when I could breath again.

They both turned my way and looked at each other. Then they began tickling me at the same time.

"Yeah," Lincoln admonished between my giggles. "Merry Christmas to *you!*"

Forty-Six

HOLLY

I stirred in the darkness, secure beneath the warmth of three layers of blankets. Between that, and the two gorgeous men snoring on either side of me, I was feeling pretty fucking toasty.

Too toasty.

My stomach growled, and not for the first time. I was hungry. Starving, even. Sometime after our tryst in front the fire, the three of us had yawned our way up to the master bedroom on the second floor... without even so much as a snack before bed.

I had no idea what time it was. In all the fun I'd had with the boys last night, and all the things we'd done afterward, time seemed to lose all meaning.

Silently I slipped downward, crawling my way out from the base of the mattress. Luckily the sheets weren't *too* tucked in. I managed to extract myself without waking anyone, and pushed open the door to the room.

A blast of cold enveloped me, and I retreated inside to grab some clothes. I wasn't adverse to wandering the house in my underwear, but not if it meant shivering.

A quick pair of sweatpants and two T-shirts later — one of them Brody's — I was on my way to the kitchen. I wasn't exactly sure what I'd find in the fridge, but the snacks we'd bought at the convenience store sounded incredibly good all of a sudden. Even Lincoln's vast selection of beef jerky.

I crossed the living room, past the sad remains of our roaring fire. A few glowing embers cast an orange pall over our makeshift sexual 'picnic', illuminating the blankets and pillows and sheets.

Double-penetration.

The phrase was dirty. Naughty. Incredible arousing.

Double-vaginal, actually.

I still couldn't believe it. Neither could my swollen entrance. I was pleasantly, satisfyingly sore between the legs, to the point where I was being careful with my steps. But it had been worth it. Every glorious, beautiful second of it...

And they want to do it again...

I chuckled as I crossed the threshold into the kitchen. I'd have to ask for some sort of a break, maybe. At least in the morning. Waking up next to them, the warmth of my womanly body pressed against theirs, I had a feeling one or both of them would be raring to go. And if that were the case, maybe I'd accommodate them. But only with my mouth...

Morning blowjobs, eh?

Actually, it sounded fun. Suddenly I was looking forward to it. Staring into Brody's face as I went down on Lincoln... seeing the lust in his eyes as I—

KNOCK...

I whirled, nearly tearing the door off the refrigerator as I yanked it open. The noise had come from the previous room. From the living room, or maybe—

KNOCK KNOCK.

My heart began racing, the kitchen floor feeling suddenly cold beneath my bare feet. It was a faint sound, a gentle sound. Maybe the wind. A stray branch, banging against the house. But as much as I wanted to believe that, the sound was also very distinct.

KNOCK KNOCK KNOCK.

Okay, *now* it was louder! So loud that it was unmistakable. It was a knock. A *door* knock, because it was definitely coming from the front door.

I abandoned the fridge without shutting it, as if the slightest noise or movement would give away my position. Then I crept backward, into the living room. The staircase wasn't far. All I had to do was cross the—

"OHHH!"

My heart leapt from my chest as I jumped a foot in the air! There was a figure standing next to me. A figure standing *beside* me, so close he could reach out and grab me and—

"EASY, Holly..."

It was Lincoln. Bare-chested and beautiful and wearing only his boxers. The half-fire cast amazing shadows over his muscles, bringing them out in stark definition. Even terrified and startled out of my wits, I found myself staring.

"There's someone at the door!" I whispered loudly.

"Someone's trying to—"

"I heard it too," Lincoln breathed. "I heard the knocking."

He walked confidently in the direction of the front door, as if it were broad daylight and he was expecting someone. But he did reach for something first... a fireplace poker. A long, heavy length of iron with a twisted hook at the end, taken from the tool set near the hearth.

KNOCK KNOCK KNOCK—

"WHO IS IT?" Lincoln demanded loudly.

A voice answered, low and muffled. Stepped on by the wind.

"I SAID WHO—"

"IT'S ME," the voice cried, finally loud enough to be heard. "IT'S DONOVAN!"

Lincoln looked back at me in shock, blinked twice, then flung the door open. Sure enough, Donovan was standing on the porch, shivering like mad, covered in snow from head to toe.

"Holy SHIT!" I cried, running forth. "Donovan! What are you *doing* here!" I ushered him in as Lincoln closed the door. He actually had to lean into it a little, to force it against the wind.

"How in the world did you you..." I stammered, brushing him off. "What did you—"

"I decided to come up," he said teeth chattering. He dropped a duffel bag to the floor with a heavy thump. "I wanted to spend Christmas with you."

Lincoln and I glanced at each other in confusion. He spoke first.

"But we're coming home the day after tomorr—"

"No you're not," Donovan interrupted. "Haven't you seen the news? Have any of you been watching the weather reports?"

We shook our heads. Lincoln slid the poker back in place as I took Donovan's snow-covered coat.

"No one's going *anywhere*," he shuddered. "This storm's going to last for days. Everything's grounded. Several feet of accumulation. Even the City is going crazy... I left not long after you flew out. Just as the first of the flakes started falling."

Lincoln put his hand on Donovan's shoulder, motioning him closer to the fire. Swinging open the iron door, he threw another pair of logs on.

"You actually *drove* here?"

"Most of the way," Donovan nodded. "I got stuck a few miles south of here, in a drift, outside a gas station. Found a guy with a plow who'd drive me up here. He plowed your driveway, by the way. I threw him some cash." He stared at Lincoln for a moment. "You gave the address," he shrugged. "You told me to come."

"Yeah yeah," Lincoln nodded. "Sure man, no problem. I— I just thought you had to stay. You said you had clients, you couldn't leave work."

New flames leapt up, and Donovan held his hands close to the fire. He rubbed them together and glanced back at us.

"I don't have work anymore," he smirked. "I just got fired from *Crunch Time.*"

Forty-Seven

HOLLY

"You got *fired?*" I cried in disbelief. Donovan's nod felt like a punch to the gut. "How'd you get fired?"

"Eddie," he replied, as if it were all that were needed.

"What happened?"

"Well, he was giving me less and less new appointments," said Donovan, "and it was starting to get obvious. He was also approaching some of my existing clients, asking if they'd be willing to switch trainers. 'Scheduling reasons,' he claimed."

Lincoln cursed under his breath. "Scumbag."

"I know, right? Anyway, he was also hitting on two or three of my female clients. Ones I knew he not-so-secretly liked. Not that they'd give him the time of day, but when I started warning them about him he stomped over to have words with me."

"Uh oh," smiled Lincoln.

"Yeah."

"So what happened?" I asked.

"Well, things got heated and he told me to fuck off. In front of *clients*, no less. So I laughed at him, and Eddie didn't like that, so he pushed me."

"And you clocked him," guessed Lincoln.

Donovan nodded. "One punch, right across the jaw. He went straight down, like the sack of shit he really is."

"Good for you," said Lincoln.

"No," I protested, pushing forward. "No, *not* good for him! Because of this he has no job, Lincoln. He has no home gym, no place to train anyone. He's going to lose his clients!"

"Some," Donovan agreed unhappily. "Maybe most. I don't know. That place was... well it was *ideal*, really. Good location, central to the village. Such a great place, except for Eddie."

I stared at Donovan, and he stared at the floor. As for Lincoln, he looked thoughtful. He was rubbing his chin again.

"Well I'm glad you're here," I said hugging him. "We all are."

Lincoln smiled. "True enough, bud. Me casa es su casa."

The fire crackled. Already it was getting warm again, although nowhere near as hot as before. I could see Donovan looking around, taking the place in. Realizing, as Brody and I did, how picture perfect it was.

"Where's Brody?"

"The kid's upstairs sleeping," Lincoln replied. "Snoring like a lumberjack."

Donovan's gaze shifted to me. He raised a

mischievous eyebrow. "You wore him out?"

I made a pouty face. "He wore *himself* out," I said. "If you can believe that."

"On you?" Donovan joked, knowing it was probably less of a joke and much closer to the truth. "Yeah. I can believe it."

We stood huddled around the fire for a while, feeding it well, watching it grow. Donovan talked all about his long ride here. He also told us about the storm, and how we'd likely be stranded here for a while. Maybe a long while.

As the two men laughed and got along, I took a step back to admire them. They were beautiful on the outside, of course — more physically amazing than anyone I'd ever dated. But they were also handsome on the inside, where it really counted. Each of them was smart, driven, funny. Personality-wise they were incredibly sweet also, each in his own unique way.

And Brody...

Slumbering upstairs, Brody added a bright optimism and youthful energy to everything he touched. It was one of the things I loved most about him. That, and his remarkably talented mouth...

Slowly I came to the realization that being stranded here — with my three incredible lovers — wasn't exactly the prison-sentence Donovan was making it out to be. In fact, it sounded like the best Christmas ever.

"Sun's coming up in a a few minutes," said Lincoln, staring into the flames.

"You thinkin' what I'm thinkin'?" Donovan asked.

"Coffee?"

My personal trainer laughed and nodded. "Shit yeah, coffee."

"And breakfast!" I chimed in. My stomach rumbled its full agreement. "I almost forgot why I came down here. I'm starving!"

"What *kind* of breakfast?" Donovan squinted.

Lincoln started counting off on his fingers. "Eggs, toast, bacon, potatoes with onions..."

Donovan wrinkled his nose. "Got any unsweetened, steel-cut oatmeal?"

"Sure," laughed Lincoln. "It's out in the detached warehouse, right next to the Maserati."

"The blue one or the red one?" Donovan grinned.

"Right next to the 'fuck you' sign. Over by the—"

"Will you assholes *stop?*" I laughed. "Holy shit, if we don't make something soon I'm going to chew my own arm off." I pointed at Donovan, then at the kitchen. "It's Saturday now. That's your cheat day. Get the hell in there and start scrambling some eggs before I stick a foot in your ass."

"Foot in my ass," he nodded, grinning. "Got it."

"But first..."

I leapt into his arms and kissed him, before he could say anything else. Donovan's strong arms slid around me. He held me tightly as his lips churned against mine, kissing me back firmly, passionately...

"Welcome to the weekend," I finally winked.

Unwrapping Holly - Krista Wolf

Forty-Eight

HOLLY

"And I say if we're going to have Christmas here, we've *gotta* have a tree..."

Brody's statement was punctuated by him stuffing a quarter of a pancake into his mouth. His jaw moved vigorously, trying to win the ensuing battle.

"I just don't have one," shrugged Lincoln.

"Not even a fake one, up in the attic?"

Our host shot my youngest lover the dirtiest of looks. "A fake Christmas tree is fucking blasphemy," he said. "Might as well install the Yule Log app on your phone and we could sit around watching it, rather than light the fireplace."

Scraping the last egg off his plate with a fork, Donovan laughed. "I don't think that's quite the same thing, bro."

"Whatever."

It was truly hilarious, the breakfast conversation so far. We'd debated the power of vampires vs. werewolves, whether or not Tom Cruise actually found (and refuses to disclose the location of) the fountain of youth, and which was more 'real' pirates or ninjas. The guys had argued over best pizza toppings, bottled water vs. tap water, and which of the *Rocky* movies was the best. The latter at least they agreed upon unanimously: *Rocky IV.*

"So if you don't have a tree, let's go out and get one," Brody was saying.

Lincoln walked over to the window and yanked the curtains back. "See that?"

"No," said Brody.

"Exactly. And that's because it's whiteout conditions out there. Usually the view from this window is quite beautiful. But right now?" He peered again. "I can't even see past all the snow caked on the glass."

Donovan nodded and poured another mug of coffee. "Storm's supposed to rage all day and into the night. We couldn't get out if we wanted to, even if we had three shovels."

Lincoln was still staring out the window. His expression was almost restless. Finally he let go of the curtain and turned back to face us.

"I have *two* shovels."

Brody smiled optimistically. He'd slept more than anyone. I could almost feel the energy radiating from his body, like an electric aura.

"Nothing's gonna be open," said Donovan. "Trust me. The guy that drove me here said it was going to be the worst storm in—"

"You wanna try to shovel out anyway?"

The words just came out. I didn't know why I said

them, but something about playing outside in the snow with my three boyfriends appealed to me.

"I mean, what *else* are we gonna do today?"

All three of their gazes turned to me. I sighed and rolled my eyes, but deep in my tummy I felt a warm tingle. "Besides *that*."

The soreness between my legs was less pain and more a pleasant reminder of last night. Still, there were *three* of them now. A little breather certainly wouldn't hurt, especially if we spent a lot of our energy outside.

"Donovan's probably right," Brody said glumly. "Nothing's going to be open. I guess we could make a snow-tree outside, sort of like a snowman. Sounds lame, but it's better than—"

"I know a place we could try," Lincoln interjected. We all looked at him hopefully. "About three miles from here there's one of those cut-down-your-own Christmas tree farms." He shrugged. "I know the guy who runs it. Even if it's closed, we could stuff an envelope in the mailbox. Take what we want, and—"

"I'm not killing a perfectly happy tree," I jumped in, "just so we can stand it up in your living room for a couple of days."

"We wouldn't have to."

Donovan laughed. "You wanna just decorate it right there, or—"

"No, they have a bunch of pre-cut trees already, for people who aren't into the whole Clark Griswold thing. We could grab one of those."

Brody's eyebrows came together, until we explained to him who Clark Griswold was. When he mentioned he hadn't seen any of the *Vacation* movies, everyone groaned.

"So it's settled?" asked Lincoln. "Dig out, shoot down the road if we can... see if we can make it?"

Brody nodded eagerly, and I found myself following suit. But Donovan crossed his arms.

"And what if we *don't* make it?"

Lincoln smirked back at him. "How's your cardio?"

"Godlike," he said proudly.

"Then three miles shouldn't be much of a problem."

Forty-Nine

DONOVAN

It really was a magnificent tree: big and full and without even a bad side to it. It was also taller than any tree I'd ever had growing up, but then again we'd never had twenty-foot ceilings.

"Damn, it's *still* not straight."

It had taken us the better part of the morning, just to dig out. The snow was at least three feet deep, five at the drifts — and this even after the driveway had been plowed. Luckily it was still light and fluffy, and not the soggy, water-logged snow that always seemed to weigh a ton.

Even running two shovels non-stop, and trading off whenever someone got tired, it wasn't until sometime after noon that we actually reached the main road. And the road itself sucked.

"Push... no, no, on this side," said Brody. "There you go. Hold it right there. Don't let it tilt."

Still, all the shoveling was great exercise. I'd been a little panicked at the prospect of missing a few workouts, and secretly even *more* worried about what would happen when we got back to the City.

No more Crunch Time...

I'd left gyms before, but always voluntarily. Always with something better already lined up, and after having informed my clients way ahead of time. Usually my new home gym would allow a trial period for anyone I brought with me; a free month to enjoy the facilities, on the hope that they'll switch over.

Only right now I had no home gym. I had no plan...

"There, twist it tight. Both sides. But don't let go yet."

I waited until the tree was fully screwed into its stand. Then we all let go at once — tentatively at first — before taking a few steps back to admire it.

"Damn good job," Brody declared. He put his hand out. Lincoln smirked and slapped him a high-five.

"I can't believe we didn't slide off the road," I said.

"Me neither," Lincoln swore, "if I'm being perfectly honest."

It was stupid, really. Risking ourselves for a tree. Driving through a roaring blizzard, swerving around drifts and watching out for the lights of incoming snowplows. The roads had been treacherous, to say the least. Yet we'd all piled into Lincoln's Bronco and braved the trip together, excited and nervous and still fueled with the adrenaline of having shoveled out a quarter-mile of driveway... or at least it sure *seemed* that long.

"Hot chocolate's up!"

Holly re-entered the living room, carrying a tray of

steaming hot mugs. She looked radiant, all rosy-cheeked and flush with the combination of outside and inside, of cold and heat. My heart jumped a bit, just seeing her. I'd driven more than four-hundred miles, with the image of her burned into my brain...

And now she was here, smiling and winking at me. Handing me a cup of hot chocolate.

"No marshmallows?" lamented Brody.

"Sorry man," laughed Lincoln. "Can't have everything."

"We have a Christmas tree at least," Brody agreed. "Even if we don't have ornaments."

Lincoln sank into a nearby chair. Before he did, he kicked a dog-eared box his way. "Got lights though."

In a way it was perfect timing, getting here when I did. Getting out of the City just as the storm hit, and racing it all the way through New England. I'd been very lucky. I'd caught the roads at exactly the right time, just as people had been scared inside due to the upcoming storm. The highways were virtually empty, all the way up.

"Aw crap, they're tangled."

I'd been in the City so long now, I'd forgotten what it was like to drive without traffic. It was just me, the radio, and visions of Holly. She'd made such an impact on my life in such a short time, I couldn't imagine Christmas without her. And not that I was jealous of her spending the weekend with Brody and Lincoln... that part I was totally cool with. But the thought of her spending Christmas without me saying what I needed to say?

That was just too dismal.

"Wanna nap?" Holly laid her head on my shoulder as she snuggled into me on the couch. "I know you drove all night. You have to be exhausted."

I smiled and wrapped my arm around her. I couldn't nap. I couldn't miss any of this.

"Come upstairs with me," I said, grabbing my bag. "Help me unpack."

She smiled and nodded as we set down our mugs together. Brody and Lincoln didn't even look at us as we left. They were too busy arguing over the best way to untangle the tree lights.

We entered one of the guest bedrooms, made up as nicely and clinically as a bed and breakfast. It was amazing how easily you could tell when a room was actually lived in, as opposed to when it was not.

"Something up?"

I looked up to find her leaning against the doorway, looking all breathless and sexy without even trying. I dropped my bag without unzipping it.

"Yes," I said, pulling her into the room. "Come here."

Her mouth went suddenly serious, her expression laced with concern. Even so, she melted into my body. Didn't resist as my arms slid around her, and in fact, pulled me into her own space as well.

"What is it?" she breathed, our faces so close we could kiss at any moment.

For several long seconds all I could do was stare at her,

admiring her beauty. Her perfect, angelic face. Her almond eyes, shining tiffany blue.

"Donovan *tell* me," she whispered. "What is it?"

"It's you," I breathed.

"Me?"

"I think I'm in love with you."

It came out as a sigh. Not of disappointment, but not of abject happiness either. Of somewhere in between.

It was a sigh of *longing*.

My hand came up, and I held her by the chin. My thumb brushed her lower lip, ever so lightly.

"Before you say you something," I whispered, "you need to know I don't expect anything in return. I know your position. I can't even imagine what's going on in your head, but I realize—"

"Hey..."

Holly took my face in her hands. She cradled it gently and leaned forward, until our foreheads were touching.

"I love you too," she breathed. "Totally. Completely. Every bit as much as you love me, Donovan. My feelings for you are all there."

She kissed me, and a fire passed through her lips. I felt it surge from her body into mine, consuming me, lighting me up from within with all new hope and love and reverence.

It made me feel *alive*.

"I'm not expecting you to give yourself to me," I added quickly. "Or make your decision, or feel any differently about the others."

Her expression changed. It grew deeper, maybe a little sadder. But it still held the same amount of love.

"I appreciate that."

"Because I know," I went on, "that we put you in this position ourselves. That in not asking you to choose, we've actually been selfish."

"No..." she murmured, stroking my face. "It's not like that."

"Yes," I went on. "Yes it is."

Holly's lips were pouty now, and it only made her prettier. But there were lines on her forehead too. Worry lines that weren't there before.

"In giving ourselves to you, individually and together, we've made it impossible to separate your feelings for us. And that's not fair. Because if you're looking to make a choice, how can possibly—"

She shushed me, moving one slender finger to my lips. I stopped talking, even as I stayed helplessly locked in her eyes.

"I'm not looking to choose," she said simply. "I love you *all*. If anyone's been selfish here, it's me. I'm the one who hasn't been fair..." Her voice cracked as she finally looked away. "But Donovan, I *can't* choose! I don't know what to do! I came into this thinking it would be fun and easy, but that eventually one or more of us just wouldn't click. Only we *all* click. We all click together so damned well..."

She was becoming upset, and getting her upset was the last thing I wanted. I had to shift gears.

"Look, I just needed you to know how I feel," I smiled happily. "I love you Holly. Alone, together, as a threesome or a foursome — I just fucking *love* you." I pulled her tighter against me, giving her ass a couple of firm squeezes. "And I gotta say, this right here is shaping up nicely."

Her eyes were glassy, but she wasn't crying. If anything, they were brimming with tears of happiness.

"Thanks," she said, squirming deliciously into my palm. "I've got a kickass personal trainer."

"He must work you out often," I replied mockingly.

"He does," she grinned, her own hands now wandering. I jumped as her fingers closed over the crotch of my jeans. "But sometimes I work him out too."

Fifty

HOLLY

It was late by the time we'd finished dinner, and dessert, and second dessert. It seemed that either Lincoln had a sweet tooth, or those responsible for stocking his cabinets did.

When we were finished we retired to the living room, where Brody had the fire going stronger than ever. It was so warm that the windows no longer accumulated snow. Whatever flakes landed on the outside panes quickly melted.

Our little Christmas party consisted of the four of us, two Santa hats, and a bowl of pretty incredible eggnog whipped up, surprisingly, with all the necessary ingredients found in the kitchen. The latter had been well-fortified with brandy and rum, to the point where it might even be flammable.

The tree looked utterly fantastic, even without bulbs or ornaments. Top to bottom, the guys had done a great job wrapping it with an over-abundance of colorful, twinkling lights. A third Santa hat had been planted on top as a makeshift star. It made the whole thing funny, but Christmasy, too.

For an hour or two we just lounged around, drinking

our fill of eggnog before each switching to something lighter. Lincoln and Brody had beer. Donovan was mixing vodka with club soda, which was typical considering how closely he watched his diet.

The conversation started off light, and got heavier as the night wore on. Eventually it went to our families, and how distant and far away they all were right now. Even Lincoln, who'd grown up not far from the cabin we sat in, lamented the obvious disconnect. The social and emotional distance invoked by long hours of tedious work, and not spending enough time with those he loved.

"Let's make a pact to include each other from now on," Donovan toasted abruptly, "whenever we're stuck in the City alone. And not just Christmas either, but any holiday we might feel lonely. Any time we can't be with our families."

I raised my glass immediately, and so did the others. The moment was actually quite beautiful. All four of us were smiling.

It was not long after that the flirting got heavy.

No matter where I was in the room, I always seemed to be in someone's lap. First it was Lincoln, who cradled me with my back against him. He was content to wrap me snugly in his arms, moving my hair aside and kissing my neck whenever the mood struck him. Every time his lips touched my skin it sent shivers of pleasure throughout my body. Sensing my reaction, he of course did it over and over again.

Next it was Brody, also playing with my hair... amongst other parts of my body. His hands moved confidently and unashamedly as the four of us talked, until I was squirming and writhing happily beneath the touch of his talented fingers.

Donovan was boldest of all, touching and kissing me whenever he wanted to. Making out with me hotly in front of the others, as if I was his girlfriend, which of course I was.

Music played as we drained our phones, a mixture of everything Christmas and holiday-themed. Internet service out in the wilderness wasn't all that great, and there were long stretches of silence as songs buffered to completion. It was still romantic though. Still very Christmasy and beautiful.

"I wish we had our presents," lamented Brody at one point. "I actually got you guys some stuff."

It was adorable to me, imagining Brody shopping by himself. Buying gifts not just for me, but for his fellow suitors too.

We're friends, I realized absently. *You might be the only one sexually involved with all three of them, but they're socially involved in each other's lives as well.*

For some reason that made me feel better about the whole thing. That as much love and attention I'd been getting all to myself, maybe it hadn't been *all* to myself after all. For example, I'd learned Donovan and Lincoln had started working out together. Brody had hung out with Donovan on occasion as well, and the three of them had also gone somewhere they wouldn't tell me about — presumably Christmas shopping — before all going out for drinks.

In that respect, the relationship was more circular and interconnected than I originally realized. I wasn't just the hub, and my boyfriends the spokes of a slow spinning wheel. They were also connected to each other by the rim of the wheel itself. By an inherent camaraderie that came with sharing me together, both inside the bedroom and out.

"Well I've got a present for you," I said slyly.

"For who?"

"Pretty much for all of you."

All of a sudden I had their full attention. Donovan sat up. Brody sat down. Lincoln's legs, slung over the arm of the couch, stopped rocking restlessly for a moment. A bottle of beer still dangled, playfully, from between two of his fingers.

"And when do we get it?" asked Donovan.

"Get what?" I asked innocently.

"This present!"

I rolled my eyes to the ceiling. "Oh, I don't know..." I chewed my lip as I pretended to consider. "Whenever you want?"

Donovan and Lincoln were leaning forward. Brody's mouth was a devilish smirk.

"And what if we want it now?"

I took my time answering, teasing them a little. "That's doable," I shrugged. Slowly I traced the top of my wine glass with one finger. "You'll have to leave the room so I can set it up though."

The three of them scrambled quickly to their feet, which was funny considering how stretched out and relaxed they were only a second ago. I pointed toward the kitchen.

"Why don't you boys freshen your drinks in there," I said, turning and heading for the staircase. "I'll call you after Santa comes."

Fifty-One

BRODY

"Okay, boys!"

Holly's voice called from the living room, all sexy and sultry and sweet. Entirely on its own, my heart started racing. I actually *did* feel like a kid again, on Christmas morning.

"You can come on in..."

Donovan pushed open the door eagerly, with Lincoln and I right behind. The lights in the living room were low, competing with the fire's warm glow. Between that and the twinkling lights, everything was bathed in warmth and shadow.

But under the tree...

Resting just beneath the Christmas tree, flat on her belly, Holly had her hands crossed casually beneath her chin. She was wearing a Santa hat... and not much else. And she was smiling sweetly. Sweetly, but also impishly...

"Merry Christmas, boys."

Holly lifted one of her legs, revealing red and white, candy-cane, thigh-high stockings. The three-inch spiked heels she was wearing were cherry red. Ditto for her matching bra, and red G-string panties...

"Santa stranded me here," she purred, kicking her legs slowly back and forth. One of her heels caught in her thong, pulling it upwards and open. "Something about being a little too *naughty*."

She looked like something straight out of a fantasy. A complete dream, from head to toe. I wanted to take her right there, to ravish her the way we'd ravished her last night. I wanted to be on her, kissing her. I wanted to be *inside* her...

"So are you just gonna stand there?" she giggled, rolling onto her back. "Or are one of you going to unwrap me?"

The three of us all appeared to be in the same trance. Donovan broke it first. He dropped to his knees, crawling over Holly and lowering his mouth to hers. He kissed her slowly, softly. Sensuously...

Don't just stand there!

I was jealous, but only because I hadn't acted yet. It was a simple thing to place myself under the tree. To slide down below her, where my hands could find the warm strip of flesh between the tops of her stockings and the lacy edge of her G-string bottoms.

She felt *warm*. Wonderful. I wanted to bury my face between those beautiful thighs, to throw her stockinged legs over my shoulders and devour her endlessly.

"Unwrap you?" Donovan laughed finally. "You look pretty well unwrapped to me." His hands went to her breasts, kneading them, running his palms over her barely-covered nipples. "Besides, we're not taking any of this stuff off you.

You look too damned good with it *on*."

I was in total agreement with him. Shifting between her legs, I slid Holly's G-string to the side. Her pussy was already drenched, probably in anticipation of what we were about to do to her. And she to us...

"Mmmmmm..."

She moaned into Donovan's mouth as I finally went down on her. I was licking, sucking, dragging my tongue up and down through her glistening wetness. Savoring the sweet, musky taste of her, I pushed even deeper. Holly responded by spreading her thighs so I could scoop out her golden, honeyed nectar.

"Oh *fuck* that's amazing..."

Lincoln's voice. I looked up for a moment, to see that she was blowing him. She still had the Santa hat on, her beautiful brown hair spilling out the sides. One cheek was bowed outward by the head of Lincoln's cock, even as she glanced down at me to deliver a slow, dreamy wink.

She's perfect.

She was. Holly really was the perfect woman; the antithesis of anyone I'd ever dated. Her sweet, thoughtful nature was punctuated by a sharp wit and an intoxicating laugh. She was selfless and loving. Nurturing and caring. And at the same time, she was strong. Stronger even than when we'd first gotten together with her.

Most of all I marveled at how quickly we'd fallen for her, all three of us. Each of us taking her as our own, and yet also accepting the fact that we were taking her together. None of us seeming to mind that we were splitting our time, because it never felt like splitting at all. If anything, it felt like multiplying our fun, rather than dividing it.

Few girls could've handled such a thing. Maybe one in a million. In any other circumstance there should be infighting, jealousy, favoritism... and yet, every time I was with Holly it felt like the first time. Each date we went on she felt like my loving *girlfriend*, and the starstruck way she looked at me made it seem like I was her entire world.

"*OHHHhhhHHHhhhHHHhhh...*"

I was brought back to the moment by Holly's fist in my hair, rolling her knuckles so deep that I was drowning inside her. My tongue was further than it had ever been. And I was moving my head up and down, forcing my upper lip over her swollen clit...

"Damn, bro," I heard Donovan say. "Save some for us?"

I laughed into her, and the vibrations caused her to moan even louder around Lincoln's cock. She was sucking him hard now, pumping him with her fist. The light from the fire glowed on our bodies, and I could feel her stomach rising and falling quickly, as her breathing grew rapid.

I slipped two fingers inside her, just as she came. Holly's ass left the floor as she went ballistic, pulling Lincoln from her mouth so she could scream out loud. It was amazing, watching the final outcome from between her legs. Enjoying the fruits of my labor as her eyes crossed and her thighs trembled and her pussy exploded with contractions around my fingers and tongue.

I moved my hands beneath her, cradling her ass as she rode out her orgasm on my face. Holding still, I let her control the pressure. Between her fingers wrapped in my hair, and the up and down grinding against my chin, I let Holly dictate everything, leaving her as the architect of the remainder of her climax.

I could do this forever.

That much was true. So true, I had to wonder if Holly was considering the same thing.

"I'm going first," said Donovan, taking his mouth from her breasts. "You guys had your fun with her last night."

I slid away reluctantly, giving her over. Watching as he took her slender, quivering legs and hooked them both around his trim, sculpted waist.

Then he pushed himself against her sopping wet entrance, and Holly's gasp sucked half the oxygen from the room.

Fifty-Two

DONOVAN

She was so warm, so wet, she took me all the way inside her on one stroke. I had Brody to thank for that; whatever he'd done to her, I'd never seen her this worked up. Never seen her *this* much in heat.

"Oh God... Oh fuck..."

Holly was thrashing her head back and forth, her Santa hat all crookedly cute. Her stockings felt smooth wrapped around my flanks, as she screwed her body downward to grind me deeper.

Damn...

It was totally insane, how *good* it all was! How incredibly tight she felt as my balls clapped against her writhing ass. I thrust forward some more, the pressure signaling that I'd reached bottom. That I was finally buried inside her all the way to the absolute hilt.

Lincoln grinned at me, then went back to feeding her his cock. I took her slowly at first, with long, controlled strokes that made her chest bounce and her body rock. Of all the things I loved most, it was fucking her with her G-string on. There was something extra sexy and wonderful about leaving her panties on and just yanking them to the side. About feeling the lacy fabric rub gently against my shaft, every time I plunged in and out of her.

Brody had joined Lincoln on the other side of her head, and now she was trying to go down on them both. She had one hand on each of their cocks, alternating between sucking and stroking them. Her head flailed left and right as I fucked her, blowing one while pumping the other. And all the while, whimpering softly as I picked up the pace.

I think I'm in love with you...

My own words rattled around in my brain. They were difficult to arrive at, and even harder to form. But they were also the truth, and they'd felt amazingly cathartic when I'd finally told her.

The car ride from New York City to Maine had been eleven hours of freedom, honesty, and self-reflection. I'd not only decided I really *did* love her, but that I'd probably loved her all along. That strange day in the coffee shop, meeting the others, had somehow been the beginning of something much bigger than I'd ever imagined. And the more I tried to deny its magnitude, or attempted to tell myself it couldn't possibly be as deep as it was?

The more I realized I was just flat out lying to myself.

Holly was switching between her other two lovers again when she stopped halfway. Looking straight up at me, still bouncing gently with my every movement, her eyes met mine.

I love you... she mouthed with her lips. She said it lustily, and with an unapologetic smile. Most of all she said it in full view of Lincoln on one side, and Brody on the other.

Not caring if either or both of them saw.

That could only mean one thing: Holly had told them she loved them too. In which case they'd professed their own feelings for her, which I obviously already knew because I'd had conversations with the both of them.

All the cards are on the table then.

It was a big realization. A huge step in the direction of total transparency. But it was also a welcome one, because it meant that all four of us were being completely honest.

What if she really does love you all?

For the first time, the possibility cemented itself in my head. It was suddenly concrete, totally real. Sharing her with the others wasn't just something we were trying out — it was something much more permanent. Our group dynamic suddenly didn't seem like so much of a temporary competition for her ultimate affections, but more like... more like...

More like a stable relationship.

I shifted her legs higher, until her calves rested on my shoulders. Then I began to really pound her out. Holly's eyes flared, her whimpers coming louder and more frequently as I fucked her harder and deeper. She looked over-the-top sexy in her Christmas lingerie, and I found myself quickly losing control.

"Switch off..." I breathed, just as I felt the come rising inside me. It was boiling in my balls now. Begging me to release it, deep in her tight, beautiful channel.

Could you all continue to love her?

It was an amazing question. The million-dollar

question.

Love her without reservations, without jealousy... like you're doing right now?

Holly spread her thighs again as I passed her over to Lincoln, watching him position himself between her legs. It was such a turn on, watching her fuck. Watching her *get* fucked. Watching her suck me, or Brody, or Lincoln, or—

Yes. I could.

Strangely enough, I found myself answering my own question.

With these guys? The way things are now?

I sighed as Holly's hand wrapped around me. Her warm mouth closed over my manhood, as she took me deep against the back of her throat.

Yes.

Fifty-Three

LINCOLN

For some reason she felt different this time, more eager, more frenzied than ever before. It could've been because there were three of us now. Or maybe it was because we'd been teasing her all day, and the anticipation of finally bedding her together was just too much to bear.

It didn't hurt, of course, that she was dressed like one of Santa's naughtiest helpers. Holly's eyes screwed shut as I sank into her, her nipples stiffening upward as her back arched.

"Fuck me..."

She murmured the words from around Donovan's cock, nuzzling hard between his legs. I could see her perspiring now, and even that was cute. It could've been from the fire, or it could've been from being so thoroughly, satisfyingly fucked.

God. Just look at her.

Visually, I'd never been more turned on. Holly's outfit was hotter than anything I could've imagined, and seeing her all dolled up beneath the Christmas tree was a memory I wanted to tuck away forever. She looked magnificently flawless — almost too good to touch.

Almost of course, but not quite.

"Mmmmmmmm..."

She moaned again, twisting beneath me. I'd entered her missionary but now I'd rolled her onto one side, straddling her bottom leg, fucking her scissor-style with one sexy thigh curled upward. It was a position I loved because of the depth, but also because of the way it made her look. Her breasts came together, forming a beautiful valley of unblemished cleavage. Her smile widened, as she looked over her shoulder and caught my eye.

"Like that," she grinned, her eyes dripping with lust. "Just like that..."

I put both hands on her upright hip and plowed away, drilling her so hard the others had to hold her steady from above. Brody placed a pillow beneath her head. Lincoln bent down and began kissing her passionately, kneading her breasts as their tongues dueled.

You've wanted this forever.

I really, *really* had. I could admit that now. After years of denying myself any sort of meaningful connection with someone, I could finally come clean about wanting something like this. Some*one* like this...

She's everything, Lincoln. If you could make a girl from scratch, put her together piece by piece...

It was true, all of it, every word. If such a thing were possible, that girl would most certainly be Holly: funny, sexy, adorable, and so overwhelmingly smart. She was the full package, all rolled into one. The girlfriend I always imagined I'd have, if only I could keep one girl happy...

But you can. Now.

In truth, nothing much had changed. I was still busy, still overwhelmed with work. Business was expanding faster than I could keep up with — so fast in fact, that it had taken me far too long to realize I was missing tons of money. And yet Holly had been there for that too. She'd dove in headfirst to help me find out why, arriving at a crucial moment to help me stop the bleeding on a very messy and uncomfortable situation.

Firing Kathy had been one of the worst experiences of my life. If she'd left angry I could've handled it. If she'd stomped out all indignant and outraged, those were emotions I was prepared to deal with. Instead, she'd cried. She'd cried and sobbed and packed up her stuff and left without even explaining to me why she'd taken so much for so long.

Still, it was finally over, and I had Holly to thank for that. Holly, my gorgeous new girlfriend. Holly, who knew more about my accounting than even *I* did...

"Faster... *Harder...*"

I almost couldn't hear her, she was talking so low. Her lips were moving in a whisper as I picked up speed, clawing her hip harder with my hands. I drove my cock like a piston now, eliciting high-pitched grunts and groans from all new octaves as she buried her head in the other's laps.

But instead of glancing back at me looking for mercy, she begged me to push the envelope even more.

"Lincoln..."

I pulled her upright, full doggie-style. Set her on her hands and knees, where I had total control over her from behind.

"YES..."

The penetration was glorious. I could feel her squeezing down around me with every interior muscle she had.

"Oh *God* yes..."

The others perked up, getting ready for whatever came next. I was really laying into her now, giving her the entire length of me with every stroke. All the way in, all the way out. Brody was holding her face. I could see tears forming at the corners of her eyes.

"Oh fuck... oh fuck..."

Holly's ass looked amazing, bouncing hard against my lower stomach. Everything was sopping wet, so totally drenched...

"Ohhhhhh fuuuuuuuck...."

I inched the ball of my thumb forward, pressing it tightly against her beautifully puckered second hole. It was hot to the touch, all glazed and slick with wetness...

"*OHHHHHH!*"

Her whole body convulsed as I pushed my way in.

Fifty-Four

HOLLY

I arched my back as Lincoln's thumb slid into my ass, adding a whole new level to the pleasure I was receiving. No, I hadn't expected it. I hadn't prepared myself for it. Yet it was still dirty and hot and amazing, just the same.

Oh my God...

Three of them. It was so radically different than two. The dynamic felt like it had gone almost from private to public, the addition of a third lover adding an element of camaraderie and teamwork to our sexual adventure that just wasn't there when it had been a simple threesome.

Simple threesome? Is that what your sex life has become?

In short, yes. Because in dating these three beautiful men, and accepting them as part of my life, I'd opened the door to them accepting each other. Limitations had been lifted, mentally and emotionally. And now, with Lincoln's thumb in my ass, physically as well.

Holy fuck that feels good...

I grunted my approval as my lover continued screwing

me from behind. His thumb felt amazing buried inside me. I could feel it pressing downward, pushing against his cock. Making everything *that* much tighter inside me, for the benefit of both him *and* me.

"You like that, don't you?"

Brody, growling in my ear. I could tell by the thickness in his voice, he was getting hotter just watching.

"*Yes.*"

"Want us to go further?"

I thought about it, but only for a second. Then I clenched my jaw, swallowed hard... and nodded.

"Good."

He cradled my face and kissed me, holding my head up. Keeping me steady while Lincoln continued fucking away. In the meantime, Donovan had slid beneath my body. He had my bra down, swirling one nipple with his tongue. Kneading my other breast in his eager hand, while positioning his legs downward.

"Slide her up... onto me."

Lincoln followed his lead, taking hold of my waist and shifting me further forward. Soon I was straddling Donovan's washboard stomach, drooling over the way his abs looked while I sank backward in the direction of his cock...

Oh wow.

The substitution happened flawlessly, like they'd rehearsed it a thousand times. Lincoln slid away just as Donovan arched forward, slipping inside me. One hard member traded for another.

"Easy, go slow now."

Donovan pulled me against him, chest to chest, face to face. It was almost like last night, only this time Lincoln was there...

... and he was replacing the thumb in my ass with something much, much bigger.

Holly... really?

It was crazy. It was dirty. It was most likely a physical impossibility, considering their size, their girth, the positioning...

But holy fuck, I wanted it anyway.

"Please..." I said pleadingly. "Just... just go slow..."

I trusted them, and that was the thing. I could see it in Donovan's eyes, in the way Brody held me steady with his arms. I could feel it in the way Lincoln guided himself, ever so gently against me...

Breathe, Holly. Breathe.

I lay there motionless, one lover buried comfortably inside me, the other one ready to screw me straight up the ass. Two muscle-bound men, as strong as they were gorgeous. About to double-penetrate me for the first, and probably not even close to the last, time.

"Ready?"

I laughed, nervously. "What do you wanna hear?"

"That you're ready for us," Lincoln breathed. "That you've always dreamed of this, and it's finally going to happen."

"Oh yeah," I chuckled. "Every girl's dream."

I joked, but in a way it was though. Every friend I ever knew had secretly admitted to a fantasy like this. I just happened to be living it out.

I felt a gentle pressure, then a push. Remembering to relax, I could feel myself slowly opening for him. Accepting him. Taking him in...

"Easy," Lincoln instructed, as I felt myself go even wider. "Don't tense up."

The head slipped in, and my whole body jolted. Donovan held me steady, by the waist. I looked down and found him grinning.

"Feel good?"

My legs trembled as Lincoln pushed in another inch. Then two. Then even *more*. It was a little frightening, but eventually the discomfort was outweighed by a pleasant, familiar fullness. After all, I'd been fucked in the ass before. Just never... never with someone else *inside* me...

"Oh wow..." I heard Donovan say. "Oh my God you're so *tight* like this."

I gasped again, and all of a sudden the worst was over. He was *in*. I could feel his body firmly against mine, both cheeks of my ass pressed tightly against Lincoln's smooth well-muscled thighs.

"Here," Brody said, taking the hat off my head. He put it on Lincoln. "He's Santa now."

We stayed frozen for a long moment, the three of us, my body sandwiched hotly between my two powerful lovers. I was filled to capacity. Fully penetrated from behind and beneath.

And God, it felt *soo* indescribably good...

"I don't know how long I'll last like this," Donovan complained.

"Not long," Brody told him. He shot Lincoln a knowing glance. "Take it from us."

Slowly, testing the waters, Lincoln glided back out of me. When only the head was still inside, he pushed back in.

"This is just ridiculous," he growled.

I had to remember — all of this was new for them, too. They'd never shared a woman like this, any more than I'd been involved in the same crazy scenario.

"You alright?" Lincoln asked me.

I sighed as he continued screwing me slowly. "Better than alright," I said. "I'm... I'm a happy girl right now."

Donovan pushed upward, clenching his asscheeks to squeeze himself deeper. I could swear he was so far inside me he might break something.

"*Now* you're on the naughty list," joked Lincoln. "For sure."

I gasped and nodded. "And I'm never getting off."

"Not if Santa's watching," Brody laughed. "And he's *always* watching."

In a daze I tilted my chin upward, to look him in the face. Brody was mopping his blonde hair back. Staring down at me with two very hungry eyes.

My body shuddered magnificently as I reached out for him.

"Get over here then," I said, pulling him toward my mouth. "We might as well *all* get coal for Christmas..."

Fifty-Five

HOLLY

The night passed in dream-like slowness. It extended our pleasure, heightened our intimacy. Gave us reason to love one another, utterly and completely, mind, body and soul.

The boys took me one by one, screwing me quite literally senseless. One by one they finished inside me, Lincoln first, then Brody, then Donovan, who somehow held out much longer than even he anticipated.

From there we passed out for a spell, lounging beneath the Christmas tree. The warmth of the flames on our skin had made us sleepy, until we were a tangle of arms and legs and deliciously sated bodies.

I woke to the sound of a shower running, and joined Lincoln upstairs in the steam and heat. We splashed and laughed and soaped each other's backs, then kissed and made out passionately beneath the spray, like two teenagers sneaking away from our respective parents.

One by one we went at it again, together and alone. Donovan fed the fire while Brody pulled me onto him, running his hands up and down my shower-warm skin. I rode him slowly, enjoying the one-on-one connection between us. Rocking and moaning, feeling the weight of his palms against my breasts, I continued until I felt the warm splash of his seed inside me, my fingers clawing his chest in approval.

This was my time now. My turn to take control. I pushed Donovan onto his back and mounted him too, riding him up and down. I picked up speed and leverage, tossing my hair back and forth as I fucked him. I must've been really hot and wet, because it took even less time to bring him off inside me.

"Now you."

In a flash I was on Lincoln again, straddling him to the root. Grinding... squeezing... climaxing around him and then collapsing forward, totally spent across his chest. It felt like the world was ending. Like we were the last people left on the whole fucking planet, screwing our socks off, celebrating the end of mankind.

"The best..." I cried, half-mad with my own arousal. "You guys... are the best..."

Then I passed out and slept like the dead.

Sunday I woke to a entire breakfast banquet — all three of them had risen before me. We ate heartily and ran outside, excited to see that the storm had finally subsided.

The skies were blue, with not a cloud in sight. We shoveled ourselves back out, only this time without any real agenda or place to go. Brody started a snowball fight, which turned into an all-out war complete with snow forts, snow men, and whatever else we could think of to keep our blood pumping.

When it was finally over we tumbled inside, all caked in snow. The fire heated us from the outside, while hot soup warmed us from within. Our muscles were tired and pleasantly sore, except maybe Donovan who was actually getting *less* exercise than he was used to. During the day, anyway.

Night fell and we did everything all over again, only this time slower and more leisurely. There was tons more eye-contact. Deeper meaning. Each of the guys took me in ways they hadn't before; kissing me, loving me, bringing me to all new heights of blinding white ecstasy... all while the others looked on approvingly, or joined right in.

Every time someone left me, another took his place. I spread wide for them, taking them into my body. I threw my arms around them, crushing them against me, relishing in the distinct feel of each of my three lovers.

We were bonded now, in ways we never were before. A happy little quadrangle, inside and out. In between our lovemaking we shared our thoughts, our aspirations, our dreams. Even our fears and failures, as well as every one of our shining triumphs.

Dawn was breaking again when Lincoln gently shook us awake. We stared at him in the violet shadows, fully dressed and squatting over us.

"Pilot just called," he murmured. "There's a flight window if we want to take it — a break between storms. But we have to decide now, before it closes."

Brody stretched and yawned. "You mean we could be home before Christmas?"

Lincoln nodded. "Christmas Eve, actually. But only if we hurry."

Home. The City. Reality...

Considering the paradise I was currently residing in, it didn't sound all that appealing. And yet...

And yet we still weren't *home*. Staying here was beautiful enough, but if got snowed in for another day or two we'd probably all go stir-crazy.

No, each of us missed the City in our own special way. Some of us even had loose ends to tie up..

"Yeah," said Donovan, throwing off a blanket. "Let's do it."

Fifty-Six

HOLLY

    Christmas Eve was always a strange day. Most people had off, but so many places were still open as well. It left the City uncharacteristically quiet, with the exception of last-minute shoppers, most of which were standing in line for gift-cards; the ultimate 'I really can't be bothered to make an effort' Christmas gift.

    I of course, had everything done. I'd dutifully sent gifts to my family and friends, and even had something for Jocelyn, for our annual Day-after-Christmas lunch. I always looked forward to that, because it marked an end to the chaos. We could relax and unwind over food and drinks. Talk to each other about our holidays...

    And boy, did I *ever* have something to talk about.

    We'd all gone our separate ways upon arriving back home, with the intention of meeting up later tonight to spend Christmas Eve together. Oddly enough it was already strange, spending the day alone. Being away from the boys after having spent the last 72 hours together.

    Awww... you miss them!

I did! And that was okay. I was going to see them soon anyway. All I had to do was run a few errands, and do a little grocery shopping. I'd promised to make dinner tonight, when we all met up at Lincoln's loft.

It wasn't until I was cutting through Tompkins Square Park that I noticed him: the person walking directly behind me. I took a side path, then another, and each time I did the person made the same adjustment.

Heart racing, I risked a glance backward. He was on the shorter side, wearing a big parka with the furry hood pulled tightly over his face. I could only see his breath on the air. Nothing else.

But he was still coming. Still walking with the same unnervingly quick gait.

I looked around, trying to find someone else. Someone to walk to. Someone to get involved. But it was just me... me and the person on the path behind me, following me. Gaining on me...

Or maybe it was just my—

No! Not your imagination.

The path turned sharply, and I hustled ahead. There was a tree I knew, one with a large, thick trunk. One I could hide behind. One I could use to maybe get away from whoever was following me, or—

Or maybe see who the fuck it is?

In one quick movement I was there, pressed against it, my back cold against the hard surface. I could feel my heart pounding. The artery in my neck, throbbing, as the too-quick footsteps grew louder and louder and...

It all happened automatically, without me even thinking. In a mixture of fear and anger and raw adrenaline, I whirled on the man behind me and grabbed him by the parka.

"OOOF!"

Twisting my body sideways, I threw him up against the tree. He was surprisingly light. He went along surprisingly easily.

"HEY!" I shouted loudly, straight into his covered face. My hands jammed hard into his shoulders, and I thought I heard a cry of pain.

In an instant I had him by the hood. I whipped it backwards, pulling it off.

"WHY ARE YOU FOLLOW—"

My own words died in my throat. I was staring into the face of a woman! A short, anxious-looking woman, with dark curly hair.

"You..."

Her eyes were wild, her expression scared. I still had her by the shoulders. I could even feel her heart beating through my outstretched palm, thundering inside her chest like a frightened squirrel.

"Andrea!"

Brody's ex-girlfriend stared back at me, all shaken and miserable. She looked exactly as she had in the photo I'd kept.

"Let go of me!" she snarled, yanking my hands away. She took a half-step from the tree and straightened out her wrinkled coat.

"*You're* the one who's been following me?" I asked

incredulously, though I already knew the answer. "What is it you want?"

I got nothing but silence in return. I could sense a seething anger, though. An underlying hatred...

"WHAT DO YOU WANT?"

Her gaze dropped. She shifted uncomfortably.

"I... I was..."

"What were you going to *do*, Andrea?" I practically shouted. "Follow me around town all week? Beat me up? Boil my rabbit?"

Her thick brows came together in confusion. "B—Boil your *rabbit?*"

"Forget it!" I cried. "Honestly, what's the end game here? You terrified me last week! What could possibly compel you to follow me through the City? You've been stalking me at work, putting all kinds of terrible ideas in my head..."

Her nose twitched and then it happened: a tear formed in the corner of one eye. It rolled down her cheek, even as a second and third tear joined it on the other side.

She was crying.

Fifty-Seven

HOLLY

"I— I don't even know what I'm doing..." Andrea choked. I could tell she was totally exasperated. "I don't have a clue, really."

My first instinct was to hold her, to make her stop. To wrap my arms around her, the way girls do.

Are you kidding, Holly?

Whatever it was, she was monumentally upset. She was still a person. I wanted to fix it.

"Why are *you* crying?" I asked, my tone suddenly a lot more gentle. "*I'm* the one getting stalked here."

Andrea shook her head. More tears dropped from her jaw, dripping down her jacket.

"I just... I don't..."

All of a sudden I had a hand on her shoulder — a gentle hand this time. It was nuts! But still, something inside me told me it was right.

"Here."

I handed her a tissue from my pocket. I had no idea if it was clean or not, but she took it anyway.

"Walk with me."

Before I knew it, we were back on the path. Andrea was dragging her feet now, but we were still walking side by side.

"Look," I sighed. "I get it. It's hard, breaking up with someone. Especially if they're the one who broke up with you. But you don't—"

"I have to see him every day!" Andrea cried suddenly. "I have to look into his eyes!"

There was a lot of pain in her voice. A lot of frustration.

I took pity on her.

"I sit there miserably while he ignores me in the living room," Andrea went on. "And he avoids me like the plague whenever we're both home."

"I get it."

"No, you don't get it it," she countered. "It's torture! It's—"

"Yeah, but you can't just go all totally psycho!" I shot back. "Do you know how you *look*, Andrea? Did you see what you did to his *room?*" She stared down again, at her shuffling feet. "No wonder why he avoids you!"

We walked a dozen steps in silence, while my words sunk in. I hoped I was getting to her. It was tough to tell.

"He could go to the *University*, Andrea," I said. "You're both students, both in subsidized housing. If he took this up with them you'd get thrown out of school."

Her head spun my way. She looked suddenly terrified. "Would he.... Is he..."

"No, Brody's not like that," I said dismissively. "You know he isn't."

The girl walking alongside me let out a long, deep breath. In the bitter cold, the steam leaving her mouth looked like dragon's fire.

"I... I know," Andrea admitted. "He's great. That's part of what makes this so hard, seeing him with someone else. Seeing him with *you*."

I nodded in acknowledgment. "He doesn't know what to say to you, Andrea. He doesn't know how to act around you. It's uncomfortable for the both of you, not just yourself."

"I... I can't afford to move out. The school pays for a good chunk of the rent, and—"

"Brody isn't happy there either," I said. "And not because of you," I added quickly, "he just needs more space. Four people, one living area. One television. Ugh! How do you ever decide what to watch?"

More silence. More walking. We were almost out of the park.

"You both need to move on," I said. "It's not going to get better until you're not in each other's faces anymore."

Andrea jammed her hands in her pockets. Her expression was still miserable.

"He's staying with you, isn't he?"

"Yes," I replied. "But whatever happens next, he probably needs to get out of that apartment. For your sanity as well as his."

Out in the street, we walked a little more. A delicious aroma reached my nostrils, and ten steps later I found myself buying a hot pretzel. The street vendor smiled at us and wished us both a merry Christmas, which was funny, in an odd sort of way. To anyone looking at us for the first time, we could've been friends.

"Here."

Tearing the pretzel down the middle, I handed half of it to her. She hesitated only a second before accepting it gratefully.

"Thanks."

"Don't mention it," I smiled. "As delicious as street pretzels are, I think I bought it more to keep my hands warm."

Andrea actually laughed, and we both stopped walking at the same time. She tiled her head to stare at me.

"You know, for a bitch I really hate you're not half bad," she chuckled.

I grinned right back at her. "Well as far as psycho ex-girlfriends go, you're pretty reasonable yourself."

Fifty-Eight

HOLLY

"Alright," said Lincoln, taking the Santa hat from Donovan's head. He plopped it down on his own and pulled it tight. It barely fit. "My turn."

We watched as he took his place in front of tree, kicking aside a big pile of discarded wrapping paper. Everyone else had gone already. Everyone else had given their gifts.

"Best for last?" Brody asked hopefully.

"You'll soon find out."

Lincoln's studio apartment was bigger than five of mine, a contemporary masterpiece of steel and glass. Every piece of furniture looked clean and unused. Every smooth surface and countertop gleamed with newness. I knew it was because he seldom spent time here. That he worked so much, and so often, he barely used his place, except to sleep.

"Who wants to go first?"

I glanced up at the clock. It was almost midnight. Almost Christmas. So far though, Christmas Eve had been the most magical night of all.

"I will," said Brody.

We'd gotten together not long ago, and eaten a late dinner. My cooking was interrupted only twice; once by Lincoln carrying me into his bedroom before the guys even got there, and again by Donovan and Brody while I was making dessert.

I didn't mind that dessert came out *very* late.

"Here you go," said Lincoln, handing over an envelope. "Merry Christmas, brother."

It was cute, watching the guys give each other gifts. Brody and Donovan had exchanged sports memorabilia. They'd given Lincoln gag gifts at first — old-man joke stuff of course — before finally giving him a set of Ranger tickets, center ice. And then the gifts they'd given me... well, they'd all melted my heart.

"What the heck is it?" Brody asked, tearing open the envelope. He pulled out a sheet of paper, unfolded it and squinted.

"It's your tuition for next year," said Lincoln. "All paid up."

Brody blinked three times, then swallowed hard. "Bro... I can't. No way I can accep—"

"Yes you can," said Lincoln simply. "I'm happy to do it. I'm in *position* to do it. Plus, you deserve it." He smiled and glanced at me. "Not to mention it's another good write-off. Right?"

Seeing the awe and excitement on Brody's face filled me with happiness. "Yes," I smiled, just as Lincoln was practically decked by Brody's man-hug. "Yes it is."

We took a minute to calm down, and then Lincoln pulled out two tiny boxes. Each was wrapped with ribbon, each had a bow.

"Who's next?"

I looked at Donovan. He nodded, giving me the go-ahead.

"I— I guess I will," I said.

I couldn't imagine what was in the box! After what Brody just got...

My hand trembled as I opened it.

Inside was a single key. Attached to it was a sleek grey key-fob.

"This... This is a car key..." I choked.

"Sure is. For an Audi Q7." He paused for a moment. "Now it's not new, it's actually a company car. It was Kathy's car, up until a few days ago."

Lincoln took my hand in his. With the other, he tilted my chin up to look at him.

"The key comes with a job offer," he said. "I want you to work with me, Holly. Come be my CFO."

All of a sudden there was a lump in my throat. It felt like a bowling ball.

"W—Work for you?"

"No," said Lincoln. "Not *for* me, Holly. Come work *with* me. Help me take things with my company to the next level. As my girlfriend, as my financial officer... as my business partner." He smiled and caressed my cheek. "I can't do this alone anymore. And I can't do the long hours by myself, while neglecting the people I love."

My arm was shaking now too. No, that wasn't right. My whole body was shaking.

"Of course, it's a lot easier to work late when your girlfriend's office is right next to yours," grinned Lincoln. "Makes the whole 'got stuck at work' thing a lot more manageable."

Off to one side, I heard Brody laugh. "And fun," he added.

I was too choked up to speak, at least initially. A key. To my own car. To the *company* car. And a job offer..."

"I... I can't..."

"Yes you can, Holly. Please."

Somehow I regained control. Pushing my emotions down for a moment, to keep them in check, I gently squeezed his hand.

"No, Lincoln listen to me. I'll take the job. God knows I need it! The place I'm at now is a total dead end."

The relief in his grin told me he'd been worried. There was a part of him that didn't think I could work with him, or that I would take the offer. But I wasn't finished.

"I can do good for you," I said. "Good for us..." I smiled and opened his hand with mine. "But I can't take the car."

He looked down as I pushed the key into his palm. His face was expressionless.

"I've managed to save a little money," I said, "and I've

got my eye on a few options. For reasons I don't expect you to understand, I need to buy my *own* car. This one little thing, I need to do by myself."

His eyes flashed. My eyebrows came together as I saw the corner of his mouth twist into a grin.

"What?"

"Well I thought you might say that," he smiled again. "So I came prepared."

He took the back the key, and held out his other hand. "I'm not gonna be the boyfriend who gave you a *job* for Christmas," he said with a laugh. "Not *just* a job, anyway. So here, I'd like you to meet present number two: pretty jewelry."

Lincoln opened one big fist. Curled inside was a breathtaking gold tennis bracelet, shimmering with diamonds.

Tears flooded my eyes. He took my hand again, and I held my wrist out while he clasped it on.

"Better?"

"Much!" I nodded, tears streaming down my cheeks as I hugged him. "Pretty jewelry is *definitely* a present I can get behind!"

Lincoln laughed. "Thought so."

I was still staring at my gift, watching it shimmer with each change of the Christmas tree lights, when Lincoln tossed the other little box to Donovan. One hand snapped up reflexively, and he caught it easily.

"Pretty jewelry?" Donovan quipped.

"Not even close."

We all watched as he undid the ribbon and opened the box. Inside was another key, gleaming, shining brightly. But it wasn't a car key.

"What's this?" he laughed, but his laugh was nervous.

"That," said Lincoln, "is the key to *Donovan's...*"

Fifty-Nine

HOLLY

For a few seconds, the apartment was so silent we could hear the traffic outside. I was hyper-aware of everything: the blinking lights, the distant rumble of the building's elevators moving somewhere beneath us. A 'click' from the kitchen, as the compressor for the refrigerator kicked on.

Donovan was still staring at the key. He hadn't looked up. "You're not serious..." he breathed.

"Oh I'm quite serious."

"*Donovan's.*"

"The gym, yes," said Lincoln. "The lease doesn't get signed until Thursday, but the preliminaries are all taken care of and the building is ours." He cleared his throat. "I mean... *yours.*"

I was enraptured, watching it all sink in. Seeing the expressions on all three of their faces as reality took hold.

"Is—"

"Yes, this is the place on 5th street. Yes, Holly told me about it. And yes, I'm doing it no matter what you say, so don't even *tell* me you don't want in."

Lincoln reached out and slipped an arm around me. It felt amazing as he pulled me close. "Beats the shit out of a laundromat or a car wash," he said. "Doesn't it?"

I nodded happily, but my eyes were locked on Donovan. He was still looking at the key. Turning it over and over in his hand.

"I have three different equipment vendors coming in next week," said Lincoln. "Architect is Monday, builders after the New Year. You can sink whatever you have into this, I'll take care of the rest of the initial investment."

Donovan finally looked up. His expression was one of total and complete disbelief.

"P—Partners?"

"For now," Lincoln shrugged. "Until you buy me out, at least. Shouldn't be too long, considering the location and the space. Personally, I think it's going to be wildly successful. Between you bringing in your client base, my marketing skills... maybe some Crossfit or spin classes or—"

Donovan shot forward, and Lincoln was knocked backward by his sudden embrace. They hugged for a long time, a really long time, while Brody and I just grinned at each other.

"You have no idea what this means to me," Donovan said at last. His voice was heavy, and shaking with emotion. "I'm going to— I mean, we're going to do the most fantastic—"

"I know bro," Lincoln interjected, ending the hug with two bear-sized pats on the back. "I know."

Suddenly something flashed through the air, and

landed in Brody's lap. It was another key. A set of keys, on a small ring.

"Who the hell are you?" Brody gasped. "The keymaster?"

"Those are for *your* new place," Lincoln said, as if it were nothing. He jerked his head at Donovan. "*Both* of you, if you want to risk living together."

I'd known about the gym. It was all Lincoln's idea, based on what I'd told him about Donovan, and his need for investments anyway.

But this... this I *hadn't* known about.

"I'm *not* taking a new apartment from you," said Brody with a hesitant laugh. "It's just way too muc—"

"You will if it's part of the building," said Lincoln. "The floor *above* the gym is zoned residential only. And since we already have the lease... we may as well make use of it."

For a long moment, no one spoke.

"That floor is already done," said Lincoln. "It's a big loft. Two baths, open kitchen." He shrugged with one shoulder. "I figured one or both of you moves in there, and any rent you pay goes directly into the gym. You're living *above* the place you work, so it cuts your commute down to about fifteen seconds."

Brody's face lit up. "I could work the front desk," he smiled. "I need a job anyway!"

"You could," said Lincoln. "And you could also get away from your psycho ex. Two birds, one stone."

"Andrea," he agreed. "Can't wait. I'm on borrowed

time at my place as it is."

"About that..." I broke in, using my sing-songy voice.

Moving together, all heads turned toward me.

"You *might* have a little more borrowed time than you realize," I said. "Andrea and I... well, we sort of worked some things out."

Brody's face drained to a sickly shade of pale white. It was all I could do not to laugh.

"You *what?*"

"We had a little talk, her and I."

His whole body stiffened. Now I actually did laugh.

"You *DID?*"

"Yup. We talked. Well, actually we walked and talked. We split a pretzel on the corner of 10th and Avenue—"

"YOU SPLIT A PRETZEL WITH HER?"

Donovan and Lincoln joined me, and suddenly we were all laughing. Laughing and hugging and needling the hell out of Brody, who couldn't look more confused if he tried.

"Yeah we're cool now, me and her," I said. "At least for a little while. But don't let that stop you from moving, or—"

"Oh, it won't!" he cried. "Believe me, I'm moving!" He turned to face Donovan. "What do you think, man?" he asked. "Roomies?"

Donovan's' grin was already so wide I was worried his face would split in half. His smile was the purest, most perfect joy.

"We could take a crack at it," he said, choking back all kinds of emotion.

Epilogue

HOLLY

"Ah... you're finally here."

I called the words coyly over my shoulder, making sure to catch Lincoln's eye before going back to sucking Donovan's cock. I was kneeling on the edge of the bed, my back to him. My rear-end high in the air.

When he didn't answer, I chuckled.

"See anything you like?" I asked, wagging my ass back and forth, seductively.

"Oh yes."

"Then come take it."

Behind me, Lincoln began undoing his tie and pulling it quickly through his collar. He couldn't get the rest of his clothes off fast enough.

"Where's Brody?"

"In the kitchen," I answered.

His voice rose two octaves. "You let *Brody* into the *kitchen?*"

"Mmm-hmmm," I mumbled around Donovan.

"Holy shit... we're ordering out then. Just like we did last New Year's Eve."

I popped my mouth free and glanced over my shoulder again.

"Are you gonna fuck me or what?" I asked, raising an eyebrow. "Or am I—"

His hands sank into my hips, gripping me hard as he pulled me against him. I could feel his manhood brushing between my legs. Stiffing against me as he rubbed it up and down.

"Mmmmmm..." I purred softly. "*There* we go..."

He plunged into me, stretching me wonderfully from the inside. God, I'd been wanting him all night. Waiting for him...

Pinned between Lincoln and Donovan, my dirty little mind wandered. *A year.* A whole year! And in that time...

In that time, all four of our lives had radically changed.

Donovan's wasn't just doing well, it was actually thriving. So many clients had come over from *Crunch Time* that they were on the brink of going out of business, or so was the word on the street. Brody and Donovan had moved into this wonderful studio apartment, and I spent half my nights here as well. The nights I wasn't spending over at Lincoln's, anyway...

"Holy shit," Donovan groaned. "Watching you fuck her like that..." he sighed. "I'm gonna lose it."

"Then lose it," said Lincoln, drilling me even harder from behind. "I'm hungry."

I would've laughed, if I actually could've. As it was, I was far too busy.

I still can't believe it's been a year...

Aside from the gym doing unbelievably well, business on Lincoln's end was booming also. Or should I say *our* end. Through our combined efforts, we'd expanded his marketing firm into two satellite offices — one in California, and one in New Jersey. The west coast office gave us the opportunity to travel, which was proving to be a lot of fun.

"Ahhhh, screw it..."

Donovan grunted loudly, holding my head steady as he finished hard, down my throat. He'd held off for a while, actually. He and Brody had been screwing me off and on for the past hour, even after Lincoln announced he was going to be late.

I sucked him dry, draining him completely. Eventually he withdrew, his expression dreamy and sated, before finally pulling on his clothes.

"Get in the kitchen," Lincoln instructed, without missing a beat. "Make sure the kid doesn't—"

"Yeah yeah," said Donovan, still breathless. "I got it."

He left the room, giving us the entire bed to stretch out on. Lincoln pushed me forward and turned me on my side, flipping my legs together so he could enter me that way.

God it felt so good...

"I guess you couldn't wait, huh?" he teased, sawing in

and out of me.

"I tried to tell them," I shrugged. "But they—"

"That's okay," Lincoln smiled. "I'll still take what's coming to me."

I sighed and lay back, hooking one arm beneath my knees. Pulling them up gave him a deeper, better angle. It also felt amazing.

"I love this part," he said, his voice going thick. "When you're all wet like this. All used and ready and—"

I lost the rest of whatever he was saying, as the intensity of my own orgasm crashed over me. I let it take me, washing me in and out like a powerful tide. Grunting and moaning into the nearest pillow, even though there was no reason to be quiet.

"You're incredible you know," said Lincoln.

"Oh..." I gasped, still clawing the sheets. "I know."

"It's one of the reasons we love you so much."

I rode out the tail end of my climax with the biggest of unchecked grins. Squeezing down hard, I waited until I felt it... until Lincoln was flooding my pussy with his own hot load, before I finally answered him.

"Mmmm... baby, I love you too..."

A few minutes of afterglow later, we were back in the loft's main area. Donovan had just finished setting the table as Brody pulled everything off the stove.

"You're lucky you finished," joked Donovan. "Because you know we'd eat without you."

"Oh I know," said Lincoln, helping himself to a beer from the fridge. The others already had theirs. "I'm well aware of your 'starting without me' record."

"Yeah, well you were late, so..."

Brody dropped something onto the table that looked like a lasagna. Only thinner. And more watery. And more—

"It's gonna taste better than it looks," he announced, without a hint of shame. "Trust me."

We sat down, all four of us, at the exact same time. It was so synchronous we had to pause to acknowledge it by looking up at each other.

"Here's to another year of being awesome," said Brody, holding up his bottle.

"Me, right?" Donovan toasted. "You're talking about me?"

"He's talking about me," I joked, holding out my wine glass. Brody clinked it from across the table, hard enough that everyone winced.

We toasted. We drank. I grabbed my napkin, laying it across my lap.

"In the spirit of the new year," said Lincoln, "I have a gift for everyone."

We'd already set down our drinks. Now Brody stopped sawing the lasagna mid-cut.

"We did gifts last week," said Donovan. "And as usual you upstaged us. There's no reason to—"

CLACK!

Lincoln slapped something down in the center of the table. It left the remaining three of us staring down in confusion... at another key.

"What the—"

"This key doesn't open anything," said Lincoln. "Yet."

He was right. The key had no teeth. It wasn't even cut.

"It's a blank key," he explained, "because it's the key to a new place. *OUR place*," he emphasized. "The one that the four of us all get together and pick out."

We were all staring at him now, as we usually were. Brody held a finger up.

"You mean..."

"I mean when you guys are ready," he said, "we rent this place out. We get a loft of our own. Or a brownstone. Or a building..."

Everyone sat uncharacteristically still. Smiling, Lincoln took the knife from Brody's hand and began cutting again.

"If we're going to be together," he said, "we might as well be *together*." He shrugged as he served me first. "Unless you all think we need *three* apartments."

I laughed. "Hell, I haven't been to my apartment in five days."

"I know," Lincoln nodded. "And although this place is great... the three of us are in love with the same woman. And she with us." After looking at each of the others, he shifted his gaze in my direction. "And that's not likely to change anytime soon. Is it?"

"Not a chance," I breathed.

"Good," he smiled, serving each of us in turn. "Then it's settled."

Settled. It was just like Lincoln to put things that way. And yet...

And yet the others hadn't argued. They hadn't spoken up. Donovan and Brody were staring at each other, with volumes passing wordlessly between them.

All of us. Together.

It was a goal we'd talked about, off and on. But it was always in the future. Always ahead of us.

And now...

"Sleep on it if you need to," Lincoln said at last. "But I'm thinking—"

"I'm in," said Brody abruptly.

"Me too," Donovan nodded. "Let's do it."

My smile widened. My heart soared. If there were anything more perfect than all four of us living together, I couldn't imagine it.

Then again, I couldn't imagine a lot of things a year ago. And here I was.

"What do you say, Holly?"

They were staring at me now, my three lovers. My three *loves.* The three most important men in my entire world.

I raised my fork in one hand, my glass in the other.

"Let's eat!"

Need *more* Reverse Harem?

First of all, thanks for checking out *Unwrapping Holly - A Holiday Reverse Harem Romance*. Hope you absolutely loved it!

And for even *more* sweltering reverse harem heat? Check out: *Quadruple Duty: All or Nothing*. Below you'll find a preview of the incredibly sexy cover, plus the first several chapters so you can see for yourself:

Unwrapping Holly - Krista Wolf

~ Prologue ~

SAMMARA

"Where are you going? Our bungalow's *this* way."

I stopped along the planks of the smooth wooden walkway, the crystal blue waters stretching in every direction beneath me. They reached all the way out to the picture-perfect horizon, where the sun seemed to be melting into its mirrored surface.

Bora Bora. The ultimate destination. My wildest, most insane travel fantasy...

My God, Sammara.

I still couldn't believe we were actually here.

"That's not our bungalow anymore," Kyle called casually over his shoulder. "I upgraded us."

He smiled and winked before continuing along the gangplanks, moving further out into the azure horizon. I could see his body was already sun-kissed from swimming and snorkeling all day. His magnificent shoulders looked tan and brown.

"What about all our stuff?"

"It's already moved."

"But—"

"Come on!"

He held out his hand, and I ran to take it. Kyle led me past the last of the other low-slung huts, to a longer walkway that stretched away from the rest. It ended in a tremendous, stunning pavilion, three times the size of the one we'd rented.

"We're staying *there?*" I asked incredulously.

"Uh huh."

"It's huge!"

"Yup."

My heart raced. As if I didn't feel guilty enough...

It was one thing; having a gorgeous, muscle-bound Army Ranger for a boyfriend. Over the last three years, that part I'd certainly gotten used to.

But it was quite another thing... to have *four* of them at once.

"Who'd you think would love this place more?" I asked. "Jason or Ryan?"

Kyle laughed. "What about Dakota?"

"Well he's from Iowa. It's landlocked."

"So? All the more reason he'd love it."

The walkway ended, and we stepped onto the veranda

of the most beautiful cabana I'd ever seen. White silk drapes floated in the breeze, acting as curtains. Just inside, I could see a sprawling common area with low seats and couches, covered in plush, colorful pillows and bamboo mats.

It was as beautiful as it was private. Like something straight out of a magazine.

It just didn't look real.

"I wish they could see this," I sighed, staring into the sunset. "All of them."

"Me too," said Kyle. He smiled back at me slyly. "But it's not like they haven't had their fair share of you, too."

No, he was definitely right about that. While the guys had all been deployed or traveling at different times, they'd each managed to take me somewhere exotic on their own. Jason had flown me to Italy; or rather I'd taken him, because he'd never been. Ryan had surprised me with a European tour of haunted castles last summer, scaring me beneath the covers before making love to me there each night. And I'd curled up contentedly in an ice-igloo with Dakota, staring up into the Alaskan sky to watch the amazing spectacle of the Northern Lights.

It had all been incredibly romantic — every last magical moment. Even so, my favorite trips were when some of us could be together. I'd spent the better part of a month exploring Greece with Ryan and Kyle, sailing the Hellenic coast in nothing but a bikini bottom for days on end. And I'd never forget the trip to Sweden with Dakota and Jason. After visiting a genuine Nordic village for a day or two — where they'd dressed me up like a viking princess — we'd spent the rest of the time soaking ourselves in the volcanic mud of a geothermal hot springs... among other things.

"You feel guilty?"

I blushed at Kyle. It always did feel like he could read my mind.

"A little, yeah." I shrugged. "But only because this is the most breathtaking place I've ever been. I mean... just look at it!"

He stepped up behind me as I admired the view. Two strong arms slid around my waist. My body shivered with pleasure as he lowered his lips to my neck.

"They'd understand," he said, planting a string of gentle kisses along my bare shoulder. "We all want the same thing, Sammara. For you to be happy."

Three years...

I clenched my jaw blissfully as I sucked in a long, contented breath.

Three happy, amazing years...

Had it really been that long?

I thought back, losing myself in the moment. It had been three years this month since I'd met Kyle. Three years since I'd first seen the ad, the one placed by four Army Rangers looking to share a 'community girlfriend'. They wanted wife material. Long term only. A girl who would be there for them through thick and thin, who'd still love them while they were gone and wait for them during long, sudden deployments.

A woman they'd all *share together...* mind, body, and soul. Because on an individual basis, not one of them had been able to keep any woman happy. But *four* of them...

It was crazy. Absolutely ludicrous. And yet...

And yet I'd tried it. And I'd *loved* it. And even better than all that, I'd fallen in love with *them*. Each of them. All of them.

They were my four sexy soldiers, each different in his own way. All four of them with the same common goal: to love me. To protect and care for me. To cherish me as their own, the way I cherished them.

"Come on," said Kyle, taking me by the hand. "Let's get cleaned up before heading down to dinner."

My muscles were sore, all over my body. A hot shower would feel baptismal.

I let him pull me inside, still watching trance-like as the last of the light went out of the sky. The bungalow was even more beautiful at dusk. It was lit up already by a beautiful chandelier in the center of the room, and two rows of red and white candles.

"It's gorgeous," I breathed, turning to kiss Kyle. "It's totally perf—"

I stopped mid-sentence and looked down. Scattered across the floor, a trail of red and white rose petals followed the curve of the candles... leading straight into the bedroom.

"Okay, *now* you've thought of *everything*," I quipped.

"Did not."

"Did so."

Kyle shrugged. "Okay, maybe a little."

I sighed happily and pointed down at the trail. "So where's that lead?"

My lover shrugged again. "Go and see."

I walked the trail gingerly, the petals soft and fresh against my bare feet as Kyle followed just behind. The room ahead of us was dark. No lights at all, except for the flickering of more candles.

"If there's a hot bath in there," I warned him, "you're getting the mother of all blowjobs."

Kyle laughed softly. Almost nervously.

"I'm dead serious," I told him. "I'll drop to my knees right now. I'm talking a toe-curling, butt-clenching, gotta pull the sheets out of your asscrack kind of..."

The words died in my throat as I turned the corner.

What happened next took a moment to register.

The bedroom was stunningly decorated; an explosion of soft gossamer ribbon and fresh tropical flowers. It was all so bright and fragrant, even lit only by candles. In the center, a tremendous four-poster bed lay adorned with silken pillows. The canopy was draped with lilies, birds of paradise, exotic orchids...

But that wasn't all.

I gasped, as tears rushed to fill my eyes. The room wasn't empty. Kneeling before me were three people; three handsome, gorgeous men who over the past three years had become nothing short of my whole life.

I saw Dakota. Ryan. Jason...

All three of them were smiling. All three of them were dressed to the nines: identical black suits, white shirts, ties and everything!

And all three of them were down on one knee, too. All three of them holding something...

Oh my God...

"Sammara."

I whirled, and there was Kyle. He was no longer standing behind me, he was kneeling as well. Kneeling with both hands cupped outward, his palm holding the most beautiful little wooden box...

"You probably know this already," he smiled up at me. "But you're our entire world."

My hands went over my mouth. My eyes filled with tears to the point where I could no longer see anything!

"We've always been a brotherhood," said Dakota, and I spun to face him. "But we've never *really* been whole. Not until you. Not until you made us."

His country-boy grin was broader and brighter than I'd ever seen it before. And he was nervous! It was the first time I'd ever seen him anything but totally confident.

"I'll admit, I never imagined this moment going down this way," said Ryan. I looked to him and saw his wry, impish grin. "But that's what makes this special. Our situation is extraordinary because you're an extraordinary woman, Sammara. I couldn't imagine myself — or any of us — with anyone else."

I turned to Jason last, tears streaming down both my cheeks. He smiled up at me as I blinked them away. "You know a part of me was broken," he said genuinely. "But you fixed it. Having you in our lives has brought the four of us that much closer. We can only hope to give you even a fraction of the love you've given to us."

Their hands moved in unison, opening four identical boxes. Revealing four very different diamond rings. I was weeping openly as they spoke together.

"Will you marry us?"

I couldn't breathe. I could barely see. I just kept crying and crying, wiping away my tears of joy. Smiling from ear to ear as my heart felt like it was about to explode with happiness.

My legs were shaking. I could barely stand...

"The question *kinda* requires an answer," Dakota winked.

"YES!"

They all rose at once, closing in from all sides. Kyle took my hand first. He slid his ring onto my finger; a radiant-cut, perfectly clear stone on a yellow gold band. I cried as he kissed my cheek, then handed my wrist to Dakota.

"I love you," Dakota whispered, in his sexy mid-western drawl. He slid on an identical ring, right next to Kyle's, only his band looked silver, or platinum, or—

"We all love you," said Ryan, going next. The band from his ring was a beautiful rose gold. He winked at me. "Just remember *I'm* the best."

I laughed, and a fresh set of tears made their way downward. A tender hand wiped them away, and I looked up into the smiling face of Jason.

"Bullshit," he said with a grin. "Everyone knows the best is saved for last."

The band of his ring was a little darker, but no less lustrous. He slid it snugly against the others, looking deep into my eyes the whole time.

For a long moment, no one spoke. All eyes were on my one trembling finger, now sparking in the candlelight.

"Here," said Kyle, stepping up again. "Let me show you something."

He took my hand, rotating the rings slightly until all four diamonds formed a perfect square. Then he pushed them together, ever so gently...

Click.

The four bands snapped flawlessly into each other, forming a single ring. The diamonds formed what looked like a single beautiful jewel, made up of four equal parts.

I was completely speechless. Lost in a sea of thousand emotions.

"I..."

Nothing could describe the moment. No words could ever say what I needed to convey. What I needed them to *know*, all four of them, in their hearts and minds.

"I–I..."

My throat was locked up. My eyes, glassed over with tears.

I had to try anyway.

"I *LOVE* you!" I practically yelled. I was bawling now. Uncontrollably. "I love you, and you and you and you!"

I spun around, making sure I faced them all. Then I

was reaching out for them. Hugging them, as they closed in around me.

"You've made me the happiest girl in the world!" I said, half-laughing, half-crying.

"World?" smiled Ryan. "More like *universe!*"

I laughed again at our own little inside joke, feeling their arms go around me. Feeling each of them lift me, one by one, into their strong, powerful embrace.

Oh God, Sammara...

They took turns kissing me, as they so often did. Long, deep, loving kisses. Soulful. Beautiful. So hot, so wet, so incredibly amazing...

I could feel the love and excitement radiating off them. It soaked into my body as they took turns spinning me around. Laughing, kissing, making us all dizzy...

And I could feel their relief, too. I could only imagine the planning that went into this. Getting them all here, all at once. Somehow without me knowing!

"I— I can't believe..."

"Oh you can believe it," said Dakota, pulling me against him. His heart was pounding so hard I could feel it through his massive chest. "You're no longer our girlfriend," he said, kissing me again. "You're our fiancé now!"

Fiancé!

The word rang musically in my ears. It sounded glorious. It sounded *perfect...*

"We're here the entire ten days," said Jason. "All four of us."

My stomach exploded in a flock of butterflies. All four of them, with me, here in paradise! It was unbelievable. Unimaginable.

I glanced around the wide, beautiful pavilion. No wonder they'd upgraded.

"Don't worry," said Ryan. "There are more than enough bedrooms."

"And you'll get to use them *all*," Dakota winked.

I swallowed past the lump in my throat. Just the thought forced my stomach to do a sexy backflip.

"Does this mean I get to start planning our wedding?" I asked excitedly.

"Ha!" laughed Kyle. "As if all girls don't already start planning that at birth."

He was right of course, which only made it funnier. Still, no matter how many times I'd imagined my wedding, the venue, my bridesmaids, my dress... I'd never once, in my wildest, most far-flung fantasies, imagined I would have *four* husbands.

"So I get four times the wedding budget," I quipped. "Right?"

"Sure, why not?" said Ryan. "Four times the guest list. Four times the presents..."

"Four times the happy hour," said Jason. "Four times the—"

I flung myself into his arms, stopping him mid-sentence. It was pure nirvana, closing my mouth over his. Feeling the heat and passion growing between us as Jason kissed me back, all strong and dark and handsome... not to mention, impeccably dressed.

My eyes crawled over my four gorgeous boyfriends — no wait, four gorgeous *fiancés!* — their sculpted bodies filling out their suits in only the best, most exciting of ways. Down below, in the area beneath my naval, I felt a warm, familiar tingle.

"Take me."

I bounced onto the bed. My hair fell over my face as I looked up at them with my best, most sultry expression.

"The four of you... I want you all," I breathed. "Take your fiancé *now*."

Kyle smiled and started forward immediately. But Dakota's hand on his shoulder stopped him.

"Dinner first, bro. Remember?"

My heart sank. My body was ready to scream in protest.

"He's right," said Jason. "The other three of us are starving. It was a long flight. The food was inedible."

"And we're already dressed!" said Ryan. He yanked uncomfortably at the tie around his neck. "I didn't put this thing on for nothing, you know."

I couldn't believe they were actually serious! I leaned back on the bed, spreading myself before them. Intentionally I let the towel wrapped around my waist fall away, displaying my bikini...

"You sure you don't want dessert first?" I winked. "Dinner afterward?"

Dakota stood firm. But I could see Jason's resolve slipping.

"C'mon," I purred. "I'm not *really* your fiancé until we all christen this bed together." I patted the spots on either side of me. "Those are the rules."

Dakota shook his head in disbelief. Ryan just laughed and looked away.

"Really? Those are the rules?"

I smiled and hooked a finger sexily into one corner of my mouth. "Uh huh."

Kyle moved forward again, and this time Jason came with him. I could feel my skin going flush with excitement as they crawled up on either side of me.

"You're fighting dirty," lamented Dakota. "You know that?"

I blew him a kiss, giggling on the inside. "C'mon baby," I pouted. "How often do you get to eat dessert before dinner?"

He didn't answer, so I stretched out, cat-like, across the bed. My blonde hair flowed down either side of my shoulders as I scissored my long legs.

Ryan folded under the pressure, stepping forward. Jason and Kyle were already kissing either side of my neck, their hands reaching for my body.

"I promise I'll make it up to you," I cooed at Jason, raising a hopeful eyebrow. I maintained eye contact with him even as Kyle began kissing me. Kept a steady gaze, as Jason's fingertips traced their way up the insides of my thighs...

"*Please?*"

Reaching down to my hip, I pulled on the tiny string tie of my bikini bottoms. Looking Dakota right in his crystal blue eyes, I bit my lip and offered it to him.

"Fine," he sighed finally, pulling at his collar. "But if we're gonna do this right now?"

I gulped, half with excitement, half with the breathless anticipation of what was coming next. I hadn't been with the four of them at once in *way* too long.

"You're getting every last *inch* of what you're asking for..."

One

SAMMARA

"So.... How's engaged life?"

Melissa grinned at me from her own treadmill, which she'd slowed down to what I called 'gossip speed'. It enabled us to keep our conversation low and comfortable, but still be drowned out in every other direction by the constant whir of the machines' motors.

"It's amazing," I said proudly. "Just like the last time you asked."

She chuckled, her light-hearted laugh echoing through our little corner of the gym. "Should I stop asking?"

"Hell no," I grinned. "A girl never gets tired of such a question."

I glanced down at my ring, reflexively. Or rather, my *rings*. Gold for Kyle, my sexy soldier. Platinum for Dakota, my dirty-blond giant. Rose gold for Ryan, as emotionally complex as the alloy itself, and brushed palladium to represent

Jason, so strong and beautiful.

It had been six months since Bora Bora. Six months since the most amazing engagement any girl's ever likely to have. An engagement filled with the most love, the most laughter, the most excitement...

And of course, the most life-changing, mind-erasing, four-on-one *sex*.

"You got a date all picked out yet?"

"No," I lamented. "That part's tough. It'll depend on them all being home at once, of course. And then there's the *other* factor..."

The other factor. The one part of the whole beautiful equation that nagged at me, more and more, as the weeks and months went by.

"Still nothing?" Melissa asked.

"No."

"It'll happen, Sammara," she said reassuringly. "Don't sweat it."

"I know," I said, more out of reflex than anything. "I'm... I'm really not."

A long stretch of silence passed. It almost got awkward, but Melissa smiled and swooped in.

"It's probably just stress," she said. "Stress about work, stress about the expansion. Your business is growing faster than you can keep up with it," she went on. "That's a good thing!"

A good thing. Yes, it definitely was. Since starting *Universal Designs* almost three years ago, it had blossomed from a decorating and staging service into a full-blown renovations company. And then last year...

Last year I'd brought things to a whole different level.

My ultimate goal — my dream, really — was to not only renovate, but actually *build* too. As much as I loved restoring old, historic properties, I wanted to somehow be involved in their creation as well.

And then it hit me... or rather, Kyle had suggested it one night. We were curled up on the couch together, after a particularly long marathon of old, scary movies.

"You really love renovating these old places," he'd said, "but you hate destroying them with new construction."

"So?"

"So why don't you build all new construction... of historic old floor-plans?"

By the time he'd finished saying it, my mind had already been blown.

"Think about it, Sammara. You could create one-hundred percent accurate, vintage homes, modeled *exactly* as they would've been built two-hundred years ago. Only with central air-conditioning and high-speed internet," he winked.

It made so much sense I was almost sick with excitement. I could create masterpieces of architecture that no longer existed, using modern engineering and upgraded materials. CNC machines to model even the most complicated trims and finishes.

I could build antebellum mansions! Georgian manors. Beautiful old Victorians, like the one we lived in now...

"Is Cindy still handling the other end of things for

you?"

"Yes."

"How's she doing?"

I smiled, pumping my arms as the treadmill's program randomly selected a new hill to climb. "She's kicking ass, actually."

Cindy had started as my assistant. Now she was my second-in-command. She was smart, capable, energetic — everything I needed her to be. But she'd never be my partner. Not after what happened with Dawn...

"Oh, I meant to tell you..." Melissa said hesitantly. "I uh... I ran into Dawn."

It was uncanny, how things like that could happen during conversation. Yet they always did.

"Yeah? And what'd she say?"

Melissa laughed. "You think I'd actually talk to her? After what *she* pulled?"

"No," I smiled. "You're a loyal friend."

"Damn straight!"

"I just figured... maybe she might talk to *you?*"

My friend shook her head as she wiped her brow. "She knows better than that. Besides, she looked like shit warmed over. I heard she finally got back into the business. After... well, you know..."

Yeah, I knew. Dawn had actually been the catalyst for *Universal Designs.* If she hadn't robbed me — and our interior design business — of every last piece I owned? I wouldn't be anywhere near where I was now.

That, plus the help I received from Jason and Ryan, of course. The two of them had shown me how to fight back. In the dead of night. With a couple of box trucks, and a crew of movers, and—

"So where are we *having* the wedding?" Melissa asked, changing the subject. "Do we know that yet?"

I smiled inwardly at her enthusiasm. "No."

"Destination wedding!"

"Maybe."

"Hawaii!"

I laughed. "We'll see."

"I'm still the maid of honor, right?"

"Last time I checked, yeah." I let my expression suddenly go very serious. "Unless you cross me, of course." I scrunched my face at her, making my eyes very narrow. "Do that, and I'd have to bring the pain!"

Melissa made a muscle and pointed to it mid-stride. "I've got the pain right here, bitch!"

We laughed some more, then kicked up the speed for the last twenty minutes and finished our workout. I watched my friend as she snagged some paper towels and dutifully sprayed and wiped down our machines.

Melissa was the one true friend I had, and the only one who accepted my lifestyle without judgment. Of *course* she'd be my maid of honor. She was everything to me.

We grabbed our water bottles and headed out, parting

ways at the parking lot. Before we did, Melissa laid a comforting hand on my shoulder.

"Hey honey," she said. "I want you to listen, and listen good."

I tried to smile as I looked up at her. But it was hard.

"You're over-extended. That's all it is."

"I know. Thanks."

She looked me up and down and grinned. "And with all *four* of the guys home right now?" She rolled her eyes. "I'm sure you're overextended in more ways than one."

I stuck my tongue out at her as she laughed. "Ha ha."

She leaned forward quickly and pecked me sweetly on the cheek. "Bye bitch," she said, dropping her sunglasses over her eyes. Then she turned, whipped out her car keys, and began walking away.

Damn, I loved her. She really was the best.

"Until the next torture session!" she called over her shoulder.

Two

KYLE

We'd skipped our mid-week date, but it was one of those rainy nights where you really just wanted to be inside. One of those really cool storms that made you feel snug and cozy and safe under your own roof.

Besides, Sammara and I were alone in the house for once. And while I loved sharing my beautiful fiancé with my three best brothers-in-arms, having her to myself now and then felt like a forbidden treat.

"Mmmmm..." she moaned, squirming into the bed. "Right there..."

I twisted down with the heel of my palm, giving the small of her back just the right amount of pressure. Sammara was sprawled face-down across her own bed, breathtakingly naked. She squirmed beneath the touch of my oiled hands as they glided over the warm surface of her well-oiled body.

"You're the absolute best at this," she groaned into her pillow. "You know that?"

I laughed, making tight circles with my thumbs. "I'll bet you say that to *all* the boys."

She turned her head sideways, her golden hair falling over her perfect face. "It would definitely be in my best interests to lie," she agreed. "But right now I'm telling—" She sucked in a sharp breath. "Ooohhh.. *Yes!*"

I listened to her moan a few moments longer before clearing her throat. "Right now I'm telling the truth..."

It was always hot, admiring her body. Especially prone like this, every last curve laid out at my fingertips. My gaze dropped again, back to her magnificent ass. She had a magnificent *everything* really, but I was gradually learning I was an ass man before anything else.

"Harder..."

I applied more oil, then more pressure. She jumped at both.

"Oh my *God*, Kyle..."

It was truly amazing, finding her the way we did. Plucking her from a seemingly endless sea of imperfect candidates, for our over-the-top, borderline crazy arrangement.

And yet the arrangement wasn't actually so crazy. The four us shared a long string of failed relationships. Duties, extended tours, sudden deployments; these things were a way of life for anyone in the armed forces. They put a strain on even the best relationships, even the strongest of marriages.

But for Army Rangers like us? It was an even tougher thing to deal with.

Sharing a single partner — rather than the four of us

trying to keep four women happy — seemed *just* crazy enough to work. But it would have to be a special kind of woman. Someone who could put aside the taboos associated with being shared without jealousy, someone who could grow to love four people equally, and receive their love too.

"My ass *again?*" Sammara giggled. "You're back there already?"

I smiled guiltily. "Gotta make sure I got all the knots out."

I just couldn't help it, her ass looked too good. The oil felt too slippery. Too hot.

She moaned appreciatively as I kneaded her two warm, symmetrical globes. My fingers dipped dangerously lower. As always, they began to explore.

"You know," I said nonchalantly, "every time we swap massages, it starts and ends the same way."

"It does?"

"Mmm-hmmm."

"Okay, let's hear it."

My hands glided into her thigh gap as I kneaded even lower.

"Well it always starts with you asking to go first... and promising to do me afterward."

Sammara let out something that was half laughter, half sigh. "Well..." she purred. "Don't I *do* you afterward?"

Shit. She had me there.

"Yes... but—"

"Then our arrangement is fulfilled."

I heard her giggle, so I slapped her ass playfully with one hand. At the same time, my other hand slid slowly upward... until my fingers grazed the warmth and wetness of her sex.

"One day," I said, letting my voice go low and seductive, "I'll get my massage."

Her breathing was heavier now, silent in anticipation of what came next. I decided to tease her. Ever so slowly, the tip of my first finger parted her tender folds. She was absolutely drenched.

"This what you want?"

She nodded into the pillow, eyes closed, her lips full and kissable. I leaned forward to cover her mouth with mine. To breathe her in, kissing her softly, our tongues exploring each other in slow, tentative circles.

"Please..."

She squirmed downward, but I moved my hand in the same direction. Just the tip of my finger was still inside her. Nothing more.

"Kyle... come on!"

"What?" I asked innocently, moaning the word into her mouth.

"You— You have to..."

She screwed her hips, and this time I let her have her way. Two thick fingers entered her, all slick and wet. I pushed upward, burying them deep.

"Ohhhhhhh..."

I was a sucker when it came to teasing her, and I could never last long. I wanted it just as much as she did. She knew it too.

It played out slowly, to the sounds of the rain. Sammara screwed herself into my hand while I chewed her shoulder, both of us listening to the big droplets as they pattered loudly off the old, lead-paned glass.

"Kyle..."

She breathed my name more than said it, which was always music to my ears. I loved the way she spoke my name. I loved her voice, soft and feminine. Her moans, her whimpers, so sultry. So sexy...

"I–I'm close, Kyle... I–"

My fingers had been sawing in and out of her, more rapidly as her excitement grew. Just before she came however, I pushed forward and made my hand rigid. I held it there and let her screw downward, rubbing the underside of my knuckles against her pelvic bone. She cried out in orgasmic release, while clawing the pillow with both hands in some sort of adorable death-grip.

By now, I knew what my girl liked.

I slid up alongside her as she came floating down, all grins and smiles. Her body was slippery against mine. There was oil practically everywhere.

"Okay. Your turn."

She began with her hand, stroking me up and down. Helping me out of my boxers, until I was naked on my back. I closed my eyes for a moment, focusing on the feel of her warm, oil-soaked fingers wrapped tightly around my manhood.

Dragging them slowly up and down. Squeezing gently, just beneath the head.

I wasn't at all surprised when she threw a leg over me. Sammara sank all the way down on my cock in a single, lubricated thrust. We both groaned simultaneously, then smiled.

"You're right about me not wanting to give up control," she breathed, placing a hand on my chest.

"Are you referring to our conversation from earlier?"

Her eyes closed, but she nodded. We'd been talking about work. About how she needed to hire someone else, but she was too much of a control freak to take on another assistant.

"Let me show you how much I like control..."

She reached back, and I felt her warm, slender fingers travel over my balls. I hissed through clenched teeth as she closed her palm over them.

"Shoot it in me, Kyle."

It felt incredible, the way she was rolling her hips. The gentle squeeze of her hand on my balls, coaxing me... urging me to come with my cock buried so deeply inside her.

"Put it *deep*, baby. Please..."

I could've held off, but there wasn't a point. Instead I let go, digging my hands into her hips as I came. Sliding them up to her breasts in order to feel the full weight of them in my hands...

"Awwww, yes! That's it..."

I climaxed with a guttural groan, shooting so hard and

so deep inside her I almost blacked out. And through it all she stayed there, rocking her body. Holding my eyes prisoner in her own sapphire blue orbs, while she smiled and grunted and rode me past the point of completion.

She collapsed forward when she was done, leaving us chest to chest, face to face. Her blonde hair crashed downward, enveloping our heads in a waterfall of golden curls that surrounded us on all sides.

"I love you," she smiled, and kissed me.

Control.

Yes, our fiancé definitely had a problem giving up control. But it's one of the things we loved most about her, too. Sammara was headstrong. Motivated. Totally unstoppable, once she set her mind on something.

Somewhere downstairs, we heard a door slam. We stopped kissing just long enough to look at each other.

"Ryan's home," I said, matter-of-factly.

Sammara grinned back at me mischievously. She raised one eyebrow.

"Want me to get him?" I laughed.

She bit her lip as if considering the question, but we both knew better than that.

"Please."

Three

RYAN

I found her upstairs in bed, exactly where Kyle said she was. As always, Sammara's room was warm, soft, and inviting. Especially with her in it.

"Hey honey.."

She opened her arms as she smiled the words. It was the best end to any day, but especially a long, hard one.

"Come to me."

Slowly I peeled off the rest of my rain-soaked clothes. Her lithe body was gloriously naked, stretched out across her soft down comforter and glistening in the dim light. I could smell oil. Candles. The soft sounds of music somewhere nearby, drowned out almost completely by the patter of rain.

In less than a minute I was naked, falling into her arms. Her body opened for me. Her legs spread wide...

"Oh... you're so *cold!*"

I really was. Cold and still wet with the rain.

Sammara slicked my hair back as she kissed the water away from my face. Her lips traveled my cheeks, my jaw, the tip of my nose, before finally settling over my own in a long, hot, passionate kiss.

"God, I missed you today."

The words were mine this time. They came out of *my* mouth. Three years ago I couldn't have dreamed of ever saying them... not to *any* woman, much less one I actually shared with my three brothers-in-war.

But now I was glad to. Thrilled, in fact. When Kyle and Dakota had first brought up sharing the same girlfriend, I'd wrinkled my nose at the idea. That they'd done it before didn't make it any less weird for me.

But right here... right now...

"Ohhhhh..."

I sank into her, spreading her thighs even further apart with the weight of my body. Sammara felt like warm, melted butter. It was crazy how turned on it got me, knowing she'd already been taken by Kyle.

"I missed you too baby," she purred, nibbling at my ear. A shockwave of pleasure bolted down my body. She knew what I liked, what I loved. Though she had four eager lovers to keep track of, she still never forgot it.

We rocked slowly, our bodies melding together. She was so *warm!* So beautiful and perfect and pretty...

And now she's your fiancé too, I reminded myself. *You're going to marry her...*

Again, it was crazy — the most insane of all ideas in the

world. But with Sammara, *it worked.* She was strong, independent, powerful. But she was also sweet and loving and caring. So thoughtful and amazing, that all these years later not one of us could even imagine our lives before her.

I'd thought about it over and over, and I'd come to the same conclusion each time: it had to be *her*. The arrangement might never have worked with anyone else, no matter who answered our ad, no matter how many times we might've tried. Because when it came down to what the four of us wanted and desired... what we actually *needed* from a woman?

Sammara was the perfect storm.

"Oh... *Shit yes...*"

I nuzzled into her neck as she hooked her ankles behind by my back, driving me in deeper. I could tell she wasn't letting go. That we wouldn't be switching positions, or taking our time, or anything like that.

No, I could tell she *needed* this. Even though I was certain Kyle had given her everything he had, it was obvious Sammara needed even more.

It was one of the hottest things about her.

"Drive it in..." she whispered into my ear. "God... *FUCK!*"

There was an urgency in her voice. Almost a frustration. She bucked forward while pulling back with her legs. *Damn* she had strong thighs.

"Put it all the way inside me Ryan," she cooed. "I need it..."

I went harder, if not necessarily faster. Sliding my

arms around her body, I crushed her against me while letting my weight do the rest.

"That's it," she gasped. "Ohhhh... yeah. Dig me out!"

Every word brought me closer to the edge. I couldn't last like this. Not with her body writhing beneath me, whispering deliciously filthy things. Not with the smell of her, the feel of her. The combination of her heat, her wetness, the oil...

"I— I can..."

She was delirious now. Almost manic.

"I... I can feel you all the way at the *bottom...*"

Her head lolled back, and all I could see was the whites of her eyes. Then it felt it; the spasms around me. The hard, rapid contractions of her innermost muscles as she came all over my cock, her fingernails digging painfully into the flesh of my ass.

"Oh GOD oh GOD oh *GODDDDDDD...*"

I lost it halfway through, shooting deeper inside her than ever before. Sammara's hands were like talons, gripping me tightly. Digging in like she was trying to force my whole body inside her, spreading her legs so wide I could hear the crack of her hips.

FUCKKKK...

My world disappeared, and for a good half minute I was lost in the searing white purity of my own climax. I couldn't see. Couldn't hear. It felt like my very *soul* was exiting my body, rushing outward like an ebbing tide. Traveling through the strong, raging erection I had planted between my girlfriend's beautiful legs... and nothing but undiluted pleasure came flowing back in.

When I looked up again Kyle was on the bed, holding her in his arms, keeping her steady while she recovered. His gaze met mine, and after a quick smirk of approval he tossed me a towel.

"You're bleeding."

Shit, I was. Both sides of my ass had been scratched by Sammara's nails. Twisting at the waist, I could see ten sharp indentations in the flesh of my rear end.

"That's it," I said, only partly joking. "No more pointed-nail manicures for you."

Sammara's chest rose and fell with long, deep breaths, still lost in her own euphoria. She half-nodded, half-smiled as I pulled out of her.

"Wow..."

The entire area between her legs was a sopping wet mess. A pear-shaped drop of my creamy white seed formed a pearlescent button inside her.

Absently I stared at it, fixating on it. Wondering if—

"Thank you," she finally breathed. "The both of you." She smiled warmly. "I needed my boys today. More than I even realized."

I slid up alongside her, enjoying the welcome warmth of her body. Staring down into her eyes as she lay glistening in the candlelight, stretched out between us.

That's when I noticed it. A lone teardrop... streaming down one pink cheek.

"Sammara!" I gasped. "What's wrong?"

Kyle bolted upright. Apparently he noticed it too.

Then we were holding her, cradling her against us... as both hands went to her face and she began sobbing uncontrollably.

[QUADRUPLE DUTY: ALL OR NOTHING IS NOW ON AMAZON!](#)

Grab it now — It's free to read for Kindle Unlimited!

ABOUT THE AUTHOR

Krista Wolf is a lover of action, fantasy and all good horror movies… as well as a hopeless romantic with an insatiably steamy, dirtier side.

She writes suspenseful, mystery-infused stories filled with blistering hot twists and turns. Tales in which headstrong, impetuous heroines are the irresistible force thrown against the immovable object of powerful, alpha heroes.

If you like intelligent and witty romance served up with a panty-dropping, erotic edge? You've just found your new favorite author.

Click here to see all titles on Krista's Author Page

Sign up to Krista's VIP Email list to get instant notification of all new releases: http://eepurl.com/dkWHab

Printed in Great Britain
by Amazon